THE

NAKEDS

THE
NAKEDS

A NOVEL

LISA
GLATT

Regan Arts.

Regan Arts.

65 Bleecker Street
New York, NY 10012

First Regan Arts hardcover edition, June 2015.

Library of Congress Control Number: 2014955547

ISBN 978-1-941393-05-5

Interior design by Nancy Singer
Jacket and Cover design by Richard Ljoenes
Jacket art by © Kei Uesugi / Getty Images

Printed in the United States of America

10 9 8 7 6 5 4 3 2 1

For my love, David

.

For my mother, Iris Stanton, who's gone,
but whose life and adventures
continue to make their way onto my pages

What spirit is so empty and blind that it cannot recognize the fact that the foot is more noble than the shoe, and skin more beautiful than the garment with which it is clothed?

—Michelangelo

PART 1

1

HANNAH LIVED in a Southern California beach city without sidewalks, with lawns and flower beds that went right down to the curbs, and today, because it was Monday, trash day, those curbs were lined with fat green bags and reeking metal bins. And today, because her parents were fighting, Hannah snuck out the front door and attempted to walk to school alone.

She'd stood in the dining room, listening to them scream *fuck this* and *fuck that* and *fuck you* and *oh no, mister, fuck you.* She hid behind a tall chair and watched them from between the wood slats. Her father stood in the corner, shirtless in gray sweatpants and socks, his hairy chest puffing up. "This is no life," he said. "Look at the three of us trapped here."

"Trapped?" her mother said in a low whisper. "Who's trapped?" She was only half dressed for work, cotton pajama bottoms and silk floral blouse, a gold hoop earring in one ear and nothing in the other. Her hair was sprayed stiff like a helmet and she had two perfectly rigid, solid curls twirling past each ear and down each cheek that bounced as she hollered. "Do you think I'll let that shiksa make a fool of me?"

"Enough, Nina," her father kept saying. "You're going to make this worse."

"Me?" she screamed. "Who's the dog here? Tell me that," she demanded. "Who behaves like an animal?"

Her father looked around the kitchen and shook his head. "How did we get here?"

Here was an A-frame cottage, a small three-bedroom house that her dad had always claimed to love.

Here was a home the two of them had picked out together with Hannah's childhood in mind.

Here was the weather the two of them bragged about to their friends and family on the East Coast—so many sunny days in a row, even in the winter months.

Before she'd left for school, Hannah had surveyed the breakfast table where two full cups of coffee sat cooling, where spoons and forks and knives for three splayed out in a messy, optimistic bundle. A loaf of challah, twisted and sprinkled with sesame seeds. Paper napkins. A glass bottle of milk. A cardboard cylinder of oatmeal. An apple sliced in quarters.

She took one last look at them. Her mother held a tall glass above her head and aimed it at her father's face.

"It's not worth working on. You'll see," he said.

Hannah had seen enough.

She snatched her lunch from the dining room table—a brown bag, with her name on it in her mother's messy cursive, that now bounced against her thigh—and headed toward the foyer and out the front door.

It was spring 1970. Her mother had told her last night while tucking her in that it was a whole new era. She talked about NASA's Explorer 1, an unmanned satellite, reentering Earth's atmosphere just a week earlier, after twelve years in orbit. "And soon, within days, the men of Apollo 13 are going to soar into space. Imagine that, Hannah," her mom said. "Anything is possible." When Hannah grew up she could be a doctor or even an astronaut. "You could go to the moon one day."

Hannah shook her head.

Her mom laughed. "I'm not much of a traveler either."

Now, walking down the driveway, Hannah thought about that unmanned satellite, spinning around in space for a dozen years, launching before she was even born. She waved at the next-door neighbor, Mr. Perkins, who was coming down his porch steps, carrying a briefcase. His black hair was wet.

"You like my new car?" he asked her. "It's a Gremlin," he said proudly. "Tell your dad to come by after work to take a look." He opened the door, tossed his briefcase into the backseat, and sat down behind the wheel.

After an awkward, wordless back-and-forth about who should go first, Mr. Perkins accepted her offer, pulling out and waving good-bye to Hannah behind the closed window.

She wished they lived on a street with sidewalks and that the neighbors' lawns weren't so neat and manicured. She walked on those lawns, tentatively, using stepping stones where she could find them. She waited a few minutes until the O'Briens' sprinklers sputtered to an end, and then moved through their yard. Halfway down the second block, an old woman in a nightgown and fluffy slippers stood on her porch, shaking her head. Hands on her doughy hips, she screamed at Hannah to get the hell off her lawn. "Can you hear me? I'm talking to you, little girl!"

Across the street, a German shepherd, chained behind a wire fence, barked and growled and bared his teeth.

"Are you deaf? Something wrong with you?" the woman said. "Can't you hear me? Are you deaf?" she repeated.

Hannah was many things, but deaf was not one of them.

She was shy.

She was bookish, in first grade but reading at a seventh-grade level.

She was nervous, prone to seriousness and hypochondriacal thoughts already.

She was worried about the new era her mom had mentioned.

She was quick to tears.

She was fearful, especially afraid of strangers and thunder, fog and the school nurse.

She was short, the second shortest in her class, only taller than Eddie Epstein, who had confided in her that he was taking special vitamins that were supposed to help him grow. Eddie was a nice boy, a boy who smiled when he talked to her and asked about her weekend, but still she was very afraid that those vitamins might work. When he'd returned from the nurse's office and sat down in the adjacent desk, Hannah stared at him— his little shoes and jeans, his plaid shirt and delicate shoulders, the tiny denim jacket hanging over the back of his chair—and she imagined Eddie growing and growing, sprouting right out of his desk, taller and taller, passing huge and handsome Tommy Miller, passing pretty Janet Murray, passing Mr. Henderson and the top of the chalkboard too, until his head brushed the ceiling, until he left her behind.

She was timid. She didn't shout out or complain when she should have. Like right now, that woman's voice again. "Get off my goddamn lawn, little girl. You're going to mess up everything."

The air was sweet from the roses to the left of her and sour from the garbage on her right. She held back tears and imagined her destination, the school itself, all concrete and redbrick, looming at the end of the cul-de-sac she hadn't yet reached. She imagined the hall monitor, a fifth-grade girl full of smarts and purpose with a whistle around her neck, standing at the front of the double glass doors. The last bell would be ringing in a matter of minutes, the intercom starting up, a crackling static, and then finally the principal's voice would break through.

Hannah was almost there.

She was stepping off the curb.

She wanted to be someone else, a stronger, bolder girl—a girl who might have surprised the cranky woman on the porch with a *fuck off* or *no fucking way*—phrases she'd heard lately at home and during recess. She stepped into the street and heard those words in her head, trying to call them to her throat and mouth, but they wouldn't come—her lips shut as if with paste.

And there in front of her, her two obedient feet, one black shoe stepping forward and the other one following.

"That's right, there you go," the woman said. She'd stopped shrieking, at least, but was now gloating. "Go on now." A bad winner, puffed up and sure of herself, her hand rising from her belly to shoo Hannah away. The German shepherd snarled and ran toward the fence, but the chain yanked him back so that he was on two legs, dancing, fiercer than ever.

Hannah was aware of her heart and lungs, her own breaths—a white puff each time she exhaled. She was aware of the wind too, which had picked up—her face cold and damp with sweat.

When the woman's front door slammed shut and she was finally gone, Hannah felt momentarily relieved. But there was a circular window on that door and the woman's face appeared again from behind it. She'd pulled the curtain to one side, spying, making sure that Hannah didn't change her mind and disobey, and she was mouthing something still.

Hannah didn't disobey, even when she was past the woman's house and the one next door and the one next door to that one.

She was careful, precise, curling around the trash cans—her body so close without actually touching them.

She heard the brakes.

She turned and caught a glimpse of the driver's startled face behind the wheel, and understood the screech was coming for her.

And it was a collision, yes, but a convergence too, an unfortunate union: metal to skin, fender to plaid dress, and, finally, fat black tire to bare calf, to lacy sock and perfectly shiny shoe. It was a confrontation, the briefest coming-together and breaking-apart, which propelled Hannah into the sky so that she was as far away from her warring parents and the cranky woman as possible, in the air, turning over—her two feet not even sharing the earth with them.

2

AFTER ASHER Teller hauled the three heavy, silver bins from the side yard out to the curb, he stood in the kitchen, looking out at the backyard and the dry grass he'd been neglecting lately, the pool he hadn't cleaned in a week. Hannah's pink bike stood in the corner, propped up against the fence, and he felt guilty just looking at it. He'd promised her a weekend, two afternoons of bike-riding lessons, and he'd promised her training wheels more than a month ago, and he hadn't come through. Next to the hose he hadn't uncoiled in weeks, the bike stood there, a two-wheeler with fringe hanging from the handlebars, with stickers and decals, with a bell and a wicker basket, all the unnecessary decorative accoutrements but no training wheels, and the weekends had come and gone, and he hadn't taught her anything.

He drained his cranberry juice in one long pull and set the glass down on the kitchen counter. After he left Nina for good, he'd hire a gardener to come once a week to take care of things, he told himself. He'd get Hannah those training wheels and teach her to ride. He'd give her that weekend and every weekend that came after. He'd be a better dad once he was out of there. He'd be a better surfer. Hell, he'd be a better dentist, a better everything, once he got out. Without rinsing the glass, he left it in the sink, then went upstairs and pulled out the receipts.

He was a man with a plan, a man who wanted to be caught cheating on his wife, so he'd leave those receipts on top of the dresser, next to Nina's jewelry box, wanting her to have proof before she even clasped her watch or put on her earrings. Usually the receipts hid in his wallet for months at a time and if he saw them again, they were faded, nearly illegible surprises he unfolded and held up to the light, squinting and trying to remember where he'd been with Christy Tucker, what they did and where they did it.

He knew that the circumstances of their meeting and six-year affair made him a cad, a cheat, a rotten man and father, but he was what he was and he'd done what he'd done, and worse, he had no intention of stopping or giving her up. What he wanted was to start a new, better life. He'd even been thinking lately about asking Jesus into his heart. Who better to forgive him?

He met Christy Tucker more than seven years ago. She was the young woman sitting behind the sliding window who handed Nina the clipboard and papers to fill out when they came in for his wife's monthly checkups. Nina had been irritable since conception, it seemed to Asher, and when he thought about it now, more than a half dozen years later, she was irritable well before she became pregnant with Hannah. Nina had stopped liking him a year or two into their marriage, it seemed to him, and it was hard to like someone who didn't like you, didn't like the simplest things that came out of your mouth, comments about the weather or the coffee or the tie the newscaster was wearing. A man should be able to criticize the newscaster's wardrobe without eliciting a hateful sneer from his wife.

Nina had made her ob-gyn appointments on Fridays and insisted that Asher make a new schedule for himself. He was head dentist. It was his practice. Driving her to and from the doctor's office was the least he could do. So once a month he had accompanied Nina to her appointments. She'd wanted him only as far as the waiting room, though, and had insisted he stay on one of the plastic-covered couches when she went in to see the doctor. Asher noticed other husbands accompanying their pregnant wives inside and felt foolish and rejected waiting alone.

"I feel like a schmuck sitting there," he told her in the car on the way home.

"I don't know what to tell you, Asher. Maybe it's me, maybe it's hormones, or maybe it's us." She sighed and turned from him, looked out the passenger-side window until they reached their driveway.

Still, month after month, he accompanied his moody wife, her belly growing like his fascination with the pretty receptionist. Month after month, he kept up with Christy Tucker's changes. She wore a new pale lipstick. A ponytail. A yellow T-shirt under her white jacket. She was sunburned. She was tan. Her pert, little nose was peeling, a patch of tender red skin exposed. She wore small hoop earrings and a gold cross around her neck.

At first he avoided sitting directly across from the window and instead sat on one of the couches to the left where he could still see Christy out of his peripheral vision but didn't feel as obvious. He'd stand up and walk to the wall, where he'd pull a parenting magazine from the rack, then sit back down with a huff, glancing up at her. She shuffled papers. She typed something up. She discreetly ate noodles from a Styrofoam bowl. She answered the phone. She ran her fingers through her hair. She was polite and concerned, dealing with the other pregnant women and their husbands. Sometimes she reached through the window and touched a woman's belly, but never Nina's.

One day he looked up at Christy and was surprised to find her looking right at him. He smiled and she smiled back. The next time, he was bold, steering Nina to the couch directly in front of the window. When his wife's name was called, he helped her up off the couch, but had to stop himself from giving Nina a little shove toward the door. As she walked away— struggling in her sixth month with swollen ankles and a hand against her back—he smiled and waved at Christy before his wife was even gone.

When Nina was seven months along, he knew he'd have to make a move, so he stood at that magazine rack an extra few minutes, causing Christy to look over and notice him. He smiled at her, waved *and* said hello.

At eight months, he added, *How are you?*

And at nine months, two days from his wife's due date, Asher said, finally, *It's good to see you, Christy. It's always so good to see you. I want to see you.*

Now the receipts he pulled from his wallet were new, the information crisp and perfectly legible, black ink on yellow paper. Each one had a memory attached to it. Bentley's Bright Eyes Café: French toast, hazelnut coffee, and Christy's understandable insistence that he make up his mind. *It's been nearly seven years, Ash. I'm almost thirty,* she had said. Market Seafood and Ale: clams and garlic butter, white wine, her foot on his foot under the table. The La Jolla Inn: Christy's thin, tiny-breasted body reclining in the bathtub, the lemon soap he lathered on her back. Thinking about that bathtub and Christy in it made him hard and he adjusted himself before heading downstairs to start the coffee.

Asher believed he could go on forever like he'd been going on for all these years, with the fake business trips and long workdays, the nights out with the guys or other dentists in the office down the hall or those buddies from work who didn't exist, but he was tired of his imaginary friends and it took effort describing cities he'd never seen. He'd told Nina and Hannah about Monterey and Sacramento and San Clemente, researching landmarks and restaurants, bringing home souvenirs, silly trinkets purchased from the pharmacy around the corner.

And more, he loved Christy and wanted to marry her—he wanted to spend days with her on the beach and improve his surfing, he wanted to keep the surfboard he'd been hiding in Christy's garage in his own garage, right there next to the washer and dryer, and he wanted to wax the board on weekends or whenever he felt like it, and he wanted to wear a Hawaiian shirt out to a restaurant with a woman who wouldn't ridicule his taste, but share it.

He wanted to switch gods, goddamn it, and move to Orange County.

3

NINA TELLER was a woman who had known, on some level, that her husband had been stepping out on her from the beginning, but had been able to deny it—to her friends back East, who said they had a feeling; to her brother, who said he had a feeling too, repeatedly harping that Asher's many business trips didn't add up; to her mother, who had also said she had a feeling, and echoed Nina's brother, saying, *What dentist travels so much? Don't people come to him? Don't they bring their mouths and sit in a chair? Where does a man like that have to go?* And Nina had denied it to all of them, especially her mother, who never liked Asher despite the fact that he was a Jewish boy from a good Jewish home.

Nina herself had all sorts of feelings but had been able to stuff them down inside of her until they were barely recognizable as feelings and surfaced instead as unjustified, irrational bad moods or minor physical ailments: headaches for which she swallowed double the recommended dosage of aspirin, stomachaches for which she sipped hot tea and nibbled on dry toast. There were long naps that she needed after teaching high school English all day, so that by the time she woke up from one of them, dusk would be making its way through the curtains and it was almost time to say a real good night.

The obvious clues had been warnings from women's magazines and *The Phil Donahue Show,* the most common being a lack of interest in sex with one's spouse combined with a new attention to grooming or getting in shape. With Asher, who'd always been in shape, there was the unexplained tan, manicured nails, and the many nights he yawned dramatically, loud and obvious, before turning off the light. The way he said *I'm beat* or *Sleep well* before Nina had a chance to even kiss his cheek.

Asher had been acquiring new clothes for years, but what struck her lately was a whole immature style, which had been evolving since Hannah's birth, that Nina had mistakenly attributed to ambivalence about fatherhood or fear of aging. On his side of the closet was a mound of flip-flops on the floor that especially irked her, a rainbow mountain of rubber shoes. Hanging up, a ridiculous assortment of juvenile T-shirts with band names printed across the front and Hawaiian shirts—garish, bright-colored fabrics with flowers and palm trees and coconuts and hula girls in grass skirts that insulted her own sense of style.

One morning she'd found him at the closet taking his Beach Boys T-shirt from a hanger. "Maybe that shirt's a little young," she'd said.

"I'm thirty-four—I'm not ninety." He scowled at her, pulled the shirt over his head. He popped his hands and arms through the short sleeves, smoothed the sides down with more force than was necessary, and avoided her eyes.

Occasionally she'd find a *Surfer* magazine on his nightstand or on the bathroom counter.

"Do you want new hobbies? Is that what this is about? I'll go to the beach with you. Hannah and I will both go," she said.

"I'm not going to the beach," he said. "Who's going to the beach?"

"You're tan, Asher. How come you're so tan?"

"This is California," he said. "I sit outside on my lunch break and eat a sandwich. I point my face toward the sun—it's a good feeling."

"It's your chest that's tan," she said.

He was adamant in his denial, claiming only a mild interest in what he called *California culture*. "It's good to know what's going on. We're not in Philly anymore. We need to acclimate."

He said that his interest had to do with work, that many of his young patients who needed fillings or root canals were surfers, and that he wanted to be able to talk to them, distract them from the pain he was about to inflict with his knowledge of waves and barrels and slabs, paddling out, taking off, and *the ride*. He said it was important that he know the difference between long boards and short boards, the waves that broke in Huntington Beach versus the waves that broke in Newport or Laguna, before he came at a nervous surfer with his needle or noisy drill.

But then there was sand, and sand was harder to deny, each bit a tiny but very tangible thing left behind. Grainy in their bed, in their sheets, visible in his hair, wet, gray puddles of sand in the shower, and, she was sure, itchy sand in the crack of his ass.

And now, just an hour before her unconscious daughter, Hannah, would ride in an ambulance to the nearest hospital emergency room, Nina's denial smacked her in the face—there, on the dresser, the receipts Asher purposefully left out for her, among them one from a new restaurant in San Diego she had heard was good and told him she wanted to try, suggesting a weekend in La Jolla for the three of them, and another from a Huntington Beach Surf Shop, where he'd purchased for his girlfriend an expensive board, a year's worth of surf wax, and a fancy pink leash. This was how Nina became a woman who knew, a woman reaching into the sink and snatching the glass streaked with cranberry juice and throwing it at a philanderer's cheek—the gesture, the glass itself, as much about collision and breaking apart as the car that hit her daughter.

4

BEHIND THE wheel of his now dented Chevy Nova, Martin Kettle hollered and sobbed. Too afraid to come out and see what had become of the girl, he frantically locked the car doors, as if she were capable of rising from the street to give him a beating, as if she were not an injured girl at all but a monster with great strength.

He leaned over the stick shift, the seatbelt cutting into him, and stretched his fingers to reach the passenger-side lock. Clumsily, he tried to unclasp the belt, unsuccessful the first time and then finally getting it, cursing himself, and then turned around, flopped between the two bucket seats like a man without bones, and stretched to the back locks. Finally he situated himself again in the front seat and pounded on the lock closest to him. He wanted to die. He wished he'd run into one of the fat trees that lined the street and only hurt himself. He put his hands over his ears, his face to the steering wheel, and made his decision.

A year ago, on this very street, Martin hit a cat. He remembered the smack, the animal in the air and then landing on its feet very much alive. He remembered the cat had hissed at the car before limping off. And six months later he'd hit a dog. It was after midnight and the dog was a big puppy, a lanky Great Dane. After Martin hit him, he pulled over to the curb while having a panic attack, which he believed to be an actual heart attack—and a young man dying inside a car had every excuse to stay right where he was, in the front seat, tearing at his shirt's collar. There was little he could do for the puppy anyway, who probably would have taken a chunk out of his hand had Martin been a mentally healthier young man, a young man who might have been able to open the car door and soothe the animal during his last moments. Instead Martin sat in the car, wide-eyed and gasping. And the puppy barked and squealed and whimpered until he was quiet.

Unlike the cat, the dog and the girl felt similar at impact—something weighty pushing against something weightier, the shock of something where

15

nothing should have been, a horrible resistance where just air and space and wind should have allowed the car through.

Martin thought that the girl he hit might be dead and if she was, he planned to kill himself when he got home. There were only so many accidental acts of violence a guy could commit before he committed one purposely on himself, he was thinking. He wondered about pills or blades or driving off a cliff and played out the gruesome scenarios in his head, the logistics, the pros and cons: sleep, the ease of access, stomachaches, blood, twisted metal, and the open blue sky.

He wondered if it was possible to get enough pills from his friend Tony Vancelli, whose dad was a pharmacist and whose medicine cabinet was always stocked with colorful capsules and tablets that he handed out like bubblegum.

Up until the point when he hit the girl, Martin had been drunk, and the hours right before the accident were lost to him. Still, the impact itself was more than clear: the punch, the blow, the pressure, the sound, a body in the air, then falling to the asphalt like a doll.

He remembered going for a taco run with Tony just after midnight and talking to his friend about quitting drinking and maybe starting junior college in the fall. He remembered Tony snickering and handing him a green and white capsule that Martin gratefully accepted and swallowed dry. He remembered Tony telling him that painting houses wasn't so bad, that it wasn't what he thought he'd be doing four years out of high school but it wasn't jail either. "It's not fucking prison. At least I'm outside," Tony had said.

"I'm starting to feel that pill," Martin said.

"My mom still thinks I'm going to be a pharmacist, but fuck that," Tony said.

"Maybe you already are."

Tony laughed.

"At least you'd have access."

"I have access now."

Martin remembered the pile of tacos wrapped in paper in his lap as he headed back to Tony's place, the skill it took to unwrap and eat a taco one-handed while driving, the mushy meat and orange grease, how quickly they went down, how his lips tingled from the hot sauce. He remembered focusing, navigating the road, and Tony begging him to pull over so he could throw up in the gutter. When his friend stumbled back to the car and sat down, his stained shirt smelled sour. Martin was surprised when Tony leaned toward him, reached over the emergency brake, and snatched a taco from his crotch. "Hey man, that's mine," Martin said, but he let his buddy have it.

What Martin didn't remember were the hours in between. He didn't remember that Tony got a second wind and that the two of them listened to Janis Joplin and Jimi Hendrix and drank more beer—one bottle after another, until they were tripping over bottles. They smoked pot out of a bong Tony had fashioned out of a toilet paper roll. They played air guitar, air drums. Tony was dancing, having air sex with an air girl. Martin laughed until his stomach hurt and his eyes watered. Tony was singing into his fist one moment and then sleeping in a chair the next.

While his friend slept, Martin sat on the floor with his back against the couch and tried to read one of Tony's girlfriends' magazines, but he was too fucked up to focus; he looked at the pictures instead. Pages and pages of foxy chicks—one chick in a bikini, one in a red silky dress that might have been a nightgown, he wasn't sure, one in bell-bottom jeans and just a black bra. Then he got to what they called *instructional pages*, and maybe it was one of those same girls getting her eyebrows plucked. It was weird to see a set of eyes that close up and the tweezers coming toward them— but not nearly as sexy as seeing her in that silky nightgown-thing.

He closed the magazine and put it aside.

He watched the dawn come, the sun rising just outside the window.

He had another beer.

Sometimes he was like this, unable to sleep, an insomniac on and off since seventh grade—and he found it was better not to fight it. He sipped his beer and thought about Tony. He thought it was good that the two of them had remained friends after high school and then again he thought it wasn't so good—maybe Martin would be doing other things, impressive things, if he didn't have Tony's shit life to compare to his own shit life.

He missed his ex-girlfriend Margo, who'd left California for some college in Iowa, but he didn't miss her enough to ask for her back or to fly off to the middle of the country for a visit. "Too much cheese in Iowa," Martin had told her on the phone when she invited him out.

"It's corn," she had said—and he could have sworn he'd heard her eyes rolling.

"Too much of something, right?" he said, feeling stupid, holding the receiver away from his ear a second and giving it the finger.

He watched Tony sleep and decided that, yes, he'd register for fall classes at Manhattan Beach Junior College. He'd take a full load, in fact. He'd tell his parents that he could wait tables at one of their restaurants only on the weekends. If he went to college, even junior college, he'd damn well know which state was known for its cheese and which one was known for its corn. Margo wouldn't roll her eyes. Maybe he'd go ahead and major in business management or restaurant science—it wouldn't be so bad to go into his parents' line of work. He was thinking that it might be cool to feed people, own his own place, be the boss, the one who goes from table to table making his father's sort of small talk, when Tony farted in his sleep—a loud one. And smelly. Martin was surprised the bass of it didn't wake Tony up. He picked up the pack of matches they'd used to light the bong and ignited one, waving the flame around, waving it toward Tony's ass, which was pointed directly at him. He wished his friend would adjust himself so that his ass faced the wall.

You stink, man, Martin said. *Fuck, you* stink, *Vancelli.*

Tony thrashed around, opened his eyes, startled, and then closed them again.

Martin popped open another beer.

And another.

And then he got up from the floor and stumbled into the kitchen. On the counter sat a moldy loaf of bread and a fruit bowl with one lone apple. There was a line of busy ants on the counter, and a dense, red circle of them right in the middle of a sponge next to the sink. A perfect bull's-eye. The sink's paint was peeling and a horrible smell like old meat emanated from the drain. Martin thought he might vomit and stepped away from the sink, bumping into the fridge. He turned around and opened the freezer, where he found a nearly full bottle of vodka. That's what he needed—a little vodka and Seven Up to settle his stomach, and he'd be on his way.

Martin didn't remember leaving his friend's house, but he remembered hitting the girl. Hitting the girl was like Tony thrashing around and waking up in the chair—it was being thrust into time and space, after being unconscious.

He wasn't there and then he was.

She wasn't there and then she was.

Now Martin wanted sleep and he wanted his bed and he wanted his sheets and blankets, and he wanted to bury himself there, he wanted to close the three little windows in his studio apartment, pull the shades, and block out the light, and he wanted to escape the car, the bucket seats, the seatbelt, the windshield, and the dusty dashboard, and he wanted out now, so he pressed his foot to the gas pedal and sped away.

5

THE OXYGEN tent was a transparent canopy tucked under the mattress, a clear cube that went over Hannah's face and shoulders and covered the top half of her chest. Asher and Nina stood by her bed in the ICU, both of them red-eyed and weepy. Every now and then one of them reached inside the tent and stroked Hannah's cheek. When drops of water gathered on the tent's walls, Nina reached inside and wiped them clear.

"It's like fog. My baby hates fog," she said to Asher before she remembered that she wasn't talking to him.

He moved to touch her arm, but she stepped back, away from him. "Don't," she snapped.

Asher had bought Hannah a present at the gift shop downstairs, a ceramic lamb with fake flowers and plastic green leaves shooting out of its back, and now he held the gift out to her. It was a dumb gift—what kind of a freak lamb grows leaves out of its back? And even dumber was the gesture, holding the damn thing out, as if she could take it from his hands, hold it herself, and thank him. The leaves scratched at the oxygen tent and Hannah turned her face toward the sound, opened her eyes briefly, and then shut them.

"What's she going to do with that?" Nina said angrily. She squeezed the tissue in her fist and barely looked at him.

Asher didn't answer her. He couldn't imagine a worse thing happening on a worse day. His daughter hit by a car on her way to school and the bastard who hit her not even sticking around to make sure she was alive, to take the slightest responsibility. It was all too much. He held the lamb tight at his side, trying to hide the dark oval spots of sweat he felt growing under his arms.

There was one oversized vinyl chair with puffy armrests sitting empty in the corner of the room. A couple that wasn't on the verge of divorce might have squeezed into that chair together, shared the space, and comforted one another while their daughter slept. At the foot of the bed, a plastic rolling tray with cold metal legs held an orange plastic pitcher of ice water, fat drops of condensation slowly rolling downward.

Asher had a pair of deep cuts on his left cheek. The gashes, two distinct lines, were so red and thick and fresh that the young nurse wondered out loud if he was the one driving the car that hit Hannah. "No offense," she said. "I was just wondering. He's hurt and she's hurt, that's all."

"He's her father, her flesh and blood," Nina said, annoyed. "How could you think such a thing? Do you think I'd let that monster stand by my daughter's bed? What kind of mother would I be then? He's her father," she repeated.

"Oh," the nurse said.

"It was a hit and run," Nina said, her voice rising.

"That's terrible." The nurse arched her eyebrows, interested.

"He left her in the road like an animal," Nina continued.

"When I find him—" Asher began, but Nina cut him off.

"You?" she said with a sad laugh.

"That's right." He stood up straight, nodding vigorously.

"*Please*," she said.

"Bastard left her there," he said.

"She could have died," Nina said.

"When I find him," Asher said again, seething.

The nurse leaned down and fiddled with the dial on the IV bag before pointing at Asher's face. "What happened there? It looks like you might need stitches. You're bleeding."

"He's fine," Nina said dismissively.

The nurse looked at her, confused.

"I'm worried about my baby—that's who I'm worried about." Nina gestured at Hannah in the tent.

"I understand that," the nurse said. "But he's bleeding."

"Asher would know if he were really hurt, is what I'm saying. He'd be the first one running to a doctor." Nina looked at Asher and shook her head. She didn't care whether he stood right there and bled to death. She imagined prying the damn lamb from his grip, backing up into the hall, and aiming the stupid thing at the opposite side of his face. She'd like to split him open one more time before the day was over.

It was strange to Asher that Nina and the nurse were talking about him like he wasn't in the room. He felt like a big, dumb sweating child. He looked out the window and toward the parking lot, still holding Hannah's gift at his side. Outside, an orderly helped a very tall middle-aged man out of a wheelchair and into the backseat of a car. Unsteady on his feet, the man swayed in the wind like a drunk, and the orderly held him around the waist, swaying too. Finally the man dipped into the car and disappeared. Asher wanted to disappear. He lifted a hand to his face and felt the blood. It was drying in raised bumps. He probably looked hideous, scary—maybe even insane, not giving a shit about such an obvious injury. He turned from the window and looked at his wife, who was now leaning toward the nurse, getting a look at her nametag.

"He ran into a door. Clumsy him. Silly him. Can't see what's right there in front of him, Penny," Nina said.

The nurse turned to Asher. "You should really have your face looked at. At least get checked out. You don't look so good. A wound like that could get infected. Maybe get a tetanus shot. Do you want some water?" she asked him.

"I'm fine," Asher said.

"He's said he's fine," Nina snapped. She'd had enough of Penny and her meddling. It was her marriage. He was her husband, at least until he wasn't anymore. His face was their problem. Hannah was the one who needed attention, not her cheating asshole father.

"I'm a nurse," Penny said, stating the obvious.

"I know what you are," Nina said, wearily, but she wasn't looking at Penny. She was looking at Asher, who was physically standing there, yes— he had just let go of Hannah's hand and was now wiping the misty tent— but seemed to have mentally stepped away, out the door and down the hall and into the elevator and out to the parking lot and into the car and down the street and onto the freeway and to *her* house, whoever she was, and into her shiksa arms.

Asher sighed. He thought about putting the lamb down on the nightstand but couldn't let go. He held on tighter. He had no idea why. With his free hand he reached for Hannah's again.

Leaving Nina was something he'd been doing more and more often, leaving whatever room she was in, sometimes literally getting up and walking off, sometimes picking up a magazine or book or turning on the stereo, leaving that way, and sometimes doing what he was doing now: two feet planted firmly, but vanishing still.

Nina started to cry again. She reached into her purse and rummaged around for more tissues. Her nose was running; she could feel wetness above her lip.

Penny hurried over and opened the drawer by Hannah's bed, pulling out a box of Kleenex. She popped it open, plucked out a few sheets, and handed them to Nina. "Here," she said.

Nina gratefully took the tissue and blew her nose.

The nurse set the box of tissue on the nightstand, apparently putting their past behind them. "I'm sorry," she said.

"I know. I know you are. It's not your fault. Of course it's not you," Nina said sincerely.

Women never ceased to amaze and confuse Asher, the way they could hold one opinion of each other and then a gesture or a short, innocuous conversation could instantly change their assessment. He stared at Nina and the nurse, perplexed, imagining that soon they'd be greeting each other with overwrought hugs and cheek kisses.

"I'll just leave the three of you alone." Penny paused at the door. "Mostly she'll just sleep now, but if she wakes up and wants anything, needs anything, ring that buzzer like I showed you," she said before turning away.

"It's so cold in here," Nina stammered when the nurse was gone. "I don't want my baby girl to be cold."

Asher imagined what a better man would do in such a situation, or a man who still loved his wife, and then forced himself to do just that. He put the lamb down on the nightstand next to the box of tissue. "I'm sorry," he said. He walked over and put his arm around Nina's shoulder—and she let him.

6

MARTIN HAD been living in a studio apartment above his parents' garage rent-free for the last four years. It was one room, but it was many rooms to him, his living room and den, his bedroom and kitchen. It had even been his guest room when Tony got too fucked up to drive home and stayed over, sleeping on the floor without a pillow, with a towel for a blanket, and when Margo had lived around the corner. It was where they played house, where they made coffee or mixed margaritas from a sugary powder and fumbled through drunken sex. Now, though, the studio was the place where he was always alone, where he hid with his secret, where, when he slept, he was exactly parallel with his Chevy Nova, which was beneath him in the garage and covered in a white sheet like a dead person.

Martin thought about other people who didn't drive: blind people, people with muscular diseases who couldn't control their limbs, really old people. Lots of people used public transportation, he told himself. He took the bus or rode his bike. No one had to convince Martin to stash his car key in a drawer and leave the piece of shit Nova in his garage; he just did it.

It sat there, a neglected secret. Sometimes he kicked the car. One time he spat on the corner of the hood not covered up by the sheet. He used a hammer and the fattest nail he could find to give it two flat back tires. The fucking thing just took up space. He wished it would disappear.

Pot was a secret too. He stopped buying it from Tony and instead took the bus downtown and walked the streets, 3rd and 4th, sometimes all the way to 7th, until he found someone haggard enough to approach. Most nights he couldn't sleep, thoughts of the girl kept coming and coming, and he'd smoke the sweet joints until he passed out. Drinking was a secret now too, something he only did alone, like masturbating or picking his nose. "I don't drink anymore. And I don't smoke pot either," he lied to Tony.

"What did you do, find God?" Tony said, laughing.

Martin tried to laugh with him, but what came out was a stilted chuckle that made both of them stiffen.

"Hope we can still hang out."

"Yeah, sure," Martin said.

"You don't sound sure."

"What do you want from me, a promise?"

Tony shrugged.

"Don't be a pussy," Martin said.

"*You're* the pussy," Tony said. "No drinking, no smoking. What else is there?"

Martin's parents had owned two restaurants for the last decade and had just recently purchased a third. When Martin didn't have a shift at one of them, he started drinking vodka as soon as he woke up. He'd stay in bed all day in a ratty T-shirt and pajama bottoms with a short glass balanced on his chest, trying to rewrite his own personal history. He'd close the windows so that day looked like night, and he'd smoke pot, joint after joint or bowl after bowl, until the room filled with a sweet, thick gray smoke that burned his eyes.

Since the accident he'd complained to his mother a couple times a week about a headache that didn't exist so he could skip work and stay home. It seemed he couldn't sleep enough—eleven, twelve hours a night, waking only to pee or drink water—and then there were naps, long, three-hour binges in the afternoons that he was thankful hurried the night up.

Martin tried not to think about the girl. He tried to forget. But he knew that trying to forget was really just remembering.

His secret followed him to the shower, where he used the hottest water, where he scrubbed so hard and with so much vigor that his skin turned pink, but only the dirt came off.

He brought his secret with him to his family's breakfast table. He had decided against another bowl of cereal alone and come down from the studio because he wanted to see his parents smile at him and raise their coffee cups in hello. They knew nothing about the terrible act that now defined him; they thought he was just their son, the same morose young man he'd been since puberty.

His sister, Sandy, only played with her food. She folded the slices of bacon over so that they looked half-eaten. She spit her orange juice into her teacup when she thought no one was looking. What wouldn't she do, he wondered, to escape a calorie?

Sandy was a cheerleader and knew everyone. She knew, in fact, someone who knew someone who knew the girl who was hit by a car, so while she wasn't eating her breakfast—just changing the shape of her scrambled eggs by rearranging them on her plate, altering their mass with a quick press of her spoon that only Martin saw—she recounted the event as if she were there and saw the whole thing. She told her family that the girl's name was Hannah Teller and informed them that she was six years old and on her way to school. First grade. Kennedy Elementary. "Too little to be walking alone," she said.

"Terrible," her mother said.

Sandy told them it was trash day and reminded them that the streets on that block didn't have sidewalks. "I'm glad we live where we live. We're lucky," she said.

"It's a safe block," her mother agreed.

Sandy elaborated, telling them that the girl nearly died, that she still might die. Hannah Teller was really, really, really sick, her insides all messed up. "Organs had to be removed," she said.

"We're eating." Martin glared at his sister. "Well, some of us."

Sandy ignored him and went on. "Someone hit her and left her there. She'll probably die. That's what people are saying, anyway."

Martin's father reassured Sandy that medicine had come a long way. He reached over and patted his daughter's hand. "If she didn't die last week, she'll most likely survive," he said, confident. "Isn't that right, Emily?"

His mom nodded energetically.

Martin shifted in his chair and felt like he might break apart. He imagined his body crumbling into pieces.

"Eat something, Marty." His mother spooned scrambled eggs onto his plate. "Have some bacon," she offered.

Martin accepted the eggs but shook his head no about the bacon.

"Who would hit a little girl and just leave her there?" Sandy said.

"Horrible thing," his father said, spreading marmalade on a piece of wheat toast, dark crumbs flying.

"I overheard a couple of women at the supermarket talking, and apparently someone saw a very old man in a truck driving around erratically one block over," his mother said.

"Figures," Sandy said. "Some senile guy from Senior World snuck out with the car keys."

"What kind of car?" Martin said, trying hard to sound normal.

"A truck, Marty. I said that," his mother said. "One of those ridiculous trucks with the huge wheels. They said the man was very old, bald, wrinkled. One woman said he had a patch over one eye. Imagine, driving with such limited vision."

"Whenever I see someone in one of those trucks," his father interjected, "I think *asshole*. I think *dickhead*. I think—"

"It's a little early for that kind of talk," his mother said.

His dad shrugged, picked up his coffee cup, and took a sip.

"Anyone who drives with a patch over one eye is as bad as a drunk driver," Sandy said. "We should lock people like that up."

"We should," his mom agreed.

Martin saw then how rumors flew, how bogus information was validated and confirmed. He took a bite of his eggs and considered his mother's eyebrows—two thinly painted arcs. He considered the wrinkles above her top lip, how they gathered together when she was angry or irritated, as she was now, and how they relaxed again, like an accordion. He considered how his father's vocabulary had been changing since he and Sandy had become teenagers, how the change seemed like a pathetic attempt to go backwards and become one of them. He thought his dad looked sort of fat and dopey, sitting at the table with bacon grease around his mouth. He considered how his dad could still be scolded like a little kid. He considered his sister's clavicle, her pointy chin, and the straps of her yellow nightgown hanging from her knobby shoulders. He wondered if she'd eventually become one of those girls who was hospitalized and force-fed from a tube.

"What's going on with you, buddy?" his dad wanted to know.

Martin shook his head. There was nothing to say.

"Hey, buddy," his dad said.

He hated it when his dad called him *buddy*. Why not *son*? Or better yet, his first name.

"The new restaurant is beautiful," his mother said to him. "Wait until you see it, Marty."

"You'll love it, buddy," his dad said.

7

MARTIN TOOK the bus to the new restaurant. If his parents saw him getting off at the bus stop or wondered why his car wasn't in the lot, he'd planned to tell them that he was saving money and didn't want to spend it on gas. If they pushed it, he'd blame the squeaky brakes or transmission.

His parents wanted this third restaurant open to the public by midsummer. They planned to have a grand opening, a buy-one-dinner-get-one-free party.

Three little rooms and a tiny kitchen, it was obviously smaller than their other restaurants but in a better location, just a short block from the Manhattan Beach Pier. It was two o'clock in the afternoon and already his mom and dad were drinking gin and tonics, sipping from plastic cups that they left on counters and then frantically searched for. "Where is it? Which one's mine?" his father said, laughing, already tipsy. "I thought it was here," his mother said. "I thought I put it down right here." She was pointing to an empty spot on the counter. "Where did it go?"

They wouldn't be asking about his car this afternoon. They'd probably pass out before sunset, resting up, as they liked to call it, on the two cots they set up in the tiny room in the back of the restaurant for just that purpose before coming home.

He helped them find their drinks. It was easy to identify which one was his mom's because she often chewed her straw into an unrecognizable mess.

She thanked him and took the drink from his hands. "You smell the sea?" she said, inhaling dramatically.

"The ocean," his father said. "We're practically on top of it."

"We're going to serve up some fresh fish, that's for sure. Halibut and salmon, scallops too." His mom's voice was excited.

"I've stopped drinking," Martin lied.

"Why would you do that?" his mom asked, obviously taken aback.

"I don't like the taste," he said.

"The taste? *Please,*" his dad said. "Restaurant people are social people. You're a restaurant person, Marty. It's in your blood, buddy."

"You could always drink those sweet things, like daiquiris or strawberry margaritas," his mom suggested.

"Too much sugar," he said.

"Hmm," she said, attempting to suck something out of her mangled straw and obviously getting nothing.

Martin picked up the trash can by his feet and moved it toward her.

She plucked the straw from her glass and dropped it into the can. "Thanks," she said.

"Most parents would be happy," Martin said, putting the can down.

"We're not *most* parents," his mom said, laughing.

Martin helped them pick out tile for the kitchen, chairs and tablecloths for the main room, and suggested a piano player *without* a singer. He told them that the place was great, but too small for a singer. If someone was singing and a customer wasn't in the mood to listen or didn't like the singer's voice, he couldn't escape.

Martin considered the word *escape.*

He considered moving to Mexico or New York, where he could be a waiter, a restaurant person in someone else's restaurant.

He could go to college in another city.

He could study business or astronomy.

His parents stared at him.

"Your skin looks a little pink." His mom reached up to touch his cheek and Martin recoiled. "OK, then," she said, insulted.

"The place is too small for a singer," he said.

"You think the place should be bigger?" his dad said.

"I don't mean small," Martin clarified, although that was exactly what he meant. "I mean cozy. It's fine."

"Cozy, huh?" His mother looked around the room as if she'd never seen it before.

"Oh, god, it's fine," Martin said, feeling like he was about to cry or confess—but he kept quiet, following his parents over to a big desk in the corner, where he gathered himself together, even helping them pick out a soap dispenser from a shiny, fat catalog—one that promised to spit out a perfect circle of lather with just a tap. He voted against the seashell wallpaper his mother wanted for the women's bathroom. He admired the stoves his father had already installed.

"State of the art. It'll all be yours one day, buddy. When I die, it'll go right to you."

"To you *and* your sister," his mom said.

"That's right," his dad said.

"Don't talk about dying," Martin said. "Please."

"Let me show you the canisters and the coffeemaker," his dad said then, putting his arm around Martin, leading the way.

Martin stood there, nodding and smiling, feigning interest in every shiny thing. He thought about his secrets, the weight of them, and how that weight was sure to double and triple, how he felt it in his arms and shoulders and back, how he was certain it would one day break him. He thought about his sister turning into nothing—surely soon she'd be just air and a set of clacking teeth. He had the urge to take off his shoes and socks, to leave them in the center of his parents' new restaurant, and walk away. He wanted to take off his shirt too, and his jeans, his underwear. He wanted to run naked out the door and down to the beach. He would take the sand quickly, and when he reached the water, he'd wade right in and keep going, ignoring its pressure to hold him back, until the water was deep enough to take him under, and then he'd swim out, mile after mile, until there was no going home, until he lost his opportunity to decide.

"You sure you won't join us for one little drink, Marty?" His mom frowned, disappointed.

"We're celebrating," his dad said, trying to lighten the mood. "Smart purchase, don't you think?"

"Yeah," Martin said.

"What's wrong with you, buddy?" His dad lowered his voice. "You don't seem like yourself."

"And your skin is pink. It's so pink," his mom said.

8

ONCE INSIDE the mall, Martin headed to the food court, where he ordered a Coke and nachos with extra jalapeños. He put his food down on a little round table, eased himself into a plastic chair, and thought about buying a gift for the girl. It was eleven a.m., a Wednesday, and the shopping center was mostly quiet. Faint music came from speakers he couldn't see. The smell of popcorn and pizza and egg rolls permeated the air. Every few feet sat huge planters with trees in them that Martin had always assumed were real, but now, up close, he realized they were fake. The Eyeglass Hut and Pretzel Palace were to his right and KC Records and Books to his left, and a shoe store directly across from him.

A couple teenage girls obviously cutting class stood just inside the shoe store and Martin watched them as he ate. The taller girl held up a rust-colored go-go boot—the kind Margo used to wear—and turned it over to check out the price tag on the bottom, and shrugged. She kicked off her own shoe to try it on. The shorter girl was chewing gum, nodding enthusiastically. A big pink bubble covered half of her face.

A security guard eyed Martin as he passed by, which made him feel as though everyone knew what had happened, what he'd done, even strangers at the mall. Martin looked down at his food, the orange cheese already hardening in front of him. When the guard was out of view, he pulled the tiny bottle of vodka from his pants pocket and poured the last of it into his Coke. He ate the chips and cheese and jalapeños, one fat ring after another—including the seeds he usually avoided—until his mouth felt scorched. He resisted the urge to touch the fake green leaves to his right and tried not to cry. He was always trying not to cry these days and felt like a pussy. He watched the tall girl walk around the shoe store in both boots, pausing a minute to check herself out in the long mirror. The girl with the gum was talking to a very fat guy behind the counter, flirting, tossing her hair over her shoulder and blowing those bubbles, keeping the poor loser occupied while the tall girl made her way out of the store in her new boots.

31

Martin looked around to make sure no one was watching him, then pulled a plastic leaf from the tree and stuck it in his pocket. He took a last sip of his Coke and got up from the table. He knocked his tray against the lip of the bin and watched his trash slide, deciding that buying a gift for the girl was the least he could do.

At Spencer Gifts, Martin headed to the aisle with the stuffed animals. Bears and rabbits and monkeys, a unicorn and a zebra, all of them ultimately reminding him of roadkill, so he went to the next aisle where he found a row of birthday cards and wrapping paper, a shelf of silky ribbons that were already tied into big bows. At the end of the aisle he found a snow globe that he liked, with two bundled-up kids and a snowman between them. The kids wore matching blue parkas, snow boots, and mittens—one kid holding a carrot. When Martin shook the clear plastic bubble, snowflakes fell and the boy's arm rose to place the carrot on the snowman's face.

His buzz was wearing off, but his lips and tongue still tingled from the jalapeños. He got in line with the snow globe and stared at the head of the old man in front of him. He could see the thick gutters where a comb had made its way through the man's white hair and a birthmark or an age spot shaped like Nevada on his neck.

Martin thought that maybe he'd move to Nevada or some other state where no one knew his name.

He tried to remember if he put the orange juice back in the fridge before he left his parents' house.

He hoped Hannah Teller didn't die.

He wished the cashier would hurry up.

He imagined telling his parents that the line at the registrar's office was impossibly long or promising to go to trade school.

He wondered what else the teenage boot-thieves would steal today. Maybe they'd go to the multiplex and slither from movie to movie until it grew dark outside.

He wondered if maybe the fat shoe salesman was aware that the girls were stealing from the store and didn't care. He thought it was possible to be that lonely.

Martin stood in line, waiting, shaking the snow globe, and watched the white flakes fall on the tiny boys inside.

9

HER GRANDPARENTS in New York sent a card and a pair of soft pajamas, blue cotton with little white flowers. Her grandmother in Philadelphia sent a blanket that she knit herself. There was a trampoline her uncle had sent, which Nina kept in the box, put up on a shelf in the garage, and didn't mention to Hannah. There were brownies and chocolate chip cookies from neighbors that Nina shared with the nurses. There was a round *Get Well Soon* card as big as a globe with every first grader's signature. Some kids sent individual cards wishing her well. Eddie Epstein sent cards two weeks in a row. Nurse Penny, in an effort to cheer Hannah up, hung a corkboard on the wall so the cards could be displayed. Nina gushed a thank-you to Nurse Penny and tacked the cards to the board with colorful pins.

Her mom brought things from home: Hannah's stuffed tiger, a favorite pillow, and a family picture of the three of them at the entrance to Disneyland that she'd snatched from Hannah's bedroom dresser. Watching the hospital room morph into her bedroom only made Hannah feel worse, as if she were never going home.

When Hannah was especially cranky, she asked about her dad, and Nina would change the subject or walk over to the board and point out how popular Hannah had apparently become. There were more gifts and toys and things waiting for her when she got home, her mom said. There were books Nina read to Hannah before she left in the evenings. Hannah's favorite, *Nobody's Boy,* was translated from French, and had appeared, like some of the other gifts, out of nowhere. Mysterious paper doll sets and coloring books and a snow globe without a card or note attached.

Nina suspected that Nurse Penny bought Hannah the mystery gifts and didn't want credit because she didn't want to play favorites or let on how much Hannah meant to her. Or maybe it was even Dr. Roth, who looked upset when he told Nina and Asher that their daughter would be more prone to infection without a spleen. "She might be sickly," he said.

"Sickly? That's a terrible word," Nina told him.

"Maybe it is," he said. "But she might be fine. We'll have to wait and see."

Dr. Roth said Hannah was a good girl, a mature girl. Penny said she was six going on twenty-six. They said she was smart enough to become a doctor herself one day.

After the first rough week, Hannah's improvement was quick and steady. The oxygen tent disappeared—one night she fell asleep inside of it and the next morning it was gone. The rolling tray that had stood at the foot of the bed now stood by her side and she could pull it to her chest at will. She poured her own water into a cup when she was thirsty. She watched TV, ate Popsicles, requested a chocolate milk shake, and wanted her hair washed.

Today Dr. Roth stood by her bed, obviously pleased. Penny was pleased too, smiling, standing just behind him. Her parents, like a pair of boxers, stood in opposite corners of the room.

"You'll have a story to tell the kids at school," the doctor said without looking up. He had just finished listening to Hannah's heart and taking her pulse and was now writing something down on a clipboard.

"It's a *mitzvah*—what you've done for Hannah," Asher said, stepping forward, moving closer to her bed. He had a patch of gauze taped to his cheek and his hair was a curly mess.

"It's my job," the doctor said.

"You're modest," Asher said.

Nina stepped forward too. "I don't know what I would have done without her."

"*We*," Asher corrected her. "What *we* would have done."

"There is no *we*," Nina said quietly, just for Asher, but Hannah heard and so did the doctor and the nurse too, who looked up at the doctor, raising her eyebrows.

"I've been meaning to ask what happened to your head," Dr. Roth said.

"I ran into a door." Asher reached up to touch his face.

"You see how bruised the area is, Dr. Roth?" the nurse offered.

Nina shot Penny a look.

"I need to be more careful," Asher said.

"You do," Nina agreed.

Dr. Roth nodded.

"I've been preoccupied," Asher admitted.

"I'll say," Nina said.

"Well . . ." Dr. Roth said, obviously uncomfortable.

"So . . ." the nurse said.

"So . . ." Dr. Roth said.

Then everyone was quiet—Hannah, watching the IV bottle's slow drip, her mother's painted lips in a tight line, her father's arms crossed, a vein on his neck blue enough to see.

Finally, Penny said, "What's a *mitzvah*?"

1 0

MARTIN STOOD in the elevator with his back against the wall, watching the numbers light up. He was heading to the children's ward on the sixth floor. An orderly with a shock of bright red hair and an empty gurney stood across from him. Martin's hands shook and he could feel the sweat at the back of his neck, but when the orderly nodded hello, Martin forced himself to make a sound. "Hey," he said.

The orderly leaned down and straightened the white sheet on the gurney and centered the tiny pillow.

"Good work you do," Martin said awkwardly.

The orderly shrugged.

"Helping sick people, I mean," Martin continued.

"I'm not a doctor," the orderly said.

"Yeah, I know, but still."

The elevator stopped on the third floor and the doors dinged open and the orderly stepped out, pulling the gurney behind him. "Catch you later," he said as the doors closed.

I certainly hope not, Martin thought to himself, grateful when the elevator began moving again and for the few seconds alone. On the sixth floor, he stood outside the elevator doors a moment and tried to compose himself, reminding himself to breathe. He took one step toward the nurses' station and then another. And once his mouth opened and the words poured out, it was surprisingly easy.

"I'm a friend of the Teller family," he told the nurse. She was old, at least sixty, he thought, and her white hat was pinned to her stiff, white hair. She was kind, listening sympathetically as he stood there lying to her. "Terrible thing that happened to Hannah. I'm a good friend of the family. I'm *like* family." He paused, standing there awkwardly. "It's been an ordeal for all of us."

The nurse nodded kindly. She adjusted her hat, pulled a bobby pin out, and then reinserted it. "You want to see her?"

"Yes," he said. "Please."

And she pointed him down the hall. "Room 614," she said. "Visiting hours are almost over. Better hurry."

"OK."

"She'll probably sleep right through your visit."

"That's great," he said.

The nurse cocked her head. She picked up a chart from the desk and looked at it.

"I mean, I'm glad she's resting. It'll be good to see her rest."

"Last door on the left," she said, without looking up.

He stopped midway and sat down on a bench. He watched orderlies wheeling dinner trays out of rooms, a couple girls about his age dressed up like candy canes, and nurses with their Dixie cups of pills come and go. He decided to move to the lounge, where he had a good view of the happenings in the hall but wouldn't be as conspicuous. He heard televisions and he heard voices, visitors saying *good night* and *we'll see you tomorrow* and *rest up now*. He picked up a newspaper from the coffee table and tried to read about Nixon's latest lie, but he couldn't focus. An old man and a young woman sat on the couch directly across from him and he tried to avoid eye contact. When the old man started weeping into his hands, Martin felt his own eyes welling up and decided he'd had enough. He stood up from the couch and decided to go back to the bench.

When the last TV was turned off and the hall was finally empty, he slinked down the hall and stood outside Hannah's room for a few minutes and watched her sleep. Satisfied that she was out for the night, he opened the door and slipped inside like a thief. He carefully set the snow globe on the nightstand beside her bed. She was smaller than he remembered, pale with long dark hair fanned out against the pillow, an IV in her little hand and some machine beeping to the left of her. One of her legs was suspended in midair. There was a rolling table and an orange plastic pan that was shaped like a quarter moon. A nasty, meaty smell emanated from under a silver lid. A television hung high in a corner. There was a curtain separating Hannah from another patient. He heard the other patient mumble something in her sleep. And he heard Hannah's snore, so slight it might be called breathing. He approached Hannah's bed and stared. The metal bars pulled up around the mattress made Martin think of jail, where he knew he belonged. He had the urge to release the bars and whisper something in her ear, an apology or confession, but just as he was leaning down, a nurse entered the room. He straightened up and backed away from the bed.

"Hi," she said, smiling. She wasn't the nurse who'd greeted him earlier but a younger, pretty nurse with silky skin and a perfect smattering of freckles across her cheeks.

"I know visiting hours are over," he said defensively.

"Take it easy," she said. "I'm not a good enforcer." She was still smiling and the lines around her eyes told Martin she wasn't as young as he'd thought, probably near thirty.

"Good thing," he said, loosening up.

"When you love someone, you should get to visit them whenever." She took the thermometer out of its sleeve and shook it. "How are you?" she asked. "You look a little peaked."

"Peaked?"

"Worn out, sort of tired," she said. "I'm Penny," she offered. "How do you know Hannah? Are you her uncle?"

He wondered if she was suspicious or just friendly, but didn't want to stick around to find out. "Really good friend of the family, *like* family." He moved toward the door.

"Oh," she said.

"I was just leaving," he said, stepping into the hallway.

"Wait, what's your name?" she said. "Who are you?" she wanted to know, but he was already walking away.

Back in his apartment he drank vodka and orange juice. He thought about Penny the nurse and beat off. He drank some more, popped a frozen pizza in the oven, and while he waited for it to cook, he beat off again. When he ran out of orange juice, he mixed the vodka with fruit punch. While he drank, he thought about how little it helped, really. There was always a guilty, anxious Martin waiting for him when he sobered up, and after the last joint was lit and the bowls had all been sucked empty, there was always his dry mouth, always his belly to feed, and always the persistent images of the crash itself—vivid enough to startle him all over again. There was always the impact, the sound and sensation, the girl's limp body by the curb, and his decision: his own heavy boot on the gas pedal.

Bay Shore Hospital was more informal than Martin had expected, loose with the rules. It wasn't just Penny the nurse who wasn't a good enforcer. Visiting hours were from ten to two and four to seven every day, but anxious relatives and friends could be found at all hours roaming the halls, bent over the nurses' station, complaining or just chatting, or sitting by a patient's bed. Even though there were signs posted around the hospital stating that kids weren't allowed, Martin had seen the same obnoxious pair several days in a row, obviously brother and sister, playing cards on the floor. They thought they owned the place, sitting with their legs spread out in the hall, and they were loud when they won or lost, like grown men at a sporting event.

Martin made up his own rules about going to the hospital, and one of them was to shave and shower before a visit, which wasn't really a visit, more like a slinking around, a skulking. Another was to always dress nice, so maybe people wouldn't recognize the skulking. He wore button-down shirts and pressed slacks, the clothes his mother bought him to wear when the new restaurant finally opened. Martin felt that it was important to show respect to the sick. Also, as much as he was drinking these days, he promised himself that he'd never show up drunk to the hospital. He didn't want to get kicked out and he didn't want to be discovered. He needed his wits about him. He wanted to slip the presents, the kaleidoscope, that French novel *Nobody's Boy* that he'd loved himself as a kid, a baby doll with blue, blinking eyes, inside Hannah's room without waking her up.

The last thing he wanted to do was to scare her.

Last week Martin was sitting in the lounge, waiting for Hannah's visitor—a man he assumed was her father—to leave, and for Hannah herself to fall asleep so he could drop off the paper dolls he'd bought. The door to the room across the way was open and Martin could see in. He watched a little boy with a newspaper in his lap, reading aloud to a sick old man. More kid visitors, he was thinking. What about the rules? What about the red sign that said *No Exceptions*? Didn't kids carry all sorts of germs? Didn't they play with bugs and eat dirt? Martin could see the boy's lips moving and the old man nodding his head. He watched as the old man lifted the oxygen mask off of his face to shout, "Nixon is a lying jackass!" The man was wagging his finger in the boy's face. "I told your mother he's a liar. Tricky Dick!" the man shouted and then started to cough and struggle. The boy shot up from his chair, letting the newspaper fall to the floor, and tried to calm the old man, rubbing his arm, and when that didn't work, he tried to pry the oxygen mask from the man's clenched hand. The old man pulled away from the boy and continued shouting. "It's not OK! How the hell can you say it's OK? What do you know? You're eleven!" he shouted, before letting the mask snap back against his face. He was taking deep, almost violent breaths, sucking in air, and Martin was thinking that some things needed to be said out loud, like condemnations or apologies, some things a man needed to say and he would skip breaths to say them.

Finally, Hannah's father came down the hall and stopped at the elevator and pushed the button. He ran a hand through his dark curly bangs, pushing them off his face, revealing a red scar on his cheek. *Ouch*, Martin thought, *what happened there?* When the elevator dinged and opened, the man stepped inside, disappearing behind the doors. Martin grabbed his bag and made his way down the hall to Hannah's room, hoping she was sleeping and alone. She wasn't sleeping, but having her blood drawn. He stood in front of the room across the hall and tried to look innocuous, staring at his watch and glancing down the hall, like he was waiting for someone. Out of his peripheral vision, he saw Hannah extending her arm, making a fist. He saw the yellowish ends of the tied tourniquet, and then the vial filling up with the darkest red.

He went down to the cafeteria and got himself a cinnamon roll and a cup of coffee. There were long empty benches against the walls with long thin tables in front of them. He sat in the far corner on one of the benches and avoided eye contact with the few people eating dinner. It was seven p.m. and the place was mostly empty. He knew there was another, better cafeteria on the third floor, one that served fresh food instead of the prepackaged stuff and day-old pastries that they served here, but he preferred this one because it was usually quiet. He pulled his cinnamon roll apart and stuck a long sweet piece in his mouth. It wasn't so stale, but warm and buttery, just what he needed. He opened a packet of sugar and poured it into his coffee, added cream, and blew into it before taking a sip.

Penny the nurse was setting down her tray on one of the tables, slipping herself into a seat across the room. She took the paper napkin in front of her and spread it out across her lap, like people did with cloth napkins at his parents' restaurants. She had long, dark red hair in a thick ponytail that fell across her shoulder, pouty, puffy lips, and eyes so bright green he could see their color even from where he sat several feet away. He thought she was pretty, but tried not to meet those green eyes. She was staring, though, so hard that he thought he might have spilled something on himself. He brushed his shirt off and tried to ignore her. In addition to catching him that one time in Hannah's room, he knew that she'd seen him on Hannah's floor more than once and was sure that she had to be suspicious. Maybe she'd tell somebody and get him arrested. Now she was smiling right at him. It made him nervous, her smile, and he pretended not to see it. He wished he'd brought something to read. He thought about taking the paper dolls out of the bag for something to look at, but decided that he'd look like a weirdo, sitting alone and looking at dolls.

He remembered he still had the brochure from the junior college his parents had left on his pillow. It was folded up and crammed in his wallet. He took out his wallet and opened it, unfolded the brochure, and spread it out next to the cinnamon roll. He stared hard at the list of classes offered, though he had the list memorized already: English 101, 102, and 103; Math 101, 102, and 103; history, and so on. Martin thought it sounded a lot like high school and wanted to do something new, go somewhere else; he wanted to start over and forget.

He glanced up from the brochure and the nurse was still staring. She raised her cup in a sort of hello that startled Martin, his own cup slipping from his fingers and splashing coffee onto his shirt. He zipped his jacket to cover up the spot, then stood and headed to the exit. He turned around one last time to look at the nurse and she was still smiling. She gave him a little wave. He thought she was probably crazy.

When he returned to Hannah's door, she wasn't there. He stood outside her room for several minutes and then made his way to the nurses' station, where he found the green-eyed nurse who didn't look quite as crazy as she had downstairs. "Hey," he said.

"You're the guy who ran away without giving me his name."

"Yeah, I . . ."

She motioned for him to come closer. "It's OK," she said. "Charlotte's doing rounds. She'll be giving little Leon his antibiotics. Leon likes to talk after taking his meds, so Charlotte won't be back for a while."

Martin smiled and stepped closer to the nurses' station.

"You're the guy who keeps bringing presents for Hannah and doesn't want to be seen," the nurse said quietly, looking around, making sure no one heard her. "Don't worry. I've noticed you and haven't said a word about it. I know you're harmless. I'm a terrific judge of character. You look very trustworthy—a little sad, maybe, but not dangerous," she said, nodding.

I was right, she's crazy, Martin thought. But she didn't look crazy. She looked pretty and sweet.

"My sister knows someone who goes to school with Hannah. One of her good friends," he lied.

The nurse nodded.

"Where is she?" Martin said, trying not to stare at the nurse's pretty lips.

"I'm sorry," she said, leaning forward, "but the poor girl's back in intensive care. I used to work in intensive care."

"What happened?"

"I don't work there anymore. I was transferred."

"No, I mean with Hannah."

"Oh," she said. "Of course. You don't care about my work." She laughed.

"What happened to Hannah?" he asked again.

"Fever spike—we think it's some sort of infection. We've been running tests for days."

He looked down at his shoes and thought about giving the nurse the paper dolls for Hannah, but decided that he'd already risked enough just talking to her.

"I gotta go," he said.

"What's your name? I can tell the family you came by."

"Never mind," he said.

"I won't tell the family. Obviously, you've been giving gifts anonymously. What was I thinking? You don't want me to tell the family. I won't tell them. I haven't told them yet, and I won't. You don't seem like a lunatic," she said.

"Thanks, I guess," he said. Then, "I'll come back when the girl gets better."

"What's your name?" she said, again. "Hey, hey," she called after him, but he was already walking away again, heading to the elevator, and pretending he didn't hear her.

11

WHEN HANNAH'S temperature suddenly spiked, the doctors and nurses seemed to morph into other people. Aggravated and impatient, they rushed around her bed with jobs to do. Their movements were quick, setting up a new IV line, taking her pulse with extra pressure to her wrist. There wasn't time for pleasantries or the compliments Hannah had grown accustomed to. They were busy and stern professionals. Hannah didn't feel so smart or mature anymore. She was crying like the baby she was. Dr. Roth leaned in close enough for her to feel his hot breath on her hot face, for her to smell whatever pungent thing he had eaten for lunch. "Where does it hurt?" he asked, speaking slowly, spacing out his words.

"Everywhere," she answered.

"Can you be more specific?" he wanted to know.

Back in ICU, she was sweating and hallucinating. The bed was on fire. The doctor was her father. The nurse was a waitress. The IV bottle was a glass of milk.

"Where does it hurt?" he asked again.

"I don't know," she said.

Test after test.

Drink this chalky mixture. Pretend it's a milk shake.

X-rays.

Handfuls of colorful pills.

That's right, swallow them all. No, no, all of them.

Come on, Hannah.

Be a good girl.

Hold your breath.

More tests.

Stay still.

Don't move.

Do you want to get better?

You want to get better, don't you?
I don't know what she wants.

Someone changed her sheets every hour. Someone dabbed at her face with a cool cloth. Her parents visited her individually, her mom during the days and her dad in the evenings, or maybe it was the other way around—she couldn't be sure of anything. Her mom sang to her, pausing to shake pills into her palm, to tip back her head and swallow them. Her mom sighed and said, *Who did this to you?* Her mom said, *Where is he?* The pills her mom had swallowed kicked in, but her anger and resolve stayed strong. *One day I'll find him,* she said, slurring her words. Her mom stared at the mute TV suspended in the air in the corner of the room. Her mom closed her eyes and curled up in a chair. Someone begged Hannah to eat, spooning salty broth into her mouth. Someone rubbed cold lotion on her shoulders and chest. Someone fanned her with a magazine. Her dad's eyes were red. He'd gotten a haircut, his curls flat now and pressed to his scalp. He wasn't wearing his wedding ring. He'd brought a blonde friend along. Maybe the gash on his cheek was closing up, healing as it should have been healing, or maybe time was moving backwards and the wound was opening up, big and red again, about to swallow her. Eddie Epstein and his mother stopped by or maybe they didn't. After Penny checked her temperature, she smoothed Hannah's hair away from her forehead. Another nurse fed her slivers of ice. Someone slinked in. Someone picked up the snow globe from the nightstand. Someone shook the snow globe in front of Hannah's face before putting it back down. Someone called her name. Someone called her name again. Someone pulled up a chair and sat down by her bed. Someone said he was sorry. Someone was weeping. Someone was blowing his nose. Someone was holding his elbows, rocking back and forth. Someone stood up and looked at her. Someone said he was sorry one more time. Someone walked away.

12

NINA THOUGHT about him at night, but sometimes during the day too. Some days every man in every truck at every red light was *the criminal*. A man without a heart. She'd look over, stare into his front seat, see his hands on the steering wheel, and feel certain there was an empty space in his chest where his heart should have been. She'd look away as the light turned green, and by the time her foot hit the gas, she'd be imagining a pocket of air surrounded by red flesh, a place where he could store his cruelty.

Nina was alone in bed, thinking about him, and Asher was in bed with Christy, thinking about him too. Asher thinking, *That man hit my Hannah and left her in the road to die.*

Asher and Christy had probably just said a prayer. They might have just had sex. Either way, Asher would start thinking about him. He'd think about how he wanted to punish him, what he'd like to do to him if he ever found out who he was.

Asher and Nina spent an increasing amount of time wondering who he was and what he looked like. They wanted a face and a name, someone to be accountable.

Asher dreamt of a faceless man in a bathtub and he killed him with a baseball bat. He talked about the man to Christy, saying, *That fucking man drove away.*

"Don't say fuck," Christy said. "I mean, don't say the *f*-word. Let's pray."

And they'd pray. It wasn't just a thing they did before dinner. It was after every argument. It was on Sunday afternoons and evenings, in preparation for the new week ahead. Christy wanted to pray for the man who'd hit Hannah, but Asher refused. "You pray for him alone," he said. "A human being stops his car," he told her.

On Nina's particularly bad days, it wasn't just men in trucks, but every man in the grocery store. He was the old man reaching for the eggs. He was the young man pulling cereal from a shelf. He was the boy with bad skin and braces bagging her groceries. He was the middle-aged man smiling at her in line. She wanted to yell at all of them. *How could you have left her there?* she wanted to scream.

13

THE NEW doctor arrived, and he was young and lean, wearing jeans under his white jacket, with a degree from Stanford. He insisted they both call him Dr. Seth, and he was smarter than the rest, her mom whispered in Hannah's ear. When he entered the hospital room, Nina nearly jumped up from the chair and smiled like she hadn't smiled in weeks. She was giddy, a girl, Hannah thought. She was sucking in the little bit of stomach she had, and straightening her skirt, and Hannah hoped her mom didn't forget to breathe.

Although the last three tests had come back negative, Dr. Seth believed that Hannah's liver was abscessed, which meant she'd undergo yet one more test. She'd have to drink another chalky ten ounces of what the technician called a milk shake, and she'd have to lie there very still while the machine took pictures of her insides.

"It's most likely in a place we can't see—a spot the scans haven't picked up," Dr. Seth said, demonstrating on her mom's hand. "Here's what we saw in our first X-rays," he said, "and here's the underside." He flipped Nina's hand over in his own and looked at her blushing face. She shyly pulled her hand away.

"We're so lucky you're here," her mom said, fixing her hair, poofing it up with her fingers.

"We'll know definitively this afternoon. I'll find out what's wrong and then I'll fix it." His voice was deep and confident.

"Hear that, Hannah? We'll know soon," she said.

In the middle of the night the rushing nurses told Hannah nothing about what they knew. They talked to each other in hushed tones. One of them inserted a new IV into her hand. Two orderlies lifted her from the bed onto a gurney and hurried her down the hall and into the elevator, where, despite the excitement, she watched the numbers light up and her eyelids grew heavy.

. . .

When Hannah woke up there was a thick tube snaking out of her waist, poking out from under the sheet and traveling across the room. It spewed the infection into a huge machine that seemed alive with its chirping, blinking, and constant hum. Dr. Seth explained that it was cleaning Hannah out, which made her wonder what kind of a girl she was—just what kind of girl gets dirty on the inside?

14

MARTIN WANTED to go back to the hospital and tell Penny his name. He wanted to bring her a plate of lasagna and a cup of spumoni ice cream from one of his parents' restaurants. He wanted to ask her questions and get to know her, but mostly he wanted information about Hannah and her progress. He wondered if an abscessed liver could kill a girl.

It had been nearly a week since the last time he'd hurried away from Penny. Now he stood at the nurses' station trying to get the chubby nurse's attention. He could have sworn that she'd spun around in her chair when she saw him coming down the hall. She was talking on the phone with her back turned to him, laughing, obviously flirting with whoever was on the other end.

What about the sick people on your floor? Someone might be dropping dead this very minute. Penny would never ignore someone, he thought.

She twirled the phone cord around her finger and said, "You didn't, did you? You did!" and then she laughed. Martin watched her fat finger going white. He shuffled around in his shoes. He sighed. He coughed. He cleared his throat.

"I gotta go," the nurse said into the phone. She hung up the receiver and spun the chair around, staring at him. "Can I help you?" she said, all put-out.

"Is Penny working tonight?" he asked.

"Nope." She stood up and snatched some charts from a shelf. "What do you want with Penny?"

"Do you know when she'll be back?"

"She's working tomorrow—the night shift."

"How's Hannah Teller?"

"Are you her brother?

"A friend of the family."

"She's still in ICU."

"I'm sorry," Martin said.

Something buzzed—two lights at once were flashing red. "I gotta go," the nurse said, turning and rushing off, her ample hips teeter-tottering away.

After peering in and seeing Hannah with the woman he assumed was her mother and a young doctor at her bedside, Martin went to the ICU waiting room and sat down. No one was there—the many couches empty, the TV on but so quiet you couldn't hear what the newscaster was saying. Damn it, fuck it. He wanted to die. His miserable sister was right. Hannah wasn't going to survive. She was still in ICU. Wasn't that where they took people right after a horrible fucking trauma, like when they were shot or had a heart attack? She'd been doing so well. He was a murderer. He was a fucking killer. A monster. He knew it. He'd known it all along. He'd known it from the beginning, he'd felt it, and now it was happening.

He'd been sitting there, berating himself for nearly an hour when he saw Hannah's mother coming down the hall with her purse over her arm, wiping her eyes with a tissue. The young doctor was next to her and they were heading toward the elevator. The doctor held a clipboard at his chest and spoke to her out of the side of his mouth. She was nodding as he talked, agreeing. Martin thought they knew each other better than they should and wondered where Hannah's father was.

Martin tried to obey his hospital rules, but the night after he'd seen Hannah's mom and the doctor go into the elevator together, he broke one. After drinking three beers alone in the park, he showed up at the nurses' station. He'd had a roast beef sandwich, an apple, and half a bag of potato chips, and he'd sipped the beers slowly, over the course of a couple hours, so he wasn't really drunk, but mildly buzzed, which ended up giving him the confidence to approach Penny, to ask her things. He'd walked down the bright hallway and popped a mint in his mouth.

"What's your name? I'm not talking to you until you tell me your name," she said.

"I'm Marty Kettle," he said.

"You're pretty like a girl, Marty Kettle," she said, softening.

"I'm a mess," he said.

"You know Hannah, don't you?" she said.

"I don't know her," he said. "My sister used to sit with her at lunch sometimes, that's all."

"Then why—" she began.

He lowered his voice and looked at her solemnly. "I live a few houses away from her. And I heard the whole thing," he tried. But he could see it wasn't enough.

Penny's arms were crossed against her chest.

"OK," he said. "You want the truth?"

"Yes," she said.

"I have another sister, I mean, I *had* another sister," he said, and as he lied, his eyes welled up. "She'd never eat and no one said anything. Not my mom or dad—it was like they couldn't see her. And I didn't help. And then she died in a car wreck."

"I'm so sorry," Penny said, looking like she meant it.

"It's been very hard," he said. "She and I were close. I feel like I lost my best friend."

Penny uncrossed her arms, dropped them to her sides. "I don't think Hannah likes the snow globe because, you know, she grew up here, by the beach," Penny told him.

"Oh," he said.

"I guess she doesn't care about snow."

Penny told him that Hannah's parents had mostly given up on finding the driver, who they'd heard was a very old man. "He probably couldn't see where he was going," she said. "Old men get cataracts."

"Yeah."

"Old women too."

"All of us," he said.

She nodded and stared at him hard. "Their eyes cloud up and they can barely see."

15

SHE'D BEEN hooked up to the machine that was draining the abscess from her liver for just two days and her fever disappeared and her cheeks were pink and her appetite was back. She ate plates of unrecognizable meat and the palest, softest vegetables and blue Jell-O or red Jell-O and little cups of ice cream that she opened herself, pulling the tab. They had moved her downstairs to the floor where the kids were just sick, not necessarily dying, her mother said.

"Katy had her tonsils taken out yesterday and she's going home today—isn't that right, Katy?" Nina pulled the curtain that separated the two girls to one side and popped her head around.

There was a fruit cup and a carton of milk on the tray in front of Hannah. A stale roll left over from lunch and a little ball of butter in a glass dish. She used her fingers to pick up a chunk of pineapple and ate it.

Nina turned back to Hannah and let the curtain fall behind her. "Katy can't say much just yet, but she was nodding. I imagine she's still in pain. Poor her."

Poor me, Hannah thought.

"Very nice girl, though—sweet as sugar," she continued. "Billy down the hall had a terrible case of the flu—I met his mother in the elevator."

Hannah used her fingers again to pick up a slippery slice of peach.

"Use your fork," her mom said.

Hannah ignored her. She wanted her mom to stop talking about the other sick kids and focus on her—she was the one who nearly died, not Katy with her sore throat or Billy with his flu.

When a nurse brought Katy a wheelchair, Hannah leaned over and whispered in her mother's ear. "Why does she need a wheelchair if she can walk on her own?"

Nina explained that leaving in a wheelchair was hospital policy and that when Hannah was discharged she too would sit in a wheelchair and be pushed out to the parking lot. She looked at Hannah's leg then, and

Hannah followed her mother's eyes and looked at her leg as well, and there it was, still in traction, still hanging there. They looked at the exposed toes that Hannah still couldn't wiggle. Her mom gave her a weak smile that neither of them believed and then they sat in silence, listening to the sounds on the other side of the curtain. A drawer opened and closed. A suitcase snapped shut. Someone coughed. The nurse said, "Easy now, careful, sweetie. That's right." They heard Katy situate herself in the wheelchair she didn't need, and the squeak one of the toys made as someone gathered it in his or her arms.

Then they were leaving, all of them, the nurse pushing Katy, and her cheerful parents following, stuffed animals and dolls spilling from their folded arms.

"Get well soon, Hannah," the mother said.

"Take care—both of you," said the father, his eyes on Nina.

And the toy, wherever it was, squeaked one last time.

Although they hadn't had time to bond or even talk to each other, Hannah felt abandoned. When Katy turned around at the door and waved good-bye, Hannah kept her hands under the blanket and barely mustered up a smile.

"When do *I* get to go home?" she whined as soon as they were gone.

"Dr. Seth needs to remove the tube first. You wouldn't want to go home with that, would you?" Her mom looked over at the machine.

Hannah said nothing. Of course she didn't want to take the horrible thing home.

They were quiet for several minutes until her mom said, "The kids at school were worried about you and they're all so relieved you're getting better. Oh, and I almost forgot," she said, excited. "Everyone in your class signed another card." She reached down into her bag and pulled out a big envelope, handing it over.

On the front of the card, monkeys swung from trees, and on the inside, it said *Get Well Soon. We want you up and monkey-ing around.* Hannah looked at the signatures and messages, spending an extra moment on Eddie Epstein's words. He'd written *I like you* or *I bite you,* Hannah couldn't be sure.

When she was finished reading the card, she handed it back to her mom, who immediately pinned it to the board alongside the others.

"Who brought you this?" Her mom picked up the snow globe and gave it a shake. "I love these things," she said. "The snow reminds me of Philly. Where did this thing come from?"

"I don't know," Hannah said. And she *didn't* know. The snow globe was like the paper dolls and the purple flowers—things that had appeared out of nowhere.

"I think the nurses are secretly giving you presents. Or even the doctors. Everyone likes you so much. You're such a brave girl."

"I'm not brave," Hannah said.

"What are you talking about?" her mother said, still shaking the snow globe. "Of course you're brave."

Just then Dr. Seth arrived and startled Nina. She quickly placed the snow globe on the nightstand and stood to greet him. She stared up at his face, smiling, fixing her hair with her fingers again. "Good to see you, Dr. Seth," she said, using a voice Hannah didn't recognize.

"Good to see you too. Good to see you both," Dr. Seth said, but he was looking only at her mom and her mom was looking only at him and they were talking only to each other. Dr. Seth asked Nina how she was holding up, how she was doing on her own now, and Nina shot him a look that told him Hannah didn't know her father had left yet. But she did—of course she did.

"Oh, *oh*," Dr. Seth said, wincing.

"It's OK. You saved Hannah's life. You saved my baby," Nina said, not looking at her baby at all, but into Dr. Seth's eyes.

"I'm happy I could help. Your daughter's a gem," he said.

"We're lucky. I was just telling Hannah how lucky we are." And then her mom was again poofing her damn hair.

Hannah couldn't look at the two of them anymore. She looked at the silent television hanging from the ceiling and turned up the volume and switched channels, impatiently, madly, until her mom finally looked at her and asked what was wrong.

"I want to go home," Hannah said. "I want to see Dad."

"Soon, honey," her mother said, sweetly now, attentive again.

Dr. Seth moved closer to her bed then. "I certainly hope so," he said. He checked under the sheets, making sure the tube was secure. He asked if anything specifically hurt Hannah, if she needed pain medicine, if she was able to sleep through the night. "That tube's nearly done its job. She's just about all cleaned out," he said, smiling.

"I want to see Dad," Hannah said again.

"Look at those pretty flowers. Look at that big card!" Dr. Seth said, walking over to the corkboard. "Who sent you these monkeys?"

"Where is my dad?" she wanted to know.

16

FOR THE last week, Martin had preferred his parents' den to his own apartment. Before hitting the couch, he'd go to their kitchen, where he'd lean into the refrigerator's cold and pull something from a shelf or he'd stand in front of their well-stocked liquor cabinet, pouring vodka or gin into a coffee cup. The shag carpet in the den was bright orange. The TV was a box with rabbit ears. The couch was brown and plaid and gave way under his body, the springs underneath him squeaky and unforgiving.

Sometimes he went to their new restaurant even though it wasn't open yet and he only took up space, walking around the two rooms, staring at things: the six ovens all in a row, the soda machine, the knives lined up on the wall.

Or he was at the hospital.

Martin knew he should go upstairs to his studio and try to sleep in his own bed, instead of sitting in his dad's recliner, listening to his sister chatter on, but he didn't want to be alone. Alone—even stoned alone or drunk alone—meant alone with his thoughts and his thoughts inevitably turned to the girl.

Sandy sat on the couch with her bare feet up on the coffee table, painting her nails. Even her fingers were skinny. She was focused, deliberate, and slow, as if those skinny fingers were the most important things in the world. It was four o'clock on a Friday afternoon, game day, and his sister was still in her stupid black and gold skirt and sweater, her pompoms on the coffee table next to her feet and an open, uneaten bag of pretzels, and what looked like a Slurpee. "You know the girl who was hit by a car?" she said.

"I don't know her," he said, startled.

"You know what I mean." Sandy rolled her eyes.

"What about her?"

"Billy Judson says that she'll never walk again. And that her leg is all deformed."

57

"Don't believe everything you hear. Billy Judson's not a doctor."

"I'd rather die than be deformed," she said.

Martin decided that secretly drinking was almost like drinking alone, especially in front of his idiot sister. He sat with a folded map of the United States in his lap, sipping his vodka and orange juice and trying to ignore her. She was oblivious, so self-involved, he thought, he could take out a needle and shoot some heroin and she probably wouldn't even notice.

"The kids at school say the girl's going to be crippled. *If* she lives," she said.

Martin was glad his parents were working late and was looking forward to Sandy leaving soon for the game. He'd have the house to himself. He could drink, beat off, and sleep as much as he wanted to. He unfolded the map and smoothed it out.

"Billy says that she's crippled. I'd rather be dead than crippled," Sandy said.

Martin said nothing. He lifted his cup and took a big swallow. He set the cup down hard, smacking the glass table next to him, startling Sandy so that she slipped, the little brush she'd been aiming at her fingernail going off course.

"Damn it," she said. "Look what you made me do, Marty." She held the finger up to him, a red line going from knuckle to nail.

"Fuck you too," he said.

"Why don't you go up to your own apartment and leave me alone? I don't know why you moved up there. You're always here." She dipped the brush back into the polish and didn't look at him.

He hated the way nail polish smelled and wondered how girls could stand it.

He hoped Sandy's team lost tonight and that Billy dropped the fucking football.

Perhaps she'd twist her ankle while doing a cheer.

He wished his parents could see through her.

He hoped they couldn't see through *him* and that they believed he'd registered for classes.

He wished he *had* registered.

He wanted to talk to Penny again.

He was sorry he was drinking his parents' most expensive vodka and he wasn't sorry he was drinking it.

He thought it was strange that he could feel two opposing things at once. Maybe he was crazy—the injured girl always on his mind.

He dreamt about her almost every night.

In last night's dream she was older than she was or he was younger than he was—and she was in love with him. She had an arm for a leg in the dream, but he didn't care, he was in love with her too. It was just a dream, but it freaked him out when he thought about it—and he thought about it a lot. He didn't know the girl and he certainly didn't love her. He felt terrible that he hit her, sure, but he wasn't in love with her. It was gross to even think about. She was a little kid and he was a grown guy. Thinking about the dream made him feel like a pervert, made him want to take another shower, and worse, much worse, gave him a boner. He adjusted himself, pushed his boner down, which he was able to do discreetly because of the map across his lap.

"You've been acting even weirder than usual lately," his sister said, working on her thumb with the little brush. "Are you even going to school? I bet you're not. Shouldn't you have bought books by now or school supplies or something?"

"Shouldn't you shove that pompom up your ass?"

"They say her liver had to be removed. I'd rather die than live without my liver," Sandy said, twisting the cap on the bottle of nail polish. "Wouldn't you rather die?" she said.

"And how long do you think someone can live without a liver, Sandy?" he said.

She didn't answer him. She leaned over, and without using her hands, without messing up her precious nail polish, took a loud sip from the straw. She sucked and sucked.

Martin stared at her lips around the straw and decided that she was fucking Billy Judson, and probably giving him head too. "You're a slut," he said.

"I'm not a slut," she said, adamantly. "A slut fucks a lot of people—and I only, well, I only *make love* to one."

"*Make love,*" he mocked. "I might like you better if you were a slut."

She held her hands up on either side of her head, her fingers splayed out dramatically, waving like a lunatic. "Go home," she said.

He picked up the remote and turned on the television. The newscaster was talking about the nineteen mountain climbers who died on Mount Fuji in an avalanche. Martin was thinking that it was dangerous enough just getting up in the morning and walking to school, let alone climbing a fucking mountain.

"They shouldn't have been up there," Sandy said. "You won't catch me on a mountain."

Martin downed his drink and thought about making another one. More vodka this time, fewer ice cubes, less orange juice. He'd feel better. His sister could chatter on and he'd have no trouble closing his eyes and zoning out. He'd be able to look at his map and ignore her completely.

Tony would be home by six o'clock and he'd call him then. He could tell him that Sandy was fucking Billy Judson. He could tell him that she was probably giving him head too, that she'd accept a mouth full of dick but wouldn't eat food.

"Mom and Dad think something's wrong with you," Sandy said suddenly.

"Yeah, well," he said.

"They're not even sure if they want you to work at the new restaurant."

"Don't exaggerate," he said.

"Well, Mom says your mood better improve if you're going to be head waiter."

"*My* mood? What about you, Sandy? Skinny, fucking you. Aren't you hungry?" he asked.

"Aren't I *what*?"

"I see you playing with your food, moving it around on your plate. Anything to keep it out of your mouth, huh?"

"Something *is* wrong with you," she said, emphatically. "No wonder they don't want you around."

"I'm moving anyway," he said, looking down at the map in his lap. There were so many places he could live, state after state after state. He ran a finger from Southern California to Nevada, and then scooted it all the way to New York.

17

HANNAH SAT up on the examination table, her bare leg at an angle in the doctor's hand. He had just removed the first cast, in which she'd spent eight weeks, and was preparing to put on a second one.

Hannah's injured leg was whiter and thinner than her right leg and Nina wished the doctor would hurry up and get the second cast on so they wouldn't have to look at it. She wanted the leg covered up, not only for her own eyes but for Hannah's too. She didn't want Hannah to ask the doctor questions about her leg's appearance, and didn't want to hear the answers.

Dr. Bell was a large man with heavy jowls. He sat on a little stool at the foot of the examination table. His body spilled over the sides of the stool and although Nina thought he looked like an enormous mushroom, she found herself using that voice with him and giving him that smile. She told herself that if Dr. Bell were attracted to her, he'd work harder to fix her daughter's problems.

He took a little wheel with several dull spikes sticking out of it and rolled the wheel up and down Hannah's calf and ankle, asking if she could feel it. He rolled the wheel on her foot, the bottom first, trying to tickle her, but got no response. Then he tried the top of her foot—again, nothing. He asked Hannah to wiggle her toes, which was something she couldn't do the whole time she was in the hospital, but she could do it now, and she did.

"Good girl," Nina said, as if Hannah had done the dishes or made her bed without being asked.

The doctor wore bifocals with thick black frames. He was jowly, his skin ruddy and wrinkled. The one oily strand of gray hair he had left was combed back over his bare scalp. "Can you move those toes up?" he said.

Hannah tried.

She tried again.

When they wouldn't move up, she moved them down.

"Move them up, not down. 'Up,' I said."

Nina squeezed her daughter's hand. She willed her daughter's toes to move up, not down, and nothing. Hannah tried again and again. Nina could see it on her face, how Hannah concentrated and focused—and still, nothing, not the slightest quiver. The doctor might as well have asked her to fly around the room or read his mind or bend a fork without touching it.

Dr. Bell looked disappointed and Nina felt afraid, biting her bottom lip. "Try once more, baby," she said.

"I can't. They won't move. They're stupid."

"Toes can't be stupid. People can be stupid," Dr. Bell said. "And you're certainly not stupid, Hannah. You've been injured," he said gently.

Two new rolls of plaster were smoking in the sink behind his head.

It was only Hannah's second cast, but Nina already knew the steps: first the gauze, then the cotton, then the plaster—she wished he'd hurry up.

Nina was mostly concerned with Hannah walking again, of course, and by not asking about aesthetics, what the leg would eventually look like, she could make her own prognosis. Certainly the atrophy was to be expected and was temporary. Of course Hannah's leg would plump right up once the last cast was removed. Her ankle, though, alarmed Nina—it was sunken and the foot itself was twisted inward, like a pigeon's.

"The toes are stupid," Hannah said again, her voice sharp. She was angry, not only at her mother and Dr. Bell, but at her toes, talking about them as if they weren't quite hers. Her fingers and other limbs behaved, responded to her internal orders, and her left leg, by comparison, was becoming her bad leg, the leg that wouldn't listen.

It was a bum leg.

It was a peg leg.

It was something separate from the rest of her, yet very much attached.

The three of them stared at her stubborn toes. "Move them up, not down," he had said. It was there on Nina's face, how important his request was, how everything depended on this one seemingly simple thing Hannah could not do.

"You can't move them up?" Nina's voice cracked.

Hannah shook her head, trying not to cry.

"It'll come back to you, I'm sure. These things take time. We just need to be patient." Nina left her daughter's side then and went to the corner of the room where she'd left her purse. She searched inside it for a minute with both hands, then popped something into her mouth. "An aspirin," she told Dr. Bell, who was looking at her.

He nodded.

"For my headache," she added, returning to Hannah's side.

Dr. Bell told them that this second cast was a special cast, one he hoped would straighten out Hannah's foot. "Let's get this on you, shall we?" He slapped his hands on his big knees and stood up. "Let's get this going."

He started with the gauze, wrapping it around and around Hannah's leg, her calf, her ankle, her foot, leaving her useless toes free. She was leaning back on her elbows, watching him.

"It's a lot like polio," the doctor said, finishing with the gauze and moving on to the roll of cotton.

"What?" Nina said, horrified. Getting hit by a car was one thing, but having a disease—a *disease*—was another.

"What's happened to Hannah's leg is what we used to see with polio cases—the nerve and muscle damage."

"Polio?"

He nodded.

"More movement will come back to her, though, right?" Nina said. "Hannah was in the hospital for four weeks before she could move those toes at all. And now she's wiggling them. You saw them wiggle. One day she couldn't do it and the next day she could. It's possible. I'm sure it's possible." She looked at him, searched his face.

He said nothing.

"Don't tell me it's not possible," she said.

Dr. Bell didn't respond, which, they both knew, was a sort of response. He stood up again and walked over to the sink. He put on plastic gloves, so tight they slapped against his wrists. He reached into the sink and scooped up the hot rolls of plaster, then carried them across the room, milky white drops falling from between his fingers. He sat down and began wrapping the first roll around and around Hannah's leg. He worked around her calf and ankle and foot and started humming.

When one roll was finished, he picked up the second one and began again.

"What are you now, Hannah? Eight?" he asked.

"I'm seven," she said.

"She just had a birthday last week," Nina said, trying to sound upbeat.

"You could pass for eight," Dr. Bell said, winking.

"She's very mature," Nina said.

Finally, he rubbed the cast up and down and sideways too, working with both hands, smoothing the plaster out with such care it was as if he was making art, a sculpture, something beautiful and permanent.

Two days later, the cast completely dry, Hannah was back on Dr. Bell's examination table. To her left, a circular saw with white dusty blades hung from a chrome-plated mobile stand. "This isn't just any cast. It's unique," he said, pulling a black marking pen from his jacket pocket.

"Hear that?" Nina said, smiling at the doctor. She crinkled the table's white paper in a clenched fist and took in a deep breath.

Hannah wasn't biting, though. She knew the little yellow bus that took the slow kids to school was unique, and she knew the kids themselves were unique too, and she knew her leg was unique in the same way.

Dr. Bell was drawing on the cast now—what looked like an outline of a huge kidney bean that wrapped around her ankle. He stood back and admired his drawing for a second before pulling the mobile stand closer, lifting up the saw, and turning it on. It whirred and vibrated in his hand. He leaned down then and began, twisting the saw, maneuvering it around his drawing.

When he was finished, he used what looked like a large bottle opener to pop the chunk of plaster out, making room for what was next. He slid across the room on his stool, the little wheels squeaking and struggling, and opened a drawer. He pulled out a metal contraption that looked like a shackle and held it up proudly for them to see. "It won't hurt. It just looks like some sort of torture device," he said.

"Hmm," Nina said.

Dr. Bell wheeled back over to them. "A little pressure at night after you twist, that's all." He fit the metal contraption into the space left around her ankle, fit a metal screw and a tiny wheel in place, and gave the two of them instructions to twist the screw an inch to the left. "It's important to do it every single night."

"Of course, Dr. Bell," Nina said. "We'll do whatever you say. Isn't that right, Hannah?"

Hannah was quiet.

"Of course we will. We want to walk, right?"

"*I* want to walk," Hannah snapped, surprising even herself.

Her mom cleared her throat and looked like she was about to cry.

On crutches, Hannah *did* walk, but it was stepping into the world in a new way: pushing off with her arms, lifting her one good leg in the air, and thrusting forward—a short flight to the next square of linoleum or shaggy carpet, the next patch of grass or piece of sidewalk. It was a steady business of effort and relief, and when her two feet were off the ground, swinging forward together, she was aware for that brief second of not being planted to this world.

Dr. Bell's hybrid was a strange contraption made of plaster and metal that was cast *and* brace, an amalgam, something she'd wear for eight months without one signature or set of initials, without one sketch or funny drawing.

And every night before bed, they twisted. Once in a while, Hannah did the twisting by herself, alone in her bedroom, but usually her mom sat with her, drinking tea and watching Hannah twist. And sometimes her mom said, "Let me do that, baby girl. Here, let me."

She'd ask Hannah if it hurt and she'd say no.

"At least the doctor didn't lie. Your father, the dentist, he lies. Once he filled a cavity of mine and said it wouldn't hurt. Well, I nearly shot out of the chair."

Hannah was twisting, trying to concentrate.

"Do you miss him?" Nina asked her.

Hannah looked up.

"You don't have to answer that," she said.

18

MARTIN, CROUCHED between a Volkswagen bus and a black El Camino, kept an eye on Hannah's front door. Three girls played hopscotch across the street. They'd drawn squares with yellow chalk on the driveway and were singing some girlie song that Martin didn't recognize. He wished Hannah was up and healthy and playing with the girls. He wondered if they missed her, if the four of them used to play together.

One girl said something about a boy named Ryan and the other one said, *Hey, he's mine,* and Martin decided that the three of them were too mature for Hannah anyway. *Let them hop around and talk about boys,* he thought. The three of them looked alike, matching shorts and shirts tied at their waists, matching blonde ponytails and bangs, white sandals with fake daisies at the center. They looked stupid, he thought, and he couldn't tell them apart, and when they hopped fast, one behind the other behind the other, they could almost have been one girl with one long pale curtain of hair flying behind her.

He'd moved from behind the El Camino and stood behind an oak tree. His bike was a few blocks away, propped up against the side of Tony's apartment building. What would happen if the girls caught him behind the tree, he wondered. They'd probably scream and think he was some sort of a pervert, which he wasn't, no matter how weird his dreams were. Perhaps if the girls caught him they'd figure out who he was and what he'd done, which was worse than if he were just a flasher like that guy Brandon Striker who dropped out of high school in the eleventh grade to roam the neighborhood and show his dick to all the high school girls who wouldn't look at his face when he was just a student. It was said that Brandon targeted the girls who had snubbed or made fun of him. He was unique that way, the cops had said, and he was labeled The Revenge Flasher, but no one ever ended up in a hospital without a spleen or with a fucked-up liver, no one ever ended up maimed for life because a guy flashed his dick at her.

This was the fourth day in a row that Martin had been here, waiting for Hannah to come out and show him that she was OK, maybe not perfect, but still a whole girl. He thought that if she didn't come out today he'd give up. He'd continue leaving presents on the porch but wouldn't hide out here like an idiot.

It was mid-afternoon when they finally came out of the house. He thought Hannah maneuvered pretty well on the wooden crutches and was impressed with what he decided was her ability to adapt. Oh, who was he fooling, he quickly corrected himself: It was summer and she was in a cast and she was probably hot and, despite a short giggle at something her mom said, Hannah was probably cranky as fuck. Her mother wore a silky dress and high-heel shoes and was even prettier than Hannah, which might have been because she was that kind of beautiful or maybe because she was a grown woman. There were flesh-colored pads on the crutches to protect Hannah's hands and underarms, and one of the hand pads sprung loose and was rolling down the driveway. Her mother rushed to retrieve it, and while Hannah stood waiting by the car, Martin got a good look at the strange cast. It didn't look like any cast he'd seen before. There was a clamp or something metal around her ankle, which told him that Sandy was right, that something was very wrong with Hannah's leg.

The girls were waving at Hannah now, but hopping at the same time, and Martin wished they were more sensitive. Couldn't they see that playing hopscotch was something Hannah could not do? Couldn't they stop hopping for one fucking minute? Finally one girl did stop hopping, but only to stare at Hannah and her mother, who was now taking the crutches from under her daughter's arms and laying them in the backseat of the car. Hannah was on one foot too, hopping, just like the stupid girls, which made Martin want to cry. She took a couple quick hops before her mother helped her into the car. She rolled the window down.

"Hey, Hannah," the one girl said with her stupid voice.

"Hi," Hannah said out the window. And her voice, he thought, wasn't stupid at all; she sounded smart and sad and older than she was.

By the time mother and daughter had pulled out of the driveway, the girls were finishing up their game. Martin heard them talking, something about Hannah's broken family or her broken leg, he couldn't be sure. Either way, he didn't like them. They were gathering up their box of chalk and plastic cups and a bag of potato chips from the ground. One girl rubbed the bottom of her sandals on the asphalt, erasing the yellow numbers and squares. Finally, they skipped up the driveway and headed toward the front door.

Martin looked around the neighborhood, poking his head around the tree to make sure he was alone. Satisfied, he crossed the street and walked up to the Tellers' porch, where he very carefully set down one more *Get Well Soon* card he hadn't signed.

He had the maps laid out on his bed at home.

He had his tip money under his mattress.

He had the bus schedule hidden in his sock drawer.

He imagined himself crossing the country, talking to strangers on the bus, and making up lies about himself.

He took a quick look back at the envelope he'd left for Hannah, and then walked back to Tony's house to get his bike.

19

THE HOUSE went up for sale—a bright orange sign dug into the front lawn. It told people, Hannah thought, that someone didn't love them, someone had left them, and that they, in turn, were leaving the house behind.

When her dad left her mom, he'd left Hannah too, moving into the home and arms of a woman her mom called *that whore shiksa* or *that surfing Jesus freak*. Worse, her dad had told her that he'd been thinking of converting to Christianity. He had left them on so many levels, left her mother physically alone in that big king-sized bed, in a house that was falling apart, and with a damaged daughter to care for, and finally he'd left their religion and culture too, become another man completely. A man who wore shorts and rubber sandals and too-bright Hawaiian shirts, a thirty-three-year-old man who was taking surfing lessons and going to church.

He calls himself a Jew for Jesus, her mom would say hatefully. *A Jew for who? What's a Jew for Jesus? A nebbish traitor, a man without a backbone, that's what*, she'd say, answering her own question.

But her mother would soon lose her religion as well, which made Hannah believe it was something they had practiced without being certain. It seemed as though being Jewish was only necessary to define them when they were together, what they were: a Jewish family from the East Coast, living on the West Coast now. But once their union of three ended, so too did their apparent beliefs.

When Hannah came home from the hospital, they lit the candles on Friday nights as they always had, but it felt pretend, false, like dress-up. It was a thing they had done as a family, and now with just the two of them sitting at that too-long table with the empty chair at the head, they were barely that. After three weeks of rushing through the prayer with less and less enthusiasm, the fourth night they just sat down with deli sandwiches and tomato soup and ate, pretending it was any other day of the week. And her mom said, "We should move, Hannah. We'll make a new start, that's what we'll do."

. . .

Soon, strangers were making their way through the rooms and halls, whispering about the weedy backyard, the filthy pool, and the gaudy bathroom wallpaper. They moved through the living room and kitchen and den, stood inside the walk-in closets and sniffed. They opened the pantry and commented on her mother's choices. "Fresh peaches are so much better. I'd never buy these things in a can," one woman said. And her husband stood next to her, nodding and tugging on her blouse like a five-year old. "Let's get out of here," he said, whining loud enough for Hannah to hear all the way from her bedroom.

They were rude, like they owned the house without even buying it. They picked things up, inspected them, and put them down—a self-help book her mom had left on the coffee table, the clock, the *TV Guide*—and Hannah didn't understand what those small things had to do with the house itself, how it could affect someone's choice to live there. Often, she watched from her room, propped up in bed, staring over the pages of whatever book she was reading at the nosy strangers and counted the minutes until they said *thank you,* until they said *good-bye,* until they stepped out the front door and out of their lives.

Sometimes they knocked on Hannah's bedroom door before entering and sometimes they pushed right through. Eyes went right to her cast. People had stories of their own: broken tibia, torn ligament, tennis elbow. This man fell out of a tree when he was eight. This old woman twisted her ankle on her wedding day. Thirty-five years ago. Walking down the aisle and then flat on the floor. *Remember that? Remember that, honey?* she said to a fat little man who only grunted and turned away from her, stepping out into the hall.

People assumed Hannah's leg was broken, but she'd tell them no, it wasn't. Despite her irritation, she was often just lonely enough to engage them in conversation when they made an effort. She would say that initially her thigh had been broken and in traction, but it had healed nicely in the hospital. Some people wanted more information and probed further, but when she'd tell them the truth—the doctors weren't yet sure what was wrong with her—their expressions changed. They grew serious, crossed their arms. When she'd tell them that she was hit by a car, they'd step back, away from her.

"Here, on this street? In this neighborhood?" one man said. He was very thin and old, with skinny cheeks that jiggled when he turned his head. He wore a light blue polyester suit and dirty white shoes. His wife, also in blue polyester, was even thinner than he was—her face was a gaunt mask covered with light powder.

"Oh, my," the wife said, clicking open her purse, then clicking it closed for no apparent reason. "What sort of crazy drivers live here?" she asked her realtor, who glared at Hannah.

"Were you playing in the street, honey?" the realtor asked.

"No," she answered.

"I heard she was playing in the street," the realtor said to the couple, talking out of the side of her mouth.

"That's a lie," Hannah said.

The realtor laughed nervously. She clutched her blouse at the neck and shook her head. "Honey . . ." she said, an admonition.

"We don't have sidewalks. There's nowhere to go. I had nowhere to walk," Hannah said.

"Bye-bye, dear," the realtor said then, steering her clients away.

2 0

HANNAH SPENT time on her back, or sitting up with her leg outstretched and resting on a pillow on the coffee table, watching television or reading books. She read whatever she could get her hands on: her mother's magazines, the dentistry textbooks her father left behind. She discovered *The 1970s Woman,* who worked out of the house and wanted everything: a man, babies, a career, a gray suit, a reliable watch, the perfect stroller, and silky lingerie. And she read about teeth, looked at the pictures of molars and bicuspids and cavities.

Limited mobility kept Hannah inside her head, inside her room, and mostly inside the house. And that first summer, things were breaking inside that house: Screens were coming unhinged; the sliding glass door didn't slide anymore; the dining room table tipped to one side, needing a shim; mothers and toasters and air conditioners were falling apart. The television was stuck on one channel, so Hannah watched the news. She was especially interested in stories about natural disasters, the earth cracking open like the biggest mouth and swallowing thousands of people, a massive wave erasing a coastal city in Thailand, a hurricane spinning villages into scraps and dust. How insignificant a house became, how little protection it offered, what pitiful shelter.

She followed the news story about the park ranger Roy "Dooms" Sullivan, who'd been struck by lightning seven times—the first strike shooting through his leg and ripping off his big toenail. Another bolt zipped through his hat and set his hair on fire, and the last one scorched his belly and chest.

She used the wooden crutches to get herself from room to room, never knowing what mood she'd find her mother in. Her mother was many mothers that summer. Now that Hannah's father was gone and Nina couldn't fight with him, she fought with herself. She'd say something one day and the very next day she'd contradict it.

She was angry and impatient, unreasonable, and quick to shout.

She was sweet and sorry, and overly attentive, painting Hannah's nails pink and braiding her hair.

She was in her robe and slippers all day, her lips pale and bloodless.

She was dressed up in clothes too young for her, hot pants and mini-skirts, low-cut blouses and tight T-shirts.

She had black hair that was shiny and full or it was dull and matted to her head.

She wore lip gloss that smelled like bubblegum.

She was awake all night, walking the halls or sipping warm milk from a coffee cup in the dark kitchen.

She was taking pills she claimed were aspirin that didn't look like aspirin at all.

She was anxious to move out, hated the house she'd shared with Hannah's father.

She didn't want to sell, wanted to stay in that house forever. It was where their memories lived, she said.

She wished it was fall so she could start teaching again, and she was relieved it was summer. Imagine if she had to recover from Asher's adulterous behavior and Hannah's accident while teaching classes.

Her mom was lonely, weeping one minute and then giddy on the phone with Dr. Seth the next. When she hung up, she was prettier and younger. She'd go wash her face, put on some blush.

Sometimes, unable to face the width of the king-sized bed, she'd sleep at the kitchen table with her head down, where Hannah would find her in the morning, shake her shoulder gently, and she'd wake up confused, asking, *How did I get here?*

2 1

MARTIN COULDN'T choose how he felt inside, but he could choose how to behave, so he did as his parents had asked and worked on his attitude. He pretended. He put on a show, moving between restaurants and consciously trying to act normal. He thought about who he'd been, remembered the conversations he'd had with customers, and instigated those same conversations again. He asked them innocuous questions and nodded politely, as they gave him innocuous answers. He stood at their tables and served them things. He smiled and smiled and smiled.

At the diner, he served burgers and ham sandwiches and golden grilled cheese. He served mashed potatoes or scalloped potatoes or French fries, big Cokes and frothy milk shakes. At the more upscale place, he dressed up in black slacks and starched white shirts, served Italian cuisine, and suggested wine pairings like the most polite sommelier.

He moved from restaurant to home and back again. Sometimes he went to the beach at dusk and sat on the sand, staring at the ocean. Sometimes he went to the hospital to see Penny, and some days to the mall to buy Hannah another gift.

He rode his bike or moved from bus stop to bus stop.

It was early fall and he was sitting at one of those bus stops now, thinking about finally visiting the college campus and checking things out, even though he had no intention of sticking around. Maybe he'd find a college in his new city, wherever that was, and maybe he'd get all A's and meet a girl like Penny.

An old woman in a colorful shawl and a long, floral skirt was walking toward the bus stop, pushing a stroller. She sighed loudly when she sat on the bench next to him, and he noticed several white whiskers on her chin and above her lip.

"Good morning," he said.

The old woman nodded and smiled. She pulled the stroller closer to the bench and Martin could see in, noticing it was empty. The woman looked at him and shrugged, then she scooted toward him, an inch or two closer than he would have liked, but still he wanted to be friendly.

"Where's the baby?" he said, smiling.

"*My* babies," the woman said in English, her palm flat on her chest. "Mine," she repeated with a thick accent.

"Yeah, OK," he said. "Where are they?"

"*Sí, sí,*" the woman said.

"Did you forget the baby?" he said, pointing at the empty stroller. He could tell from her expression that she didn't understand English, but it was the only language he knew, so he spoke it louder and slower, which was, of course, futile. He felt embarrassed for both of them and looked away. Two kids were riding one bike across the street, a boy pedaling and a boy balancing on the handlebars. It was ten a.m. and they should have been in school, Martin thought. Maybe they were late and on their way. It seemed reckless, the way they were riding—how could the pedaling boy see?

"My babies," the old woman said again.

Martin turned back to her.

The old woman smiled at him.

"I hurt a little girl," he said.

"*No comprende,*" she said.

But Martin wasn't deterred. He wanted to talk. So what if she didn't understand a fucking word he said? Maybe it was better this way. "I hit her with my car and she almost died," he continued. "She's all busted up. A little kid, walking to school. And now she'll never walk again." He shook his head and felt his eyes welling up. Not again, he thought, not in public. *I'm a fucking pussy*, he told himself.

The old woman nodded, still smiling. "Louisa," she said.

"What?" he said.

"Amelia, José, Juan."

"OK," he said, uncertain.

"Margret," she continued. "Maggie, Maggie, Maggie," she said, clicking her tongue and looking like she was about to cry.

Martin figured that the names belonged to children the old woman had lost or children she'd had to abandon in Mexico. He turned away again, wanting to see if the boys made it down the street, but they were gone. When he turned back to her, she looked angry, not sad anymore, but mad. She was speaking Spanish to him and he didn't understand one word.

"Can't help you," he said. "Look, lady, I don't understand a thing you're saying." He rubbed his palms on his jeans, shaking his head.

She turned from him then, looked straight ahead, and continued her rant, talking to no one.

Martin looked away again. There was a guy about his age holding a book bag that said *Manhattan Beach Junior College* on it, standing in front of the bus stop. He was just a couple feet to the right of Martin and the old woman. He had longish hair, wore jeans and a T-shirt that said in bold black letters: *Vietnam: Stop the Killing.* Martin had no idea how much of his conversation with the old woman the guy had heard, and he felt embarrassed. He could have eavesdropped on the whole thing. The guy turned around then. "You know what time this bus is going to get here?" he asked.

Martin looked at his watch. "About five minutes," he said. The guy was obviously on his way to class, a normal guy with opinions about the world and a destination, a place to go, a guy who didn't hit little girls on their way to school or spend time confessing to people who didn't understand him.

Martin didn't want to get on the bus and go all the way to campus with this guy. Maybe he'd do something else today and check out the school tomorrow. He'd get to his parents' restaurant early and help out. He'd figure out where he was going once he got on the bus, which thankfully had just arrived, shooting its black air into the sky, the doors whooshing open. Martin stood up and thought about helping the woman and her empty stroller onto the bus, but he really didn't want to. He was relieved when the bus driver got out and stepped down. He addressed the old woman by name. "Manuela," he called to her, speaking in Spanish and helping her and her stroller up the stairs.

The bus was crowded and noisy with chatter. Martin stood in front, scanning the rows for a place to sit.

"*Sí, sí,*" the bus driver said, helping Manuela settle into her seat, patting her arm.

By the time Martin made his way down the aisle, there was only one open seat and that was next to College Guy, so Martin didn't have a choice. He sat down and tried to get comfortable.

In front of them, Manuela was singing a Spanish lullaby.

"Lady's crazy," Martin said softly out of the corner of his mouth, but either College Guy didn't hear him or didn't like him because he leaned down, unzipped his bag and pulled out a textbook. He put the book in his lap and opened it. Martin used his peripheral vision to check it out. Apparently, he was studying astronomy. On his lap, stars and galaxies, the sun, the moon, and a blue-black sky.

"You into stars, huh?" Martin said to him.

The guy nodded, begrudgingly, but didn't look up. He obviously didn't want to talk or make friends, which convinced Martin that he'd heard everything.

The bus moved along, stopping once at the public library and another time in front of a supermarket. One middle-aged woman got off at the library and several old people moved slowly down the aisle at the supermarket stop.

When Martin saw the shopping mall in the distance, he knew instantly where he'd spend the day. He pulled on the cord and stood up.

"Bye-bye, *señor*," Manuela said.

He turned around to wave at her, but she had her head turned and was looking out the window.

"Bye," he said.

The bus driver looked at him impatiently, so Martin hurried down the steps. The doors smacked shut behind him and the bus pulled away from the curb.

2 2

THE HEAT was the big story. Record highs, the newscaster said. The hottest it had been in thirty years. One hundred two degrees on the coast, 110 degrees inland. He suggested staying in the shade and stressed proper hydration. He sipped from a glass of water to demonstrate. A young reporter with a ponytail and shimmery lipstick talked to a bare-chested construction worker, a glistening bear who complained into the microphone, his shirt stuffed in his back pocket. When he turned around to point at the apartment complex he was working on, the shirt swung behind him like a tail.

Hannah sat on the armchair in the den with her sweaty, itchy leg outstretched, the cast resting on a pillow on the coffee table. A day earlier, she'd twisted a coat hanger and used it to scratch at her calf. When she finished, she stashed it underneath the sofa. She was hoisted up on one elbow, bent over, searching for it now.

All she could think about was the itch, steadily getting worse. The newscaster reported that a woman had dropped dead in line at the bank, fell to the floor clutching her checkbook. Heatstroke, he said. He warned people to take care of their needs, watch out for their children and pets. Hannah wanted that hanger. She was feeling around under the sofa and finding dust. She found a metal button the size of a quarter, a spool of red thread, and a safety pin. She set the objects on the sofa's arm and continued searching, wondering if maybe her mom had discovered the hanger and thrown it away. Maybe she'd thought about the doctor's stern warning about scratching inside the cast, his admonition against knitting needles, hangers, and butter knives. Maybe Hannah would be scolded or maybe her mom would understand.

Finally, she found the hanger pushed up against the wall in a far corner, and then she was holding it in her hand, aiming right inside the dark tunnel, when she heard her mother's footsteps in the hall. She quickly hid the hanger behind her back, tucked it behind the throw pillow.

"What's the story?" her mom said, sitting down in the chair opposite the sofa. "What's going on in the world?" She wore navy shorts and a white cotton blouse tied at her waist. Her feet were bare. She reached into her pocket and pulled out a tube of lip gloss. She put it on without a mirror and smacked her lips together and Hannah could smell the bubblegum flavor from where she sat. "It's so damn hot. I can't take this heat," her mom said, picking up the *TV Guide* from the coffee table and fanning herself with it.

"They're talking about it on the news," Hannah said. The itch was getting even stronger, more intense, and she wished her mother would take her horribly sweet lips out of the den and leave her alone. It was the right side of her ankle specifically and she wanted to get to it. She wished her fingers were long and thin enough to reach. She scratched at her knee because it was all she could get to.

"What's wrong?"

"My leg itches."

"Try not to think about it. Think about something else. Think about the house finally selling. That would be a great thing." She paused. She exhaled loudly. "Your dad wants to see you this weekend. Think about that. Think about where you'd like him to take you. He wants you to meet Christy. I told him it was too soon. You don't want to meet her yet, do you?"

Hannah shrugged. She didn't know how she felt. Her knee was red now, but it was her ankle she wanted.

"What's that?" Her mom leaned in, staring at the pillow behind Hannah's back and the couple inches of wire sticking out from behind it.

Hannah adjusted herself, trying to cover up the pillow. "Nothing," she said.

Her mom stood up and reached behind Hannah's back, pulling out the hanger. "Oh, dear God," she said. "This is dangerous—what have you done? Have you hurt yourself?"

"No," she said.

"You could break the skin."

"But I haven't."

"You know what the doctor said, Hannah. You could get an infection. Dr. Bell said not to scratch. It's so dangerous, honey. You don't want to get all scarred up. You've been hurt so much already."

"I'm careful," Hannah said.

"It's not safe to scratch."

"You don't know what this is like. You think you're hot? I'm hotter. It's just a little scratching. I use the curved end. It isn't even sharp."

The two of them stared at the coat hanger for several minutes before her mom finally said, "How do you do it? Show me."

And Hannah eased the hanger into the opening, aimed, and reached her ankle. "Ah," she said. "Oh," she said, finally, finally scratching that itch.

2 3

DR. SETH'S house calls weren't really house calls, but visits. He wasn't worried about Hannah's physical problems anymore; it was her mother's body he came to see. He didn't give Hannah's liver a thought these days, saying hello quickly with a squeeze to the shoulder or an insincere pat on the back.

Twice a week, her mom and Dr. Seth sat together in the living room, sipping wine, eating crackers and soft cheese or little meatballs they picked up with toothpicks. Sometimes they had fat strawberries dusted with powdered sugar.

At dusk they moved to the bedroom, where, her mother told her, they listened to classical music.

Now it was early evening and Mozart sounded through the walls, down the hall, and into Hannah's bedroom, where she sat at her desk putting together a puzzle—a gift from Dr. Seth. The puzzle was a re-creation of a famous painting. A woman sat on a hill looking at a house or the woman was crawling toward the house, Hannah wasn't sure. She had the puzzle pieces spread out in front of her and was trying not to hear what was happening. The sitting or crawling woman's back was only half there and Hannah was looking for her shoulder, and her mother was moaning in the next room, and the moan sounded painful, like the doctor might have been hurting her.

Hannah found the piece of the woman's shoulder and snapped it into place and now the woman was a whole woman. The puzzle was really coming together. She leaned back for a moment, admiring her progress, while from the other room, her mother shouted: *Oh, no. Oh, God, no. OK, OK, OK.*

2 4

WHEN MARTIN stood at the nurses' station with his hands jammed in his pockets, sucking on breath mints and waiting for Penny to return from handing out midnight meds, he felt remotely human. It was the briefest respite. It wasn't redemption, which he certainly needed, but something else. He had no illusions about his gift-giving, and understood that buying toys for the girl could never absolve him of what he did and, mostly, *didn't* do—stay put and care for the child—but Penny reminded him that some small part of him was still capable of feeling something other than guilt and shame.

They were becoming friends and maybe more than friends, and it was a human thing to do, more human than hating your sister or lying to your parents about how you spent your days or ignoring most of Tony's phone calls and hanging out alone in your tiny apartment or on the couch in your parents' den. It was risky, starting to care about someone—that urge to talk, to tell too much, to confide and confess already pressing on his throat.

Penny answered Martin's questions and thankfully didn't ask too many of her own, especially about what brought him to the hospital in the first place, which was obviously an unexplained and curious duty to Hannah Teller—nor did she ask why he kept coming back, even though she had told him Hannah had been released and sent home with her mother weeks ago. Martin had imagined the little girl sitting in a wheelchair and being pushed through the big glass doors and into the sunny day with all the new, complicated physical problems that were his fault.

He worried that Penny had a sense about what he had done and sometimes felt himself pulling away, recoiling—not from her, although it probably looked that way when he took a step back from the nurses' station and said an abrupt good-bye or refused to accompany her downstairs to the cafeteria for her break.

Perhaps Penny was suspicious but was choosing not to acknowledge it—the way Tony Vancelli was telling him now that his new girlfriend,

Veronica, a seriously religious girl, the daughter of a local minister, was oblivious to his heavy cocaine use. Sure, she'd asked Tony, who was a sloppy user, about the white powder under his nose, and sure, she noticed his mood swings, but she trusted him, Tony said—that's all that matters finally, he told Martin, that a chick sees what she wants to see.

"How does she explain it to herself?" Martin asked. It was a rare occasion—Martin had let Tony talk him into leaving the studio and venturing out somewhere other than the hospital. They were in a little bar on Main Street they used to like, and, with some coaxing that involved insults about Martin's masculinity—the size of his penis, questioning if he even had one—he'd been pushed into joining Tony for a beer.

"She thinks I'm just moody," Tony said, laughing. He picked up his shot of tequila and downed it, smacked his lips happily, then popped a quarter-moon of lime in his mouth and sucked it dry. "The point is, Veronica doesn't see what she doesn't want to see. And I get my dick wet. That's what matters, right?" Tony slapped him on the shoulder. "You need to get your dick wet too, my friend," he said, looking around the room.

"I've got someone," Martin said, surprising himself.

"Sure you do," Tony said, sarcastically. "That's why you're always cooped up in that hellhole of yours—because you've 'got someone.'" He set the lime down on the bar where it rocked back and forth a couple times before it was still. He looked at Martin hard. "You know, you haven't been yourself since Margo left town. If I looked like you, if I had your pretty-boy face, I'd have the wettest dick in town. My dick would be so wet I'd need to wrap it in a towel to keep it from flooding the floor. My dick would be so wet I'd need to keep a sponge in my pants. I'd have to wring my dick out before I left the fucking house. My dick—"

"It's not Margo," Martin interrupted.

"Then who is it?" Tony leaned toward him. He wagged his finger in Martin's face. "You miss your wet dick, is what you miss."

Martin shook his head.

Tony turned and eyed the entrance, where two tall, pretty girls in miniskirts and go-go boots, in pearly pink lipstick with white-blond hair, were stepping inside, looking for a place to sit. Tony watched them slip into a booth and set their oversized purses on the table. One of them was adjusting her breasts in her halter top. "Hey, isn't that Margo's friend, what's-her-name?" he asked Martin.

Martin turned to look. "Annabelle. Yeah, that's her. You had sex with her in the backseat of my car."

"How's your car anyway? You haven't been driving."

"I told you, transmission's shot to hell."

"Get that shit fixed."

"And back tires are flat."

"Both tires?"

"Yeah," Martin said, realizing how weird it sounded.

"Maybe someone doesn't like you, man. Both tires sounds like weird-ass revenge to me," Tony said.

"The bus doesn't bother me," Martin said. "You can get fucked up and not have to worry."

"Thought you didn't even drink, man—until tonight."

"Yeah, I don't. If you wanted to get fucked up, though, you could."

"I don't know about you anymore. You're not the same guy you were." Tony was talking to Martin, but smiling over at Annabelle.

"I need to get going," Martin said, slapping his hands on his thighs. "I've got work tomorrow."

Tony ignored him. "Should I call that girl over? She's got a pretty little friend for you," he said.

"I'm seeing someone else," Martin lied.

"What's her name?"

"She's a nurse." Martin finished his drink and stood up.

Tony was waving Annabelle and her friend over, smiling like a horny dickhead, Martin thought, and barely noticed when Martin slipped out the front door.

2 5

HER FATHER wasn't there to fix what was broken and he couldn't take Hannah to the market or to the movies on a whim. He could call her on the phone and make a plan, coming over like a visitor. That's what he did on Saturday mornings, came over like a visitor—a rushed visitor who pulled up to the curb and beeped his horn, who only got out of the car when Hannah opened the front door.

At the car, he hugged her hard, helped her into the front seat, and then slipped her crutches into the back. They were quiet for the first few minutes, like people who didn't know each other. He tapped on the steering wheel and nodded at nothing, and Hannah felt uncomfortable and nervous. He was her dad, she knew, and she shouldn't feel the way she felt. Finally, he asked about her leg and the cast, wanting to know if she was in pain, if any of her friends from school had come over to visit, and if the twins across the street had stopped by since she'd been home from the hospital.

She told him that her leg didn't hurt, but it didn't work either. "I'd rather have it hurt than be so useless."

He nodded, sadly.

She told him that the twins were away at camp for the whole summer, but that before they left, they played a lot of hopscotch and mostly ignored her. She said she didn't really blame them, that not a lot of kids wanted to play indoors in the summer.

"I'm sorry," he said. "You'll be moving soon anyway. You'll make new friends when you move."

He took her to her favorite place on Main Street for breakfast, a café with blue-and-white-checked tablecloths and matching napkins, with big windows and the best banana pancakes in town. They sat where they always sat, at the same table with the same three chairs.

"Christy wants to meet you." Her father leaned back and stared out the window.

Hannah noticed that the gold Star of David he had always worn around his neck was now replaced by a shimmering two-inch cross.

"Well?" he said, turning to her.

"What?"

He picked up his napkin and wiped his mouth, though there was nothing on it that she could see. "I'm sorry—about all of it. I know it must be hard on you. The accident, the timing—I know it's terrible." He reached across the table and rubbed her arm.

Hannah wanted to pull her arm away but knew that her dad would be hurt, so she left it on the table between them. She was aware of the awkwardness of his touch and how he seemed as uncomfortable as she was. She wondered what his life was like now, if Christy had children who he was pretending were his own.

When the waitress came up to the table, Hannah's dad ordered banana pancakes and eggs for the both of them. And for the first time, at least in front of her, he ordered himself bacon, which surprised her because he was the one who had always insisted on keeping a kosher house. He even offered Hannah a slice, held an oily strip out to her—the limp thing flopping over his hand.

"No, thanks," she said.

"People always said bacon was tasty and I didn't believe them. I thought it was just salty, but it's really tasty," he said.

"Mom's got a boyfriend," she told her dad, when really she knew that Dr. Seth wasn't her boyfriend at all but a married man who rushed out the door before dinnertime.

"Really?" Asher said, and she couldn't gauge his reaction, his face giving nothing away. Hannah was nervous, found herself answering questions he didn't ask. "Mom's doing fine. She takes good care of me. When the house sells, we're going to start over."

"As long as you don't forget about me," he said.

"I won't," she said.

"What are you doing tomorrow morning?" He was chewing and talking at once, a drop of grease on his bottom lip. "Want to come to church with us and then afterwards we'll take you to the beach? You can watch me surf. Would you like that?"

Hannah cut into her pancakes with the fork and lifted a bite to her mouth, looking at him. She gathered up her courage and asked the question before she could change her mind. "Dad, aren't we Jewish?"

"Some Jews find Jesus," he said, scratching the scar on his cheek. "Some Jews find Jesus and ask him into their hearts."

She wasn't hungry anymore and she wasn't sure who this man sitting across from her was, smiling like he meant it, talking about Jesus and the big swells of Huntington Beach. She didn't know who he was, eating slices of pig, and she wanted her other dad back, even if he looked unhappy most of the time.

"This bacon sure is tasty," he said again. "Are you sure you don't want a piece?"

After breakfast, they went to the park. Hannah was staring at the swing set, her favorite thing, remembering when her dad used to stand behind her, pull her to his chest, and push her into the sky.

Her crutches were leaned up against the bench, just to the left of her cast. When they'd first approached the bench, Asher had reached for the crutches, offering to take them out of her way.

"No," she said, pulling them back, needing to know where they were at all times and insisting they stay within reach. She wanted them right by the bed when she slept. She wanted to be able to reach over and fiddle with the rubber hand rests, to scratch at the rubber blades that went under her arms, as she was doing now.

"Isn't that your friend from school? Eddie something-or-other?" her dad said, pointing. Eddie and his very tall friend were climbing up the slide that was meant to look like a snake.

"Yeah, that's him."

"He's so short. Isn't he little for his age?"

"I guess," she said.

"Good-looking little guy, though."

Hannah thought that maybe those pills weren't working after all and felt guilty for hoping that they didn't work in the first place. "He's growing," she said unconvincingly. "He takes pills. They're going to make him grow. They're going to cure him."

"Doesn't look like they're working," Asher said.

"You don't know that," she said.

He shrugged.

They were quiet for a few minutes.

"He'll probably be a mensch," her dad finally said.

She looked at him.

"All he's going through now, it'll build character."

Hannah looked at the pink scars on her father's cheek and thought that they looked a lot like the scars on her stomach.

They were quiet again, watching the kids play. Eddie's friend so outweighed him that he was having a difficult time on the teeter-totter. He was stuck several feet up in the air and starting to cry. "OK, OK," his friend was saying, popping up from his seat, sending Eddie to the ground with an audible thud. "Don't be a fucking baby."

The two boys walked to the jungle gym then, the taller boy leading the way and Eddie sheepishly following behind.

"Did that big kid just say the *f*-word?" her dad said.

"They all do," she said.

Asher said nothing.

There were two different boys on the snake slide now.

A young pretty woman pushed her little boy on a swing.

A pair of girls in matching bathing suits played in the sandbox.

"You could do that," her dad said, pointing at the girls.

"I'm not allowed near the sand."

"Oh, yeah, that's right," he said. "Remember when I used to push you on the swings?"

She nodded.

"I'll push you again," he said, putting his arm around her.

Just then Eddie looked over. He was once again at the top of the snake slide, waving at Hannah, all enthusiastic, standing taller than he could ever hope to be, and then he was on his stomach coming down fast, flying right out of the snake's mouth and onto the grass. He stood up, wiped off his little chest and knees, and made his way over to them.

"Can I sign it?" he said, excited, having not yet seen the cast, the metal cuff in the middle nearly twisted all the way to the left.

"I guess," Hannah said.

Eddie looked at her leg and changed his mind. "Oh, I, I don't have a pen," he said.

"My dad does. Don't you, Dad?"

Asher was reaching into his pocket when Eddie's voice stopped him. "It looks weird," the boy admitted.

"It's only temporary," Asher said, angrier than he wanted to sound.

"Didn't you move far away, Dr. Teller?" Eddie said. "My mom said that you're not a Jew anymore or at least you don't want to be one. She said that us Jews don't really have a choice, though. We are what we are—that's what my mom says."

"Is that right?" Asher said.

"She said that you're never coming back, that you're running toward the hills."

"Well, I—" her dad began, but he was interrupted by Eddie's friend, who looked annoyed, standing by the teeter-totter with a hand on his hip, screaming Eddie's name.

"I got to go," Eddie said. And then over his shoulder, "I'll see you at school, Hannah."

As soon as Eddie left, Hannah asked her dad, "If my leg's not broken anymore, what's wrong with it?" She kicked at the air with her good leg and didn't look at him, but stared straight ahead.

"These things take time," he said.

And that was becoming the phrase she hated more than any other phrase because she knew it was a lie and that when people said *these things take time* they really meant *these things might take time* or *these things might not happen at all*. What they were saying is that you needed to be patient regardless, and Hannah thought that was wrong because people shouldn't be told to wait for what might never come. It was like waiting for her dad to call out to her from the other room when he wasn't even in the house, when he didn't even live there anymore.

2 6

MARTIN WAS walking toward the nurses' station and thinking about
Penny's hips. And then there they were, and the rest of her too, coming down
the hall. There she was in her white nurse dress and boxy nurse hat and
spongy nurse shoes. Just as he was imagining her naked, she approached,
slapping his chest playfully with patient charts. "What are you thinking
about, Marty?" she said, coyly.

He shrugged, smiling.

"Thought so," she said, smiling too.

He asked about the boyfriend she had mentioned the last time they had
talked.

"He doesn't love me anymore," she said matter-of-factly.

"Then he's a fool," he said.

"Peter doesn't listen to a single thing I say. I'll be talking about a patient and he'll be staring at his fingernails like he's never seen them before,
or he'll be reading the instructions on the coffeemaker. He makes the coffee every morning and still he'll be studying those stupid instructions like
they're the key to his damn future." She paused. She looked at him. "One
door closes and another one . . ." her voice trailed off.

"What do you mean?" he said, although he knew exactly what she meant.

"There's you standing here," she said.

Did it occur to Penny that he was the one who hit Hannah that morning? He
wasn't sure. He thought that maybe she'd thought of it and then pushed it
away, that she didn't admit it to herself on any conscious level, or maybe
she admitted it but, as is the way with attraction, was able to ignore it or
pretend it wasn't so, so that only the good feelings surfaced. Obviously, Penny
knew he was a guy who kept coming around the hospital even though he
didn't want anyone to know he was coming around, and that he had left
gifts for Hannah, although he didn't want anyone to know that he had
left those gifts.

Penny had told him that gift-givers always wanted credit and that they rarely left gifts without some sort of card or note attached. She said that not wanting credit was one of the most attractive things about him.

"Wait," Penny said now, stepping in front of Martin to get to the little gate that gave her access to the nurses' station. She tapped the gate open with a swaying hip and dropped her charts on the counter. She walked over to the far side of the station, and then stood on her tiptoes, getting something from a top shelf. He watched her calves flex and thought about kissing her. She pulled a white bag from the shelf and scooted it over to him.

"What's this?" He opened the bag and immediately smelled cinnamon. "You remembered," he said.

He liked the way her face was older than his face, with faint lines that only made her more beautiful. He liked the way she talked and walked. He liked what she knew about bodies—and how she talked about her patients. He liked her optimism, the fact that she believed they were very near curing cancer when everyone knew that they were nowhere near curing it. And he liked the way she talked about curing cancer, saying *we*, as in *we're* very close—as if she herself, Nurse Penny, was at the forefront of the research. "We're just this close," she said, putting her two fingers an inch apart.

"You keep coming around here," she said. And again, "You're pretty like a girl, Martin Kettle." She used both his names which seemed to him old-fashioned or charming, and her face wasn't like any face he knew, certainly not Margo's face, which seemed like a dumb girl's next to Penny's.

"Why nursing?" he asked.

"Because it's a good thing to do with your life," she said, looking like she meant it. "I was thinking about becoming a veterinarian because I like animals, but, you know, I like people more."

Martin smiled.

"I know you wait tables at your parents' restaurants, but what else? What are you going to be?" she asked him.

He shrugged and turned away, looking toward the hall where a patient on a gurney was struggling with a couple of orderlies. It was nearly one a.m. and Martin asked why the guy was even awake.

"They're on their way downstairs," she said, twirling a finger by her ear to indicate the guy was crazy.

"Oh," Martin said.

The guy was trying to get up off the gurney, he was screaming about his wife, who, Penny told Martin, had long been dead.

"I want to see my wife," the patient said, and then he fell back on the gurney and seemed to fall asleep.

"What do you want to be?" Penny asked again.

Martin thought about the question.

I want to be a better man.

I want to be the man who didn't hit the girl.

I want to be who I was before I hit the girl.

I want to be a man who hit the girl and then got out of his car to make sure she was breathing.

I want to be a man who didn't hit the girl, but stopped by the side of the road, and held her, a man who gave her mouth-to-mouth and brought her back to life.

"I'll probably go into the restaurant business. Like my dad. It's in my blood," he said, trying to sound convincing. He took a bite of the cinnamon roll, which wasn't warm, but it was tasty anyway.

A buzzer went off and Penny jumped to attention, looking at the blinking panel in front of her, figuring out what patient, what bed. "Mrs. Ryan probably wants a pain pill," she said. "She had spinal surgery a few days ago. Sweetest woman. Hardly ever complains. I'll be right back." Penny snatched a chart from the counter. "Wait here, eat that," she told him over her shoulder.

When she returned from attending to Mrs. Ryan, Martin asked her questions about Hannah and Penny answered them. She told him that Hannah had just turned seven, on July 16, and that she'd gone through a lot: a ruptured spleen, a fractured femur. And worse, something too complicated to explain was wrong with her leg, Penny said, something more serious that would afflict the girl forever. Hannah would limp really badly or, more likely, never walk again. When Martin heard that, he felt sick and guilty all over again. He took a step back. It was one thing to hit the girl, but another to maim her for life.

"Do you know her, Marty?" Penny said, suspiciously. "I thought you said you didn't know her."

"I don't," he said, adamant.

"Hmm," she said.

"I swear," he insisted.

"Don't swear."

"My sister, Sandy, knows her, that's all."

"Feels like something else," she said.

Martin got himself together, made himself stand up straight and look her in the eye. "It's just sad if the kid can't walk—will never walk again. Any kid," he said.

27

THIS TIME, there was no music, no crackers or soft cheese, no little meat-balls to stab with toothpicks. From where Hannah stood eavesdropping in the hall, she could see the coffee table, an unopened bottle of wine, and two empty glasses. Dr. Seth's jacket was thrown over the arm of the couch, his black leather doctor bag at his feet, and his shiny shoes. She could see her mom's shoes too, trendy platforms, her pretty ankles crossed. And she could see the shag carpet that, despite her mother's mad rush to vacuum, looked tired, matted down, and dirty.

Earlier in the day Dr. Bell had removed her cast and made her another one, which was brand-new, bright white and smooth.

Earlier, Hannah and Nina were hopeful for a good ten minutes, thinking that Hannah's foot was all straightened out.

Despite the twisting of the little wheel at night, despite the fact that Hannah never forgot, not once, to do it, her foot turned and moved right before their eyes, flopping back out, the toes pointing away from Hannah and her mother and Dr. Bell too, as if they knew they were guilty and were trying to get the hell out of there.

"I don't know what will happen to her," her mom said now. "If that ri-diculous cast didn't work, why would this one?"

"These things take time," Dr. Seth said.

Hannah rolled her eyes. Why was everyone saying the same dumb thing?

"I need to talk to you, Nina," he said then.

"The house finally sold," her mom said, cutting him off.

"Good, good," he said, absently.

"We'll be able to buy the house in Long Beach now. Long Beach has sidewalks. And there's a house I've already got picked out. It's got a cottage in the back for a housekeeper, or maybe I'll rent it out to a college student, someone to drive Hannah to school."

Hannah couldn't see Dr. Seth's face, but she could tell from his silence that he wasn't giving her mother what she needed, the sort of attention he'd given to her when Nina stood by Hannah's hospital bed, when he didn't really know her yet.

"I need to get home by dinnertime because Evelyn's cooking. And my daughter has a summer-school project she needs help with."

"I understand," she said.

"The kid's always waiting until the last minute—she's like her mother that way."

"Sure," she said. There was a long silence. "Could you look at the air conditioner before you leave, Seth? It'll just take a minute."

"I don't think I . . ."

"Please," Nina said. "It's so hot. It's terrible for Hannah in that cast, stuck in the house all day."

"I don't know much about air conditioners," he said.

"It'll just take a minute. Please," she said.

Hannah peered around and saw that her mom was wearing hot pants, the short, silky tie-dyed things that embarrassed Hannah. She had the same ridiculous outfit in red and blue. Dr. Seth had said that he liked the blue outfit better than the red one, and so her mom had been buying lots of blue these days. Blue blouses and blue nightgowns and blue jeans and blue T-shirts. She heard her mom get up from the couch and she heard Dr. Seth get up too. She heard him sigh. She heard her mom leading him into the family room to look at the air conditioner, and so she followed them.

"Hey there," her mom said.

"How are you doing?" Dr. Seth asked, turning to glance at Hannah. "Getting around on those things OK?"

"Yeah," she said.

"Hannah's doing really well. I'm so proud of her," her mom said.

"Don't know much about air conditioners," Dr. Seth said again.

"Please," Nina said. "Just look at it."

"Let's see here," he said. He was huffing and sighing and sweating. He shook his head.

Nina offered to get him a screwdriver, but he refused. "Asher left his tool kit in the garage," she said. "If you—"

He exhaled heavily, obviously burdened.

"His tools are there and I'm sure—"

"Hey, listen," he interrupted her.

"OK, you don't need it." She held up her hands. "OK, OK. You don't need to use his tools. I understand." She was nervous, talking fast—time was running out and she had so many words to say. "You'll do just fine with what we have here. I'm sure you will. You'll make do. If anyone can do it, you can. I know you. You're so smart," she said, "you can do anything."

"Look, I need to tell you—" he began.

"Don't say it," she said.

"No, I need to—"

But she cut him off again. "Please," she said. "Please, Seth. Please, please." She looked as if she was about to cry, her eyes welling up.

Hannah felt sorry and embarrassed and angry at her mother. She went back to the living room and tried not to listen to them, but she couldn't escape their words or her mother's voice cracking or Dr. Seth's voice becoming louder and deeper and more impatient.

And moments later, he was banging on the air conditioner with a fist. He was looking hard at Nina. "I'm going to tell you something," he said.

Nina said nothing. She sat down at the dining room table and didn't say a word.

"I'm a doctor, a surgeon, a professional, not a technician—you're going to need to get someone else to fix this damn thing."

"Seth," she said. "Please," she said.

He ignored her, stomped back to the living room, where he ignored Hannah too, and picked up his black bag from the carpet.

"I can't fix it," he said at the front door, and somehow, it was certain, he couldn't fix anything. And he wouldn't be back again even to try.

28

MARTIN AND Penny sat together on a bench in the nurses' locker room. It was dinnertime at the hospital and Penny was on her break. They could hear orderlies rolling their carts down the hall and the muffled voices of visitors saying good-bye and making their way to the elevators.

Martin warned her. He told her he was leaving California and had no intention of ever coming back. He admitted he'd been saving his tips for years in a shoebox underneath his bed. "I want to start fresh," he said.

"Start fresh, huh?"

"If I were willing to stick around, it would be for you," he said.

"Me?" She perked up, hopeful.

"*If*," he stressed. He shook his head. "*If* I were willing to stick around. But I'm not. I can't. It was a decision I made before I met you."

She looked down at her watch. "I've only got a few more minutes."

He asked if he could touch her face.

Yes.

He asked if he could touch her hair.

Yes.

He asked if he could kiss her.

Yes.

And then they were standing, hugging, kissing, and her back was up against the lockers. She smelled lemony and medicinal at once. He was hard, pulling at her skirt. Her nurse's hat shifted to the back of her head and she reached up to make it right. She looked at her watch again. "Wait in the lobby until my shift ends," she said. "Come back up here at nine o'clock. I'll be waiting for you."

There was an empty bed and Penny was holding his hand, leading him toward it. There was a comatose patient in the room, a boy with a shaved head and a perfect circle of black sutures forming a band around his skull. His name was Jack, Penny told him. He was two months shy of his eighteenth birthday. Jack had been riding a motorcycle without a helmet on his way to San Diego to see a girl. His brain had burst right through his skull.

"You can be on the 405 freeway one minute and here the next," she said solemnly.

And then she was pulling the curtain closed.

And then she was stepping out of her white shoes and white uniform, unpinning her nurse's hat and setting it on the nightstand.

And Martin was stepping toward her.

And then Martin was having good-bye sex with Penny in 6A, just four doors down from where Hannah Teller had spent most of her time in the hospital.

While he moved he could hear Jack's breathing machine, the horrible suck and push of air. He was thinking about the boy, about catapulting into the air, popping from your bike like a piece of hot corn. He was thinking about Penny too, and how their good-bye sex was also their hello.

Hello, he thought. *Hello, hello, hello.*

"Is your sister really dead?" she said afterward.

"No," he said.

"You can't do what we just did and not tell the person true things," she said.

Martin turned his head, looked at the wall, and said nothing.

"You can't get naked with a person and not tell them the truth," she said.

"People do it all the time," he said softly.

"Yes, but not us, Martin—not people who feel like us." She leaned back on the pillow. "What if I told you I already know?" she said.

"I'm going to New York."

"Say it out loud, Martin."

But he didn't say it, and she put her arms around him, and he started crying, and Penny was kissing his face, his lips, and then she was climbing on top of him, demanding only that. "OK, be quiet then, don't talk," she told him. "You don't have to say a word."

PART 2

1

HANNAH'S CASTS were continuous—one after the other, year after year after year. Second grade into third into fourth into fifth, through the summer and through the fall—and here Hannah was in eighth grade and still wearing one. This was supposedly the last one, and it was the biggest one yet, a toe-to-groin, plaster from her toes' second knuckles up to her pelvic bone.

She had signatures and drawings on the cast from her best friends, Rebecca and Megan, even from Rudy Evans, a boy who stuttered and whom she'd been arguing with about evolution since the sixth grade. Rudy had written across her knee in bold, black letters *God Made the World,* to which Hannah added an equally bold red question mark. Her favorite signature, from Pablo Parker, the guy she'd had a crush on since grade school, was accompanied by one of his abstract drawings. She'd spent time in her bedroom with her eyes fixed on Pablo's lovely cursive and his sketch of an unrecognizable something. She'd run her finger along the rough surface, trying to figure it out. *I'm into abstract art,* was what he'd said when he'd leaned down in the quad to sign and draw.

The casts dried and settled and aged.

The skin inside the tunnel flaked and itched.

And while one was being removed, there were rolls of plaster smoking in the sink behind a doctor's head.

Hannah had learned which casts offered partial mobility and which were the most confining. She knew which ones the kids at school were most likely to sign, knew how they'd line up excited with their colored pens and markers, and which ones they'd most certainly stay away from, like that one from long ago, the one she and her mother had to twist at night—that thing that was both cast and brace.

Hannah adapted. She didn't hobble about slowly. There were days she raced home from school on those crutches with especially exciting news: the highest grade on a science project, a speaking part in the school play, or an invitation to the movies from the popular girls. She'd whiz past the neighborhood girls then, whose two legs worked, however leisurely, in unison—she must have been a blur of aluminum crutches and plaster and long dark hair. She liked to believe her speed was impressive.

Most casts came up to just below her knee—and one of them, a walking cast, was her favorite. In it, she was almost normal. With its rubber heel plastered to the bottom, she was able to lean her crutches against the wall and walk without them. She could ride a bike and carry her own schoolbooks.

Hannah had spent the years since the accident mostly in a cast and on crutches, but sometimes she was forced to wear a big metal brace attached to the most hideous orthopedic shoe. The shoe was heavy and awkward, a bright, shockingly white leather, and, of course, she had to wear its ugly twin on her perfectly functional right foot. Hannah did her best to hide the silver clamps that came down the side of her leg with too-long pants or bell-bottom jeans, which only improved the likelihood of tripping, stumbling to the floor, and exposing everything: the horrible vice-like contraption forming huge metal parentheses around her skinny ankle and calf, the clunky unfashionable oxford.

At least when she was wearing a cast, she could wear whatever one shoe she wanted to wear. She could also pretend to new kids and strangers that her leg was merely broken—something that happened to a lot of kids and implied you were a risk-taker, a rebel, propelling yourself out of a swing in midflight or climbing some fence you had no business climbing.

If a kid at school broke a limb, he or she seemed to feel an instant affinity with Hannah. Their newfound immobility made them curious, nudged them toward her, as if she had every answer. It signaled a time to make new, similarly immobile friends, however temporarily. In fifth grade, a girl in a short cast that barely covered her ankle sat down next to Hannah at lunch for the very first time.

"Mine comes off in six weeks," Kelly chirped. She opened her bright pink lunch pail and took out a sandwich.

"You're lucky," Hannah's pal Rebecca said.

But Kelly didn't seem interested in Rebecca or Megan either. "Want my apple?" Kelly said, eyes fixed directly on Hannah.

And for six weeks, Kelly offered Hannah her fruit. A banana. A bag of Bing cherries. And, once, two of the tiniest, sweetest tangerines Hannah had ever tasted. Kelly made Hannah's group of three into a group of four, but when that ankle cast came off, Kelly carried her tray of Tater Tots and a corn dog right past the three girls, ate her own fruit, and didn't look back.

A couple years ago, Rudy Evans, the religious boy who stuttered, showed up to school with his arm in a sling, complaining about his b-b-bike's shitty brakes. Rudy changed desks, settling in next to Hannah in science class, and asked her to be on his d-d-dissection team. They worked for several days on a frog, and because of Rudy's broken arm, Hannah did the dirty work. She sliced the frog's belly and pinned his slippery skin, marveling at the spleen, the liver, the tiny set of gray kidneys.

During Nutrition Break, Rebecca and Megan would head for the swings while Hannah and Rudy sat on a bench in the quad, eating cookies and drinking juice. They talked about everything: movies, how much Rudy loved ch-church, how kids didn't judge him there. They talked about their parents' divorces, what it felt like to wear a cast and what it felt like to have one put on, how warm plaster was when it was first applied. It was easy for her to pretend he didn't stutter, to try to minimize his discomfort. She'd watch his lips when the words came easily, but when they started to bubble and struggle out of his mouth, she'd look away, patiently, nodding *I'm listening, I'm listening.*

What effort, she thought.

It's like me getting from here to there.

It's like walking.

It was hard, admitting how much she wanted it, and when Hannah thought of *walking,* it wasn't a verb, but a noun, something she could hold in her hand like a book or clock. And when she imagined herself doing so, she wasn't limping. In her dreams, her gait was perfect, balanced, and lovely to behold.

She'd been through a series of doctors, each one enthusiastically welcoming her and her mother into his office, full of new ideas, only to shake his head in frustration a few months later and admit he didn't know what to do with her. It was nerve and muscle damage that even the best of them didn't seem to recognize, so she was shuffled from one bespectacled man with plaques on his wall—with a cupboard full of rolls of plaster, with a whirring saw in his hand—to another. Always her mother by her side, whispering, *Hannah, it's a new day. You're the one, Doctor. I can feel it.*

I'll do my best, Mrs. Teller, he'd say.

Call me Nina, she'd say, smiling, coy, and it seemed to Hannah from where she sat on the examination table, vulnerable and often pissed off at the pure repetition of these visits, that it was important to her mother that the doctor find her attractive. He could be old and jowly, bald and doughy, he could have had more hair sprouting from his nose and ears than from his head, as was often the case, and still her mother would light up when she saw that white jacket and swinging stethoscope. She'd lean in, nodding— eyes big, lashes long and black with mascara—and listen intently to every word he said.

Hannah's father had left her mother for someone younger, blonder, and more athletic, and even now, years later and remarried, her mom continued to need so much male confirmation. What magnified Hannah's annoyance was how easy it was to contrast her mother's beauty—her smooth skin and good bone structure, her figure, those firm and shapely legs—to the mess in front of them: Hannah's damaged leg, how skinny it was without muscle, atrophied and pale, how the toes she could barely move had curled into claws.

After each round of casts or braces or surgeries or a combination of the three, a doctor would prop her up and ask her to walk across the room. And she'd fail, the beginning of her own somersault, left foot giving way.

I'm out of ideas, this one said, and sent her to that one, his colleague or a doctor whose reputation preceded him or someone he'd met at a party who'd won prestigious awards and specialized in children's orthopedics.

Initially a cast was bright white, as clean with possibility as a sheet of paper, and the doctor's face was full of challenge and determination, an excitement that was contagious. Her mother's face held hope, her eyes lit up, and she'd squeeze Hannah's shoulder, offering a silent thanks to the God they no longer had time for.

At the end, though, the cast was gray and dirty, the cotton fraying where it opened at her toes. After it was removed, it was a thing cracked in half, sitting beside Hannah on the examination table, open like a split hard-boiled egg. Each doctor reacted with the same resignation and visible disappointment when faced so bluntly with what he could not fix: a girl clinging to the wall, a girl who needed so much coaxing, a girl falling to the floor, a girl finally refusing to even try.

Hannah's last surgeon, Dr. Russo, had been optimistic and had gone so far as to make promises. "I'm not saying you won't limp—you will, mostly when you're tired, though. But you'll walk. I've had patients with even more nerve damage walk right out of here," he'd said. It was all so simple, putting one foot in front of the other, and making it across the street. It was like breathing or sleeping, something most people didn't think about.

It was all she wanted.

Girls her age wanted other things.

Those first years, they wanted to skip and play hopscotch and swim at the community pool. They wanted bikes with banana seats, with colorful fringe hanging from the handlebars. The girls wanted recess, tetherball and tag, wanted boys to chase and tease and pinch, and even in skirts, they'd climb the monkey bars. They'd swing from fat silver hoops, transported, showing off their cotton panties.

Now her peers' steps carried them through malls, to football games and skating rinks. They sauntered in groups, so many lean legs working together, to parties and dances, to Carnation Park East, where the boys had become guys with faint mustaches and cracking voices, guys who waited with cigarettes and joints, with brown bags of fruity wine, purple enough to stain the girls' teeth.

Last week, her crush Pablo Parker broke his leg during football practice and the whole school was abuzz. A complex fracture, they said. He might not play for a year or more. Maybe he'd never play again. Today, wearing his own toe-to-groin, Pablo joined Hannah on the bleachers, where she was doing her math homework and waiting for Megan to finish up sixth-period PE. She looked up from her notebook and watched Pablo dramatically maneuvering, getting situated, and finally sitting down with a cranky huff. His cast was on his right leg and hers was on her left, so their two free thighs were just inches apart. She tried not to think about it. He gestured with his chin, saying, "This fucking thing will be gone in three months.

Better be off by Christmas break. I'll die, man. I can't surf. I can't take a fucking shower."

"Yeah," she said.

"My mom says I have to take a bath. Guys don't take baths," he said.

"A bath isn't so bad. I take baths," she told him, immediately embarrassed. "I mean, I have to. You know."

They were quiet for a couple minutes, him looking to the field, where the other players had made their way out for practice. She had her head down, was pretending to read from her notebook, but she couldn't focus on fractions and decimals. She was thinking that perhaps she'd said too much, that maybe he was imagining her bathing like she was imagining him stepping into the tub, naked, except for his own toe-to-groin.

He stuck two fingers in his mouth and whistled so loudly it made Hannah flinch. His able-bodied buddies turned and waved—a couple of them shouting *Hey, Pablo* through their helmets. When they resumed practice, Pablo turned to her. She looked up from her notebook.

"What's wrong with your leg anyway?" he asked.

"I don't know," she said.

"You can't dance or anything?"

She laughed. "I don't think I'd be a dancer either way."

"You'd be great."

"Why do you say that?"

He shrugged. "I want you to sign mine. Remember, I signed yours," he said, dark eyes playful. He reached into his book bag for a pen.

"I'll have to hop over you," she said, tentatively.

"Be my guest." Pablo leaned back, making room for her, and she was aware of his broad chest and his T-shirt pulling at the shoulders.

"It'll be weird."

"It won't be weird."

She put her notebook on the bleachers and used her arms to lift herself up. She stood, and then hopped in front of him, with her back to his chest, thinking that he had a very good look at her ass, if he wanted it. Finally, she sat down next to him, their two plastered thighs knocking. And then she was leaning over, pen in hand. She held the pen in the air a moment, trying to decide what to write.

"Write anything," he said.

"I'm thinking," she said. And then she leaned in closer so that her hair brushed his lap and she had to remind herself to breathe. He smelled like soap and boy and familiar plaster too.

"Fully engage," he said.

"What?" she looked up, aware of how close their lips were, and quickly looked down again.

"When I signed yours, I was fully engaged," he said. "My art teacher tells us all the time to 'fully engage.'"

She was writing by then. "Three months will fly," she wrote. "And then you'll fly too."

After she was finished, she leaned back, aware that something had switched and changed and flipped between them. She couldn't put it into words, but she knew they wouldn't be the same. They might be more comfortable and get to know each other as friends or they might be awkward, speechless in the school corridors.

He bent forward, looking at her signature and words. He nodded his approval. "I want to ask you something," he said then. "What do you do about the itching?"

"Wire hanger," she said. "But you have to be careful. You could hurt yourself."

He moved closer to her and their casts clacked again. "How can you stand it? Year after fucking year," he wanted to know.

She shrugged, not knowing what to say.

"It's your whole life," Pablo continued. "I mean, for you, Hannah, there's no end in sight."

"There's an end," she said, not at all sure. And her feelings about his comments were mixed. She felt irritated that he'd reduced her life to this one big and continuing problem, but also she felt excited: He'd said her name out loud, and his observation, however reductive, meant he'd noticed her, year after year after year.

2

BELMONT HEIGHTS was a place with sidewalks and palm trees and beachy bungalows, a cheerful neighborhood where sweet-faced retirees donned orange vests and silver whistles, where they held up stop signs and cheerfully led the schoolchildren across the street.

Their house was Spanish-style, a modest two-bedroom, two-bathroom, lots of redbrick and terra cotta tile, hardwood floors and arches introducing the dining room and kitchen. In the big backyard, there was a tire swing hanging from a tree and a one-bedroom apartment that Hannah's mom called a cottage. It was where Hannah's stepfather, Azeem, lived briefly as their tenant before he and Nina became a couple.

When they first moved in, Nina furnished the cottage with a bed and a dresser, hoping to find someone to take Hannah to school in the mornings. She put up fliers at the university near their home, offering free rent in exchange for Hannah's transportation. The cottage didn't have a shower or a stove, which meant that the prospective tenant would need access to the main house. Nina had hoped for a college girl, someone who might become a big sister to Hannah, but only young men had applied, and after interviewing several of them, she settled on Azeem, a clean-cut Arab student, who said he was studying psychology.

Yes, he *was* studying psychology, like he'd said in the interview, but once he'd moved in and Nina asked about his studies, he told her, proudly, puffing up, she thought, that his emphasis was in human sexuality. Even Azeem's earliest conversations with Nina were peppered with all that he'd been learning.

When he talked about Masters and Johnson, the sexual revolution, and intimacy therapy, his face lit up.

He'd drop the word *penis* into a conversation and it was like he was holding his own out to her.

He wanted to join a nudist camp, he admitted one morning, and she couldn't help but picture him naked. He was sitting at the table with a bowl of granola and Nina leaned against the kitchen counter with a cup of coffee.

"There's a great place up in Topanga Canyon. Would you ever want to go?" He lifted his spoon, held it in the air a moment, and looked at her.

She took a sip of coffee but didn't answer him.

"Does a place like that interest you?" he pressed.

"I don't know," she said, "but I've never been shy about that sort of thing, either."

He smiled at her, then dipped his spoon into the bowl, lifting a hearty bite of cereal to his mouth.

It was the worst sort of flirting, she thought, as if they were naked together already.

He told her he was writing a term paper on what he called *the orgasm*.

"A whole paper?" She laughed nervously. How much was there to say? But even as she teased him, she imagined herself having one right there at the kitchen table.

He'd only been living in the cottage for a week, running into Nina in the house and having those short, charged conversations, and the tension between them was undeniable. He was eleven years younger than she was, a student, a kid, she had told herself. Still, in the kitchen a few mornings later, he reached up into the cupboard for a bowl and Nina was reaching for a cup, and their fingers brushed, and they both laughed awkwardly, moving away from each other. The next morning when she entered the kitchen, it was he who was nervous, knocking over his box of granola with an elbow. Clusters of cereal fell from the counter to the floor, almonds and raisins and dates.

"I'm sorry if I surprised you," Nina said. "Here, you eat in peace. I'll be quick." She poured herself a cup of coffee and carried it into the living room.

From where she sat on the couch, she could see his hunched body, the white T-shirt taut against his strong back as he cleaned up the cereal.

And that night in the hallway, there they both were again, each offering to let the other past first—*no, you go, you go, no you go*—until finally they both stepped at the same time, bumping chest to chest, and squeezed by. Nina couldn't sleep that night, tossing fitfully, and hoped that he wasn't sleeping in the cottage out back, either.

She stepped on an almond sliver the next day and smashed a lone raisin several days later that he'd missed. She was peeling the raisin from her bare foot, thinking about him, when he entered the kitchen. "I was just thinking about you," she blurted out.

"And you me. I mean, me you," he said.

And that night he moved himself into her bedroom, and within the week, his clothes joined her clothes in the closet, and that weekend, they were heading up to The Elysium, the nudist camp in Topanga he'd told her about, to take off those clothes, and within the year, they were married. They had one ceremony at the courthouse downtown, where Nina wore a light-blue dress and cream-colored shoes, Azeem wore jeans and a gray button-down shirt, and Hannah, in her walking cast that month, followed them up the steps into the building.

And two weeks later, they had a second ceremony at the nudist camp, where they stood naked with all the other naked people, and said their vows on the lawn.

3

HANNAH'S MOM and Azeem wanted her to join them on the weekends at the nudist camp, but she refused. They tried begging. They tried bribes. They wouldn't let up. They described the camp as a paradise. The rolling lawns and clean air. Los Angeles pollution disappeared once you left the city and went up into the mountains, they said. There are tennis courts, volleyball, and all the nudist kids. There's a wonderful brother and sister, Mitch and Mica, who so want to meet you, her mom said. They're just your age, twins. They're in the gifted classes too. They like the same music you like. They read and write, and the boy keeps a journal. He likes science and insects just like you do.

Hannah pictured a naked fourteen-year-old boy on a green hill writing in a little book, drawing spiders. She shook her head no.

"It's a family camp," they reminded her.

"Naked family," she responded.

"Fine," her mom said. "We'll bring the camp to you."

And on Fridays, Hannah's mom and Azeem stepped out of their pajamas the minute they woke up and did just that. They turned up the thermostat and moved around the house. Her mom did laundry, scooped the clothes they were not wearing into the washing machine. Azeem pushed the vacuum in the living room. He sat down at the desk in the den and studied. Her mom dressed for work, but the minute the day was done and she returned home, the skirt and blouse came off.

It was a lot to see.

It was more of them than Hannah wanted to see.

While the one thing Hannah could *not* see was her own body—at least not all at once. There was her leg covered up with plaster, sometimes to the knee, but today to her crotch. Unlike her mom and Azeem, she was never naked. Even stepping into the bathtub with a trash bag twisted and tied around her cast, she was partially covered up. She was always hidden. She was always trying to scratch a part of herself she couldn't see. She wasn't whole, not really. She was a girl in pieces—there were her arms, muscled from using crutches in a way other girls' arms were not. Her biceps and forearms were sharp angles while other girls her age still held on to a thin layer of baby fat that made their limbs soft. That softness was only one of the things she envied. She had mismatching legs, one lean and muscular from all the extra work it did and the other one thin and atrophied.

If I'm a girl in pieces, if I'm fragmented, if I'm imperfect parts that do not fit together, my mom and Azeem are whole bodies, was what she thought, watching them on Fridays.

The first Friday was startling despite the buildup and warnings—*remember what we're doing on Friday,* her mom had said early in the week; *don't forget,* Azeem reminded her on Thursday while they watched the news. Ten more hours, they said when kissing her good night. Still, watching them make breakfast was a surprise, and dinner too—the ease with which they handed each other the spices and utensils—the pepper, the cumin, the spatula, the plastic basting tube that her mom used to squeeze the hot fat onto the chicken's back. She tried to look at their eyes when they talked to her but it was all too much. Azeem stirred the pot of couscous. After a quick taste, he stood on his toes to reach a top shelf for the pot's lid. Her mother leaned down, opened the oven, and hot air shot into the room, pushing her back while her breasts swung, big and heavy, in front of her. Hannah was aware of her T-shirt, the fabric covering her shoulders and chest, she was aware of her jeans, the waistband cutting so slightly into her stomach, one denim leg cut off completely for the cast to make its way through, and she was aware of her tennis shoe and one sock.

At the table, she tried unsuccessfully to ignore her mom's breasts, which didn't look as good and high as they did when she walked around the house, shoulders back, aware of her posture. As her mom leaned over and spooned some couscous onto her plate, Hannah noticed a sad humility to those breasts, their loose skin and bumpy dark nipples.

She tried to ignore Azeem's chest too when he asked her questions about school, when he talked about his own final exams that were coming up, a research paper that was due the following week. "I'm writing about the history of nudism," he said.

"Tell her the specifics," Nina said, proud.

"I'm exploring how nudism is viewed in other cultures. I'm contrasting the Europeans with Americans."

"Mostly it's about how hung up Americans are," her mom said, taking a sip of her water.

Azeem nodded. He picked up his fork and knife. He cut into the chicken breast, rubbed what he'd cut in a circle on his plate, soaking up the juices, and stuffed it into his mouth.

Hannah tried not to look at her stepfather's ass when he stepped away from the table to get seconds, but she couldn't resist. He was an average man in so many respects, at least physically—average height, average weight, and on his body an average amount of hair, except for his ass, which was extremely furry. Hannah thought of two little black dogs walking away in midair. She'd seen men's asses in movies and in the books Azeem read, and she'd never seen an ass like that.

Hannah turned and looked at her mom. "This guy from school broke his leg last week," she said. "We're sort of becoming friends."

"Friends?" her mom said, smiling big.

"It's not like that," Hannah said.

Just then, Azeem, with a steaming piece of chicken on his plate, sat down. "What did I miss?"

"Nothing," Hannah said.

"Hannah was going to tell me something about a friend of hers," Nina said.

"Pablo broke his leg playing football," Hannah said.

"That's too bad," Nina said.

"Multiple fracture. His cast looks like mine."

"A toe-to-groin?" Her mom was surprised.

Hannah nodded. "He might be coming over here to study for a test. It won't be on a Friday, that's for sure," she said.

"The more the merrier," Azeem said.

"Please, *please*, don't mention the nudist camp," she said.

"Maybe he'd like to come along one Saturday," Azeem said, smiling.

"You could invite Rebecca or Megan," her mom teased.

"Yeah, right," Hannah said.

"What else shouldn't we talk about?" Azeem asked.

"Your paper on the history of nudism."

"*Oh*-kay."

"Or your sex studies. Or your nudist friends." Once Hannah started, she couldn't stop. The list was long. The three of them could be sitting at the table all night. "Or the fact that you're naked here on Fridays," she said. "That's particularly embarrassing."

"Jesus," he said, looking to Nina for backup.

"What?" Nina said, reaching for the saltshaker. "She hasn't told her friends. She tells them we like going to the beach—that's why we're tan, right?"

Hannah nodded.

"I thought Rebecca might know," Azeem said.

"No way," Hannah said.

"We embarrass her," her mom said. "You're not embarrassed of your father, are you?"

"I am *too*," Hannah said, and they all laughed.

Rebecca, Megan, and Hannah were mostly a trio, but she knew there were times when she was a burden. She could see it in their eyes, the looks they exchanged when one of them had to hold her crutches at the bowling alley while she hopped up to the green line of tape on the floor, that ridiculously heavy ball in her arms. Then there was the spectacle the three of them made at the shopping center. Hannah did her best to keep up, but her crutches were cumbersome, especially in crowds, and she knew that she took up more than her allotted space in the world. It was difficult to carry her own bags, although she tried, swinging whatever it was down the side of one crutch until Megan or Rebecca grew tired of watching her struggle. Sometimes she'd just call her mom or Azeem from a payphone, feign a stomachache, and ask one of them to pick her up.

"Maybe you *should* tell the girls about the camp," her mother said on a Monday night. The two of them were on their way to pick up Chinese food for dinner. "We're not ashamed, you know?" They were stopped at a red light and Nina was looking at Hannah. "The human body is a beautiful thing."

Hannah rolled her eyes.

"We're not ashamed," she said again.

"It's not about you," Hannah said, angrily.

At home, it was hard for Hannah to listen to them talk about their weekend plans and even harder for her to enjoy her spicy beef. Her mom and stepdad were eating mu shu chicken and planning their weekend visit to The Elysium. They were talking about Azeem's brother and his epilepsy, Azeem saying that a trip to the States might be just what the boy needs. Hannah looked at her mom's face, which seemed to tighten up at the mention of a visitor. "I don't know," she said. "You don't want Mustafa to even know that we're married. Seems like a big secret to keep."

"What? Why?" Hannah said, surprised.

"It's not him. It's my parents." Azeem dipped his egg roll into the sweet-and-sour sauce, and sighed.

"Why don't they know you're married?" Hannah wanted to know.

"They have other plans for me," he said.

She went to her room and thought about her secrets. Her mom and Azeem's marriage was a secret. Her leg was a secret, even to herself; it was something she couldn't see or understand. The nudist camp was a secret. Her feelings about Pablo, which were growing every time she saw him struggling around on those crutches, carrying his art notebook under his arm, were a secret.

She thought about calling her dad, but decided against it. Her mom and Azeem were supposed to drop her off at his house this weekend. She'd wait until then to talk to him. She hadn't seen him in two months, since her last operation, which was a record for them. When they did talk on the phone, he was reserved and aloof. She could almost see him looking out the window into his backyard, watching the trees standing still. The conversations were stilted, and despite missing him, she felt the urge to put down the receiver right after the *hello, how are you* left her lips. She tried, though. She told him about going to the mall with Rebecca and Megan, and about bowling on Saturday night. She told him that for a girl on crutches her score was pretty good. She asked her dad about her new baby brother and her stepmom, Christy, but he was uncommunicative and answered mostly with grunts. Sometimes she'd tell a whole story and he wouldn't respond at all and she'd wonder if the phone line had been disconnected. She'd sit in the silence that followed and wait until he sprung to life with a *What, Hannah, what were you saying? I'm sorry, honey. I've got a lot on my mind.*

Hannah blamed his remoteness on the argument her parents had the day of her last surgery. She was coming in and out of consciousness, drugged up on anesthesia and pain medicine, but she remembered the two of them standing by her bedside, whisper-screaming at each other. Apparently her father didn't trust Dr. Russo and her mother believed every word the doctor said. Her dad was tired, he said, of the doctors' lies and promises, angry that Hannah's ankle was bleeding so heavily that a big red circle had soaked through the plaster. Hearing that, Hannah forced herself up, leaned forward, craned her neck, and tried to get a glimpse of the bloodstain, but she was too weak and fell against the pillow.

"Horrible," he said. "How much does she have to go through? Years and years of this. Seven years of this," he said.

"You're hardly around to witness it. It's Azeem who parents her."

"Where's Azeem today?"

"He's at school."

"I bet. I know what he studies. And he's been studying it for years, it seems to me. He should be an expert."

"Azeem's going to help a lot of people when he's a therapist."

"Help them, sure," Asher said sarcastically. "I saw what you were reading."

"What?"

"I saw your book. I saw it sitting on top of your purse. *Open Marriage. Mishegas,*" he said. "It's horrible, Nina. What kind of example are you setting? You marry an Arab. You join a nudist camp. And now *this.*"

"Who are you to judge?"

"I'm Hannah's father. I'm a good man now."

"Now?" her mother said, laughing.

"I say my prayers," he continued. "I've been praying. I want Hannah to walk. What I wouldn't give . . ." He paused. He said something Hannah couldn't make out, and then said something she heard perfectly. "You should have driven her to school that day," he said.

"It's not my fault. Don't you dare," her mom said, her voice rising.

"You're the mother," he said.

"Fuck you," she said.

"Beautiful," he said.

"Fuck you," she repeated, even louder this time.

"Very nice. Ladylike. My ex-wife, the mother of my child, uses the f-word. She's a wife and she wants to sleep around. What do you people call it—swinging?"

"The f-word?" she said, laughing. "You silly little man. You silly little Jew for Jesus."

"Enough," he said.

"You're no Jew, Asher. You're an anti-Jew. You shouldn't call yourself a Jew for Jesus—it's absurd."

"What do you swingers know about Jesus?"

"I'm not a . . ." she began. "Oh, forget it."

"What do you know about Jesus?" he said again.

"*I know* that if you think he's the son of God, if you think—never mind," she said. "I want to be with Hannah."

And within seconds the two of them were focused on her, one patting her right hand and one her left, the two of them looking down at her with exaggerated concern and sympathy one moment, but quickly looking up and glaring at each other the next.

Now, in her bedroom, Hannah left her crutches on the floor, hopped to her dresser, and turned on the little black-and-white television. She put on her pajamas and got in bed, propped pillows behind her back and also put one at the foot of the bed for her cast. She could hear her mom and Azeem still talking about his brother, Mustafa. Their voices were getting louder. Azeem was saying something about the doctors in America being miracle workers.

"Ask Hannah if they're miracle workers," her mom said.

"They know plenty," he said, and Hannah was thinking that they didn't know *plenty* about her leg.

She hopped back to the TV and turned up the volume to drown out their voices. On the news, there was footage of the Birmingham tornado. Two dump trucks tossed into the air like toys, trees snapping and debarked, and twenty-two deaths.

Hannah imagined being picked up by a black tunnel of air and being carried to another town.

She imagined the twenty-two bodies flying through the dark sky.

She imagined those trees stripped bare. She thought about Pablo's lips. She thought about his smile, how his teeth were nearly perfect, except for the one in front that barely overlapped the one next to it. She loved that overlapping tooth.

When she heard her mom and Azeem's bedroom door close, Hannah got up, hopped over to the television again, and turned down the volume. She stared at the phone a few seconds before picking it up to call her dad.

4

AZEEM WANTED Nina to open her marriage. It was *their* marriage, obviously, but when he said it the first few times, he called it hers, which made it sound like she was in it alone. Usually she was quick to correct his English, but this particular mistake was appropriate and private, something he was unlikely to say in front of strangers—*Will you open your marriage, Nina?*—so for more than a month she let him continue calling it hers.

At first it came out of his mouth reluctantly, with the tiniest apology embedded in its tone. It came out of his mouth as a question directed at her, which implied that there was a decision to make, an answer to give. And then it came out as a suggestion, easy and lightweight, tossed at her in the car or over dinner or at the grocery store.

Maybe make a left at the light.

Please hand me that gallon of milk.

You might want to grab a sweater.

You might want to grab a man who you might want to sleep with.

I might want to touch you tonight.

I might want to touch a woman who isn't you.

I might want to touch her again tomorrow.

Nina knew what was coming, how the words would eventually morph and twist, becoming what they'd been since the idea's inception: an ultimatum. And she was just waiting.

Azeem had quit his job waiting tables to study full-time, and a week later, his human sexuality professor, Dr. Winter, assigned the book *Open Marriage*, which Azeem was able to read and reread with all of his extra time. Halfway into the book, Azeem converted—Nina saw it in his posture and heard it in his excited grunts of agreement. There was a visible tensing of his muscles. He nodded, squinted, deep in thought. He wanted someone on the side, a woman or two or three of them. He was ready for flight, his shoulders sharpening into wings. He pulled on his short beard and looked over at Nina, wondering about her limits, she could tell.

In the past, when he was through with them, Azeem had offered her his textbooks: *Human Sexual Response, Anatomy of an Orgasm, The Joyous Couple, Feel Him, Feel Her, and Feel Good,* and usually she read them quickly and with enthusiasm. Nina taught high school English and spent her days talking to teenagers about love and betrayal in the most euphemistic language, and she liked to sit next to Azeem on the couch after dinner and talk, *really* talk, about what one body did with another body. It felt good in her mouth to say *clitoral stimulation* and *penile response.* She felt smart and sexy knowing the physiological words for things: the filmy sheen that covered her chest and neck after she came was a *perspiratory reaction,* the grimace she made during orgasm a result of *myotonic tension.* She felt enlightened and complicated, reading those books and having those talks, like she was more than just a good Jewish girl from Philadelphia. She was grading papers, reading through her twelfth-graders' responses to Shakespeare, Chaucer, and Jane Austen, while Azeem read from *Open Marriage.* She had spent many nights just like this, in bed next to him, flipping through a magazine or doing her schoolwork. Sometimes she'd glance over his shoulder and see a particularly interesting diagram or photograph—and she'd want to do right then what the creative couple was doing on the page. Now, as he read the book, she looked at the authors' photo on the back—the smiling O'Neills, a married couple, who seemed to be mocking her with their challenge—and felt a horrible queasiness.

Nina wore lightweight pajamas, her long dark hair twisted on top of her head with a clip shaped like a seashell. Her glasses were halfway down her nose. Azeem wore dark sweatpants, white socks, and no shirt. Every now and then he'd sigh and rest his palm on his flat, hairy stomach.

"Nina?" It was the same voice he used when he wanted to choose what movie they'd see or decide where they'd go for dinner.

"Hang on." She held up a finger. "Give me a minute. Let me finish this last paragraph." As a compromise, she inched her free hand closer to his thigh, until the tips of her fingers were warmed just under his leg.

He stopped reading, placed the book between them on the bed, and looked at her. She didn't look back. Not yet. She knew what this particular book was called. It didn't take an expert to imagine what *Open Marriage* espoused: the limitations of monogamy, the unnaturalness of lifelong partnerships, how sex with others could only enhance a marriage. Selfish, self-serving delusional bullshit, as far as she was concerned.

She finished the last few lines of her student's paper and closed the folder before looking at him. "OK," she finally said.

"Do you think you might . . . ? Would you ever . . ." he began, hesitant, and then stopped himself.

"Tell me."

"You're busy. Finish your schoolwork."

Nina noticed that her arms were tightly folded against her chest and uncrossed them. She tried to smile. "Come on," she said.

He picked up the book. "It says here . . . ," he began. He adjusted himself, turning to her.

"What?" she said.

"Well, they say that a couple might want to, that a couple should . . ." He paused. "There's a chapter on *rewriting the contract*. There's one on *living for now*."

She said nothing.

She stared at him and let him talk.

"There's a group of people from Trinidad and they have an expression." He opened the book and flipped through its pages until he found what he was looking for. "Here, here," he said, excited, pointing at the words. "These Trinidadians, they say it's 'now for now.'"

"Hmm," she said.

"And what it means is that the immediate moment is all a man has— or a woman. It's all we have. These sixty seconds in front of you." He said those last words slowly. He gestured with his forefinger and thumb as if he were measuring a very small penis.

She laughed, sadly. "I've been through this before, you know. Asher wanted an open marriage too. He just didn't call it that."

"There was nothing *open* about it. He was secretive—he *lied*—and wanted someone else full-time."

Despite what she knew was coming, she encouraged him to continue. It was only talking. She was only listening. "Keep going," she said.

"If you don't make the very most out of those sixty seconds, then you're dead."

"You're not *dead*."

"Well, you're almost dead, as good as dead. That's their point." He looked at her face and studied her eyes.

"It's not very profound. Or even new, Azeem."

"Forget it. I knew you wouldn't want to talk about this—at least not yet. You're not ready. I should have known. I should have waited. In a few months it could be your idea. Who knows?" He turned away a second, but then turned back to her. "Nina, you like the nudist camp."

"So?"

"You can't say it's not sexual."

"I *can* say that, actually."

"Come on."

"It *isn't* sexual to me, Azeem. After a couple weekends of looking at them, it seems . . . normal. And it's relaxing. There's certainly nothing relaxing about having sex with other people."

"Well, the book says . . . ," he began again.

"I don't want to know what the book says. Just ask the question. *Your* question—not theirs." She looked down at the O'Neills and hated them, hated that she shared a first name with Nena O'Neill, and hated the staged photograph. George O'Neill in all black, his shirt unbuttoned, those ridiculous sideburns, and his wife in a red turtleneck and white blazer—the two of them looking into each other's eyes and smiling. They could be anyone. He could be a real estate agent, she could be a housewife, or, like Nina, a high school teacher. They were frauds, she knew it. They were like those famous marriage counselors she'd seen on Phil Donohue, Dr. and Dr. So-and-So, who spewed out their advice to sad or frustrated couples, and then got a divorce themselves after just one year. All that talk about conciliation—and what had it done for them?

Azeem took a deep breath. He leaned closer. She could smell the garlic they'd had for dinner. "Would you ever consider opening your marriage?" he said.

"I knew this was coming. Of course this was coming," she said.

"Well?"

"Well, no."

"Why?"

"We're *married*."

"Yes."

"We have a contract. We're married," she said again. "Look, Azeem, we're not dating. It's not like we just met and need to make sure. I thought we were sure—that's why a couple gets married. That and your green card, maybe."

"It wasn't my green card, Nina." His voice was stern, adamant. "It was you. I want to be with you. It's our little family. It's you and Hannah," he said, insulted.

"A man gets married because he's positive. He doesn't *want* anyone else."

She thought of her first husband and the secret girlfriend he'd had for years and felt angry at Asher all over again. "Look, Azeem, if you're not happy or satisfied—" She paused. She tried not to cry. "When a couple gets married, they've made a decision about exclusion. And loyalty. That's what we did when we stood up there in front of those people and promised each other."

"I *am* loyal," he said. "I don't want to *marry* anyone but you."

"Great," she said. "Thanks for that." She crossed her arms in front of her chest again, not giving a fuck if it made her look uptight and bitchy, and the student folders fell to the floor. "Damn it," she said, leaning over the bed to gather them up.

"I didn't think you'd want to do this yet. I knew you weren't ready."

"*Ready?* Do you realize how patronizing that sounds?"

"I knew you wouldn't want to open your marriage, Nina. At least not without reading the book. The O'Neills give some very interesting points."

Nina, angrily reorganizing the students' folders in her lap, corrected him. "*Make* points. They *make* points." She inched away from him, so that part of her leg and hip and shoulder were just off the bed. She looked at Azeem, thinking about the many ways they might break apart, him moving to his cousin Siad's apartment in downtown Los Angeles, she and Hannah settling back into their tiny family of two. She'd miss him. Despite this latest idea of his, she'd miss him. And Hannah would miss him too, perhaps even more than Nina would. She held on to the folders tightly so they wouldn't fall again.

"I thought that maybe it was something you could think about. You know my friend Bernie from school? He's from New Jersey—a city called Nutley. You remember Bernie?"

She nodded.

"Anyway, he told a group of us at lunch about living in the suburbs and a game the neighbors used to play. These are middle-class people in a middle-class neighborhood. With kids and cars and two-story houses. All that stuff. And on the weekends, they have parties and everyone brings a dish."

"I know where this is going," she said.

"Wait, wait," he said, insisting. "These married couples from Nutley get together and share food. They have a potluck, then they toss their business cards into a bowl, and at the end of the night, they reach into the bowl and pull out a business card."

She looked at him, irritated.

"That decides who they sleep with. There are winners and losers, of course," he said.

Nina thought about winners and losers. She thought about board games from her childhood: Operation and Sorry and Monopoly. She thought about rules and instructions and wanting to win. She thought about losing, about making the wrong decisions, clumsily lifting out the wishbone and the horrible buzz that followed, informing you that you killed your imaginary patient; she thought of buying too much property or not enough, running out of those little sheets of colored money. "Makes me sick just to think about it," she said. "The randomness. The running into whatever jackass you slept with the night before while getting your mail or pulling out of the driveway."

"If we did something like that—I'm saying *if*—I'd want us to *like* the people we slept with, to have more in common with them than living on the same street." He was quiet a minute, thinking, and then said, "We go to The Elysium. We take off our clothes with strangers. I wonder what it would be like if they weren't strangers to us—if we got to know them."

"We *are* getting to know them."

"It's not intimate. It's, how you say?" he paused, looking around the room for the word, rubbing his fingers together, searching. Then, finally: "Surface. We're on the surface with them."

"It's plenty intimate to me."

"All I ask is that you read the book, then." He held the paperback out to her, an offering.

"Azeem."

"It's short—you'll buzz right through it."

She hesitated.

"Please. For me?"

She looked at him and weighed her options. "I'll read it," she said. "But don't expect me to change my mind."

"We're nakeds," he said, as if being a member of The Elysium were an obvious precursor to swinging.

"Nudists," she corrected him. "We're nudists, Azeem, not nakeds. There's no such thing as *a naked*."

5

MARTIN HAD been in Las Vegas for more than seven years and he hadn't studied restaurant science or business management like he'd planned to because all he really needed to know was how to hold shit above his head and serve people, how to say hello, introduce himself, and listen up. He didn't need college to teach him how to read body language and understand people. He knew how to make a customer feel like a bigger man or a more attractive woman, and he knew when to stop with the pleasantries and move away from the table with their orders memorized. He had methods, connections he made with a face or body: *The fat one wants the trout steamed, the thin one wants lobster slathered in butter, the old married couple wants their coffee black with extra sugar.*

"Customers aren't your friends," his dad used to say. Flattery was fine, even necessary, he'd tell Martin, but knowing when enough was enough was just as important as getting their soup out quickly.

Martin had left Manhattan Beach, his studio above the garage, his job, his surprised parents, sister, and Penny, who he probably loved; he gave his car to a grateful Tony and bought a bus ticket east. He'd intended to make it to New York City or at least New Jersey, but he hadn't even made it past Nevada.

It wasn't that he liked Las Vegas, but early on, the city liked him and those first months all he did was win. Poker, craps, blackjack, and the nickel machines: He went between them, and always, at the end of the night or the beginning of a morning, a man in a white vest would be counting bills into Martin's palm or the machines would spit out so many heavy coins that he'd need a bucket to collect them. The stickmen and the boxmen knew him by name, and even the pit bosses at Harrah's and Caesars Palace patted him on the back or shook his hand hello. He felt important, like a big man, and by the end of the first month, up a couple thousand dollars, he moved into a two-bedroom apartment, bought a waterbed and a corduroy couch that wrapped around the living room. He bought pots and pans, a coffeemaker, a broom and a mop. He bought a clock radio and a color television. He adopted a four-year-old cat from the animal shelter downtown that he named Sadie.

When the two thousand dollars was down to eight hundred, Martin got a job waiting tables at one of the best restaurants in town, right in the center of the strip. He wore a dark blue uniform and kept his shoes shiny and his face clean-shaven. He was polite, reserved even, and didn't joke around at the tables too much, which was usually fine. Once in a while, though, he'd get scolded for his moodiness and he'd miss his secure position back home, the restaurants his parents owned, where he could have an off day without worrying about losing his job.

He told his mom and dad that he was getting a kind of experience he couldn't get with them, a fair and tough experience, no special treatment, and that he'd return to California one day a better man, ready to work hard and manage their restaurants, if they still wanted him to do so.

Initially his parents were angry that he'd missed the grand opening of their third restaurant, but eventually they got over it. Now that he was living in another state, they seemed to like him more. Even his sister had matured and seemed to like him.

On the phone, he told Sandy about his cat. "Four years old?" she said, sweet and concerned. "She must have been abandoned. You know you saved her life?"

He told his mom about his couch and apartment, described them in detail, which was what she wanted. He told her what he saw when he looked out the window: big hotels, orange and yellow lights, a movie theater marquee, and a liquor store.

He told his dad how good he was at blackjack and poker, how even the machines loved him, and he could almost see the pride on his father's face.

"Lucky, like me," he said. "Did I ever tell you about the time I won a hundred bucks in Atlantic City?"

"Yeah."

"A hundred bucks was a lot of money back then."

"I'm sure it was."

"Could have paid your rent *and* car payment." His dad paused. "You don't need a car there Marty? I hear you don't need a car in Vegas," he said, answering his own question. "You know you'll need one when you come back home. You *will* come back home someday, won't you?"

6

NINA AND Azeem were on their way to the grocery store and she knew there were things he wanted at the store, yes, but there was also the thing that didn't cost money but was still very expensive. She was certain it would break them. He was driving and she was staring at his profile, his strong nose and good chin, and she felt his request in the car with them, to open her marriage. It was with them wherever they went, gas station and mall and dinner table. It was there when Nina sat on a beach chair in the backyard, getting some sun, while Azeem watered the lawn. It would be with them at the market, where he'd look at various women, and then at Nina with a dumb pathetic plea on his face, a plea she'd return with a shaking head. It made her feel like a strict, unyielding mother keeping her little boy from the sugar cereal.

If Nina so much as glanced at another man, Azeem nudged her and winked, conspiratorially, as if they were in this big wide world together with their secrets and every stranger was some ripe opportunity. Sometimes it was almost funny, but mostly it was irritating. "Enough," she'd usually snap. And what was especially *not funny* was how openly he looked at other women now, in front of her, like she was one of the boys.

He called this gawking *appreciation,* and he thought he was sly and discreet, which he wasn't. And he thought it was OK, legal, and playful, since he'd sworn repeatedly to Nina that swinging was something he would not do, could not do, would never *ever* do, without her permission and, more importantly, her participation. He didn't want to cheat. He wouldn't be like her first husband and do things behind her back. He knew how much that had hurt her and it wasn't his intent. He promised. "If, at some point, we both decide to try it out, fine," he said.

"There's a revolution going on," he kept reminding her. "Let's join in. Why starve?" he'd say.

"Who's starving? We're certainly not starving, Azeem." And she'd think about all the sex they had, how they seemed to have even more of it since his request, which she didn't understand. She thought she should be physically pulling away from him, but her body disagreed and seemed to insist on holding on. That part of their life together seemed healthier and more exciting than even the active couples she read about in those books he gave her.

She carried *Open Marriage* around in her purse, but hadn't started reading it. Every time she opened it, she changed her mind and slapped the book shut. Maybe he was right, that she'd surprise herself and agree with the O'Neills. Maybe she *was* afraid. She looked at him now in the car and thought about gluttony, about having too much of anything, a horrible abundance. "I give you enough," she said.

Nina thought Azeem was wrong when he doubted her open-mindedness. When he first asked her to visit the nudist camp with him, she didn't hesitate. She wasn't shy and had no trouble taking off her clothes. That first day, before they left the house, she hummed in the kitchen, packing falafel sandwiches with sprouts and hummus, homemade tabbouleh, and purple grapes. She spent time with the sex scholars who were Azeem's teachers at the university, and didn't flinch when one of their more unusual dinner guests showed up wearing a black T-shirt that said *Fuck* in tiny red letters on her chest and *You* on the back. She did have to agree with Hannah the next morning, though, that the T-shirt was off-putting and more than a little bit unfriendly.

She went to see the movie *Deep Throat* with Azeem and had even tried out the technique she'd seen on screen when they got home. She read Erica Jong's *Fear of Flying* and loved it. She went with Azeem to seminars on female ejaculation, male impotence, and the phases of sexual response. She learned about the orgasmic phase, the resolution phase. She learned about the sex flush and myotonia, which had to do with muscle contraction. She was particularly fascinated by the carpopedal spasm, the spastic contraction of the hands and feet during orgasm. She'd often wondered about all that clutching. It meant something to her finally when she thought about why she didn't want to sleep with other men and was her private answer to Azeem's persistent question. Something about sex and love, she thought, something about marriage, was about clutching itself, it was about the opposite of release. It was about grasping, holding dear. Azeem might be studying the sex act, the mechanics, the way things worked, but it was a pity, a shame, that he didn't understand the very basic need to hold on.

In addition to Nina opening her marriage, Azeem had been talking about his family back home lately, especially his younger brother, Mustafa, who was sixteen and an epileptic. Azeem thought that if Mustafa came out to Los Angeles for an extended visit, doctors here could cure him. He wanted to send his brother home a new boy, a boy without epilepsy, and so he'd been trying to talk Nina into buying Mustafa a plane ticket. It wasn't the money, or maybe it was—things were stressful since Azeem had quit his job to study full-time—but it was also the idea of a new person in the house, a stranger, someone who she'd have to put effort into getting to know, and mostly it was the secret she'd have to keep while getting to know him: that Azeem and she were married, and together with Hannah, they were a family. Azeem had said he didn't want his father and mother to know the truth, *not yet, too soon, they're not ready,* and when she pushed him, he admitted that they had a girl, a neighbor, just nineteen, all picked out for him. It was bad enough that he intended to stay in the States forever; how could he admit that he wouldn't accept the bride they offered? He wanted his brother to come visit and he wanted Nina to pay for the plane ticket then pay for the doctors' visits then pay in a personal way by pretending they were, what, very good *friends?* What would the boy think when they went to sleep in the same bedroom? she'd asked him. And he said he'd deal with it. He said it wouldn't be hard for him to pretend, it was something he was willing to do for his brother's health. Didn't she care about his little brother's health?

He called Mustafa his *little* brother, but there was nothing little about him. He was obese. When Azeem showed Nina and Hannah pictures of his family, he'd skate right over Mustafa's image with a huff of shame. Nina would glimpse at a dark-haired boy in a big pair of jeans, but was unable to make out the details because Azeem shuffled along quickly, one picture behind another picture, his tall and pretty sisters behind his smiling parents behind his handsome cousin Ali, on whose head shot he paused, willing Nina or Hannah to comment on the young man's shiny dark hair, intense black eyes, while poor, fat Mustafa was on the bottom of the pile, the whole attractive family on top of him.

When she asked Azeem about Mustafa's weight, he made excuses. "It's the medicine," he said. "He holds water."

"*Retains* water," she corrected.

"Holds water makes sense too," Hannah said, defending him.

That's a lot of water, she wanted to say, but didn't. *That's a lake or an ocean*, she was thinking, but Nina stayed quiet because that kind of familial shame had a way of shaming everyone who witnessed it.

When Nina was alone in the house, she had searched Azeem's desk for the blue airmail envelope, thick with photographs, and found it sandwiched between a couple of his textbooks. She was careful not to disturb his mother's letter when she lifted out the pictures. She knew what the letter was about because Azeem had already told her about the girl he'd never met who was waiting for him to return, the neighbor with very good teeth and straight black hair—a girl named Raina who his whole family was anxious he marry.

"Like *Fiddler on the Roof*," she had said.

"Like what?"

"Never mind."

Nina knew that Azeem hadn't told his mother that he was already married to an older Jewish woman with a teenage daughter, that he was a nudist, that he wanted to open that marriage and invite others in, that he was attracted to almost everyone, and that what he was studying wasn't just psychology but sexuality, and that he had no intention of ever going home.

"Will you ever tell her about me?" she asked Azeem early on.

"I haven't told her about *me*," he'd said.

Mustafa's photograph was at the bottom of the pile. There he was with his legs like short trees and an enormous belly that spilled over his slacks. There he was between his mother and a washing machine, a clothesline suspended across whatever room they were in, going right over the woman's head and across the boy's fat neck. His girth dwarfed everything: little washing machine, little mom, little couch in the corner, tiny lamp, tiny cat, little newspaper or notebook.

Now, Azeem turned in to the parking lot, pulled into a space farther away from the grocery store than was necessary. "It'll be nice to walk," he said. He turned off the car and they got out. He put his arm around Nina's waist and pulled her close. "You smell good," he said, inhaling her hair, her neck.

In the vegetable aisle he suggested she open her marriage without opening his mouth or moving his lips. They were deciding between white and yellow onions. "It's good to have variety," he said, pulling a plastic bag from the roller. He licked his fingers and used them to separate the thin sheets of plastic. He shook the bag out, picked up an onion from each bin. He held them in his palm the way another man might have held a set of pool balls, solids or stripes. "White Bermuda or Vidalia?" he asked her. And then, pointing with his chin at a bin across the aisle, "The red ones are good too."

"Depends on what we're making," she said. "I like the yellow ones for soup."

"What about for cucumber salad? I was going to make falafel and tahini this week."

"Hannah's been complaining about a sore throat. I was going to make chicken soup."

Azeem looked from one onion to the other, uncertain. He looked at the red ones across the way. "We could get a few of both."

A young woman came up from behind, her arm reaching between them. "Just real quick," the woman said. "Can I grab a couple of those?" She smiled at Nina, who backed up and smiled too, giving the woman space.

"Yes, yes, of course," Nina said.

Azeem looked at the woman.

Nina looked at Azeem looking at the woman.

"My boyfriend loves these," the woman said. She was chatty and pretty, with big brown eyes and a ponytail of blond hair that bounced behind her. She wore a red T-shirt and denim cutoffs. Her legs were tan and long. "Eats them raw. It's the strangest thing," she continued, talking fast, looking only at Nina. "But it's not that great to kiss him after a couple of raw onions."

Nina nodded, uncomfortably.

"He acts like they're apples," she said, laughing at herself, placing a now full bag of onions into her cart.

Azeem laughed with her, too loudly, with too much enthusiasm, Nina thought, and the woman seemed to agree. She glanced at Azeem for an uncomfortable second before turning back to Nina. "I like him to be happy, so what do I do?"

"You buy them," Nina said.

"Good for you. Keep him satisfied," Azeem said, but no one was listening to him.

"That's right, I buy them." The woman was talking directly to Nina. "I'm Susan," she said.

"I'm Nina. She turned to Azeem. "And this is—"

But the woman interrupted her. "I buy a lot of them too. James will sit there watching the football game and eat them, one after the other. 'Those aren't apples,' I tell him. Men—what are you going to do?" She laughed again, and then patted her bag of onions before turning away and steering her cart over to the peppers.

Azeem watched her walk away. He was still holding his own onions in his palm when he turned back to Nina. He seemed shorter to her. Rejected. And worse, the two of them together seemed suddenly mismatched and ridiculous.

"She was a lesbian," he said, definitively.

"*Please,*" Nina said.

"She liked you. Didn't you see the way she looked at you? Up and down." Nina laughed and shook her head.

He took a step back. "Talking about having a boyfriend—that was pretend. How you say, *a front,*" he said.

"I think you just creeped her out," she said.

"I did not," he said. "Lesbian."

"She was creeped out."

"Lesbian."

"Creeped out."

"Maybe she was a creeped-out lesbian," he said.

Nina looked at the onions and thought that Azeem was selfish, a bad loser, a womanizer disguised as a student of science. She thought that perhaps their eleven-year age difference *was* a big deal and that he was too immature for her. She thought that his hair was thinning on top and the elaborate twirl he'd recently mastered was doing little to keep his secret. She thought the more hair he lost the more serious his need to fuck other women would become. She imagined him completely bald, hopping from one woman to the next, unable to stop himself.

Perhaps she was partly to blame for joining the nudist camp and reading those books. Maybe she was a masquerader, playing a part. Maybe she shouldn't have agreed to visit that commune up north and maybe sex with others *was* the natural outgrowth of seeing them naked. She thought *of course it would come to this.* She thought he was wrong and she thought he was right. Maybe she *was* an oxymoron, an uptight nudist, an old-fashioned free thinker; perhaps monogamy was ridiculous, or maybe he was. She thought that the onions in his palm looked like a set of mismatched testicles with their skins flaking off.

"I want the yellow ones," she said firmly, taking the bag from him.

"Why not both? And a couple of the red ones too?" he said.

"I'm the only one working now—we can't buy all the onions we want to buy. There are things we just can't have," she said, sounding like a parent, hating her sharp voice, and feeling like she was about to cry.

"They're twenty-two cents a pound, Nina. They're just onions," he told her.

"No, they're not," she said.

He looked at her, confused.

"I like the yellow ones, that's all." And then she *was* crying, plucking the onion from his palm, reaching into the bin for a couple more. And he was pulling her close. "It's OK," he said. "Whatever is bothering you, we'll fix it. I promise," he said.

"When we get home, let's buy your brother's plane ticket," she said.

HE WAS her sibling—or half sibling. A baby brother. After all this time of being an only child, Hannah knew she should feel excited, but she didn't. She worried that the baby would be what finally separated her dad fully and completely from his former life. It was hard enough that he lived two cities away, ate bacon in the mornings, and slept with the New Testament on his nightstand, the satin bookmark and red tassels holding his place.

Azeem and her mom were dropping her off at her dad's new house on the way to the nudist camp. Actually, her dad's house was in Irvine, south of Belmont Heights, and The Elysium was north, toward Los Angeles. That's why they got an early start, waking Hannah up at seven-thirty on a Saturday morning.

In the car, Azeem asked Hannah if she was excited to meet the baby and she told him the truth. She thought babies were boring.

"He can't talk to me or understand what I'm saying," she said, leaning forward, popping her head between the two front seats.

"How about if Mustafa comes to visit us and his English is limited?" Azeem said.

"Is your brother coming?" Hannah said, surprised.

"Nothing's definite," her mom said.

But Hannah had the feeling that Mustafa's visit had already been planned out without her knowledge.

"I'm not so into babies either. They are sort of boring," her mom said.

"Were you bored with that baby?" Azeem asked, gesturing with his eyes in the rearview mirror, catching Hannah's glance.

"I'm afraid so," Nina said, honestly. "There's not a lot to do with an infant except take care of his or her needs. And despite what it looks like on television and the movies, a few of us women weren't cut out for babies. I loved Hannah right away, of course, but I fell *madly* in love with her when she was about one and started to communicate."

Azeem shot Hannah another look in the rearview, raised his eyebrows.

"Doesn't bother me," Hannah answered.

Her mom looked out the window. Then she turned to Azeem. "Am I boring to you?"

"No," he said, quickly.

"Hmm," she said, turning back to the window.

When they were off the freeway and a few miles away from her dad's house, Azeem stopped at a red light and turned around to face Hannah. "Your mother and I have been having some problems, as you know, as you've probably been able to tell these last few weeks."

She looked at him, nodding.

"Well," he said.

"What are you doing?" Nina said.

He ignored her and continued. "I want your mother to think about opening her—"

But Nina stopped him. "What are you doing?" she repeated, fiercely. "This is our business. Hannah doesn't need to know these things."

"What things?" Hannah said.

The light turned green and Azeem returned to the steering wheel. He stepped on the gas pedal a little too hard and the three of them lurched forward.

"Be careful," Nina snapped.

Azeem grunted unhappily.

"Some things are just between us, Azeem."

"Fine," he said.

Hannah hated it when they argued. She reached into her backpack and pulled out a book on insects that she'd picked up from the library last week. She began the chapter on the fruit fly, *Drosophia melanogaster*. Anticipating that her mom and Azeem's squabbling could turn into a big fight, she found it hard to concentrate and had to keep rereading the first page. She thought that if they were in a different mood, feeling better and getting along, she would have liked to tell them about the fruit fly's mating habits, what the author called the male fly's "tiny, cheap sperm" and the female's "large, expensive eggs," but they were too quiet and tense up there to tell them anything.

Finally, they pulled up to the curb in front of her father's house.

"Look at that big thing—and it's two stories," her mom said. "I knew it. How's Hannah supposed to get up those stairs?" she was mumbling, talking more to herself than to anyone else.

"She'll do fine," Azeem said. "She's a champ." He left the engine running, jumped out, and ran around the car to Hannah's door to help her with her crutches. Nina stayed inside. She rolled down the window for a kiss. "Be good. Be nice to your father even though he bought this big two-story house," she said.

"I'm always nice."

"When he talks about Jesus, try to change the subject. But be gentle. Don't insult him."

"That's your mother's job," Azeem said.

Nina shook her head.

"I won't insult him," Hannah said. She was standing on one foot, keeping her balance by holding on to the top of the car. Azeem handed over one crutch at a time, slipping a crutch under one arm and then the other. He helped her with her backpack. "I'm sure you'll love the baby," he said.

She struggled up the driveway and stood on the porch. A red welcome mat with white lettering said *Jesus Welcomes You,* which made it sound to Hannah like the son of God was sitting on her father's couch in a robe and ropey sandals, waiting for her arrival.

Her mom and Azeem were still at the curb, impatient and still angry at each other, she was sure. The front door was open, but the heavy metal screen was locked. She rang the doorbell. Nothing. She turned around and looked at her mom and Azeem, who she knew were in a rush. They'd explained all that. How they wanted a good spot on the lawn, how they needed to set up their chairs and unpack their lunches. They liked to get on the 405 freeway early before the traffic hit. The nudist camp was waiting. Their naked friends were waiting.

Even from the porch, the house smelled brand-new, fake, like plastic and paint. She leaned forward and peered in. Everything was beige: the living room's shag carpet and fat sofas, the octagonal wooden end tables, and a pair of director's chairs.

Hannah turned around and looked at her mom, who was not at all beige, who was actually very tan, with dark hair and red lipstick. She knocked on her dad's screen door one more time. Still nothing. She turned around and shrugged helplessly, to which Azeem responded by revving the engine. He didn't need to rev the engine. She could see her mom gesticulating, her hands in the air, and could tell she was screaming or at least talking loudly.

She looked away from them and down at the welcome mat again. She looked at her cast and wished she were back in Long Beach, at home by herself. She wanted to call Megan and then Rebecca, talk to each of them for an hour. She wanted to call Pablo and listen to him say *Hello, hello, who's there? Who are you?* before hanging up the phone.

Country music droned from the stereo—something about lost love and a mule. Hannah peered in again. She could see past the living room and out to the backyard, where she finally spotted her father, wearing headphones and mowing the lawn, oblivious.

She picked up her crutch and used its rubber end to bang against the screen until finally he looked up, startled and surprised, like she wasn't supposed to arrive at just this time. He waved and kicked the mower off. Hannah turned to her mom and Azeem and nodded, but before her dad was even inside the kitchen, her mom and Azeem were speeding off down the street, probably still arguing or maybe stripping off those horribly confining garments along the way.

As Hannah's dad made his way to her, she thought about his beige house and beige face and beige baby boy, who would soon be spitting bubbles onto his mother's beige arm.

He wiped his brow with his wrist before opening the screen door. "Hannah," he said. "Look at you. Let me take a look at you."

"I've been here for twenty minutes," she said, exaggerating.

"You're so big," he said.

She grimaced.

"Not *big,* that's not what I mean. You're so tall," he corrected himself.

"It's only been two months, Dad."

"Two months is two months," he said. "Too long is what it is. It's a horrible thing for a father and daughter to let the days slip by." He leaned forward so that half of his body was outside, and he looked around. "Where's your mother?"

"They're gone."

"Gone?"

"They were here and then they left."

"Oy," he said, shaking his head.

"I'm fine."

"It's *mishegas*, that's what it is. She takes off her clothes and runs around."

"There's no running," Hannah said.

"It's craziness. You tell her I said so."

"I'm not telling her anything."

"A mother should wait until her daughter makes it inside the house. A mother should keep her clothes on. A mother should—" He shook his finger in the air, scolding Hannah's mother, who was long gone.

"Can I come in?" she interrupted.

"Silly me." He stepped onto the porch, leaned over, and took her backpack. "So heavy," he said. "What's in here?"

"My books," she said.

"Still with the insects?"

She nodded.

He leaned over again to pick up her overnight bag. He smelled like freshly cut grass and too much aftershave, the latter a scent Hannah remembered and once loved. Her stepmother, Christy, stood at the top of the stairs, holding a pink bassinet. Hannah wondered why the bassinet was pink and why Christy didn't answer the door. She wondered what time it would be when her mom and Azeem reached the hills, and she wondered how that nudist boy and his twin sister could really take off their clothes and walk around.

Christy was waving and smiling, all big white teeth, pale skin, and poofy blond hair. Hannah's dad kissed her cheek, one cheek and then the other repeatedly. *Sheyner ponim, sheyner ponim,* he said, the cross bouncing on his white T-shirt and brushing against her ear.

8

WHILE HANNAH waited on the porch and rang the doorbell and banged on the screen, Nina scolded Azeem inside the car. "You can't just tell Hannah that you want me to open my marriage. What were you thinking?"

He agreed that perhaps he'd said too much, but even while admitting he was wrong, his voice rose, louder and louder in that very quiet neighborhood, so Nina said, *Just go, just go,* and he sped away before Hannah's father even made it to the door.

After they'd gotten back on the road, Nina corrected Azeem that it wasn't just *her* marriage, it was *theirs.*

"All your talk about opening *my* marriage," she said, turning, looking at him. "It's not *my* marriage, Azeem. It's *ours.*"

"Of course," he said.

"You've been calling it mine and I've been letting you do so. You've been calling it mine for a month. You've been asking me to open *my* marriage and I haven't said a thing."

"If you spoke Arabic, you'd make mistakes too," he said.

She nodded, giving him that. "I feel like it's just mine, though," she said. "The marriage—I'm in it alone." She was looking out the window, feeling guilty for not insisting he wait until Asher answered the door. She thought about asking him to take her home. She felt a headache coming on. She could send him up to the nudist camp by himself and they could talk about things tonight. But she liked The Elysium and always felt rejuvenated after a day in the sun.

He stopped at a 7-Eleven and went inside while Nina waited in the car. He brought back bottled water, a bag of cashews, and aspirin for Nina's headache, which she hadn't mentioned but which he somehow knew she had. He was good about things like that, knowing when her body hurt, knowing what she needed. "Thanks," she said, taking the bottle from him.

"I don't want to fight," he said. "I just want you to read the book and then tell me what you think. Just talk to me about it. I'm not going to do anything with anyone. We have a contract, like you said, and we haven't rewritten it—and maybe we never will. That's OK. I'll live with it."

"Marriage isn't a disease," she said.

"I don't understand," he said.

She opened the pills and shook a couple into her palm.

"Let's think about something else for now. Let's try to have a good day together." He closed the car door and put on his seat belt.

When she popped the aspirin into her mouth, he reached into the bag and pulled out his bottled water. He hurried the cap off and offered it to her.

"Let's start the day over. It's sunny. It's beautiful," he said, gesturing toward the sky. He started the car and pulled out of the parking lot, making his way to the 405 freeway. Nina leaned back in the seat and rested her head on the headrest and waited for the aspirin to kick in. Once Azeem had merged safely into the freeway's fast lane, he ripped open the bag of nuts with his teeth and poured some into his mouth. She thought she could see a tiny bit of cashew in his beard but couldn't be sure from where she sat.

They made polite chitchat, like strangers, the uncomfortable spouses' effort to smooth things over. They wondered out loud about leaving Hannah on the porch, both of them expressing guilt.

"I hope Asher shows Hannah a nice time," he said.

She nodded. "I don't know why he bought a two-story house. He's got a daughter on crutches."

"She won't always be on crutches."

"It's been years. Who knows?"

They were quiet for a few minutes before he said, "Mustafa's excited to visit."

"How long do you want him to stay?"

"Long enough for him to see a few doctors, some specialists while he's here. We could take him to UCLA and up north to Stanford. There's an epilepsy specialist in San Francisco."

Nina didn't say anything. She was thinking about their finances. She was thinking about another family member, another person to feed, another hungry mouth, and doctors' bills. She was wishing Azeem hadn't quit his job and that things were more equal between them. She was wishing he didn't want to fuck other women or she was wishing that she wanted to fuck other men. She didn't know anymore—things were getting blurry. She was tired of all of it.

"They don't know shit about epilepsy back home," he continued.

"Don't expect too much, Azeem. Remember, there's no cure here, either," she said.

"Very promising treatments, though."

"And they don't work on everyone."

"If you don't want him to come, just say it."

"It's not that," she said. "I want us to be realistic. I don't want you—*or him,* for that matter—to expect too much."

They'd reached Malibu, passed the ocean and the trendy restaurants that lined Pacific Coast Highway, and were on their way up the hills into the canyon. They were passing the roadside poppies Nina loved, the orange flowers bowing down on both sides of the road. The sun was fat and yellow in the sky. When Nina placed her palm on the window it was perfectly warm and she felt, for a moment, lucky to be on her way to a place she liked to go to.

A breeze kept the temperature down but also flung a number of bugs to the windshield. Each time a bug smacked the glass, Azeem waited a few seconds before flicking on the windshield wipers, which only smeared the dead bugs into a mess. Nina looked out the passenger-side window. She saw tumbleweeds tumbling the opposite way. She saw tall cacti and more poppies. She was wondering what Hannah was doing at her father's house, if she was bonding with the baby she was so sure would bore her. She wondered why Asher hadn't bought one of those ranch-style homes that spread out all on one floor. She hoped they'd make a bed for Hannah in a room downstairs, that they'd set her up with soft pillows and blankets, that they'd put a little table by her bed for her books. Nina wondered if Asher's wife, Christy, was feeling better, or if, as Asher had told her on the phone, she wasn't quite herself yet.

Azeem mumbled something in Arabic, then turned the wipers on again.

"It just makes it worse," she said. "Look at the mess you're making."

9

THE BABY'S name was Duke because her father liked John Wayne movies and wanted his son to be tough, but the tiny boy in his pink bassinet and pink blanket was anything but tough. When Hannah called him Little Guy, Christy shot her an angry look. "Your brother's name is Duke," she said firmly.

"It's hard to say," Hannah admitted.

"I don't know why it would be," her stepmother said.

They were sitting in the living room together, waiting for Hannah's dad, who was in the kitchen preparing snacks. Hannah was on the couch with her foot up on the beige leather ottoman. Christy and Duke were sitting across from her, pressed together in the fat, beige chair. She held him awkwardly, adjusting him every few seconds. Every time Christy moved the baby from one shoulder to the other, she sighed, exasperated.

"So this is your last cast?" she said.

"Maybe," Hannah said.

"Your father says that Dr. Russo was pretty certain. He said it was your last one."

"I've been told things before."

"Yes, well."

"The doctors say all sorts of things."

"You should be more positive. A good attitude couldn't hurt," Christy said, surprising Hannah. She moved the baby from her left shoulder to her right, and he let out a squeal.

Hannah shrugged. She wanted to change the subject. "Why's everything of Duke's pink?" she asked.

"The stupid minister." Christy rolled her eyes.

Hannah looked at her, surprised, waiting for more.

"When I was six months pregnant, he said the baby was a girl. The women at church told me he was always right." Christy shook her head. More exasperation.

From where Hannah sat she couldn't quite tell where Christy's body ended and the baby's began. It was afternoon and her stepmother was still wearing her robe and slippers. She didn't look like Christy anymore—the weight gain almost a physical improvement over her formerly hard angles and edges, Hannah thought. But something was wrong with her. Soft-spoken Christy, overly sweet Christy, had vanished. Even her voice, which had always been high-pitched, was coming out sort of manly. It was as if Christy had been eaten up by a soft, fleshy man and he was sitting in her chair, unhappily holding her baby and barking his hostile thoughts out of Christy's mouth.

"Minister Clay looked at my stomach and said he knew. He's an idiot."

Hannah smiled, uneasily.

"Seems a shame not to use what we've been given, though," she continued. "And the kid doesn't know what he's wearing or sleeping on."

"I guess not."

"Your dad doesn't like it. Thinks Duke's going to get confused. Thinks he'll turn out funny because he wears pink."

Hannah nodded, wishing her father would hurry up. She felt foolish, wishing she had something to say, wishing the sticky-sweet Christy who she'd always complained about to her mother and Azeem when she returned home from a visit would appear. She thought about suggesting that they give the pink things to charity, telling Christy that maybe they should buy the baby some blue things, even if only to avoid confusing strangers, but decided to keep quiet.

"Waste not, want not," Asher said, coming into the room with a tray of tea and cookies. He sat down on the couch next to Hannah. All around them were silence and unease, the three of them nodding without saying a word. *What a long and painful night this is going to be,* Hannah thought. Maybe she should comment on the furniture or the fireplace or the lawn, or maybe she should comment again on the baby, whom she'd already said was beautiful and handsome and, even, a gift. She wasn't sure why she said that, calling the baby a gift, it wasn't even part of her vocabulary. She could tell her father was happily surprised when he heard the sentiment. And she was as surprised as he was when it came out of her mouth.

"Well?" her father said. And then again, "Well?"

It was a question Hannah wasn't sure how to answer. "Well?" she said back.

"Give me some of that tea," Christy said, moving the baby back to her right shoulder. "Asher, pour us some tea, would you? And hand over those cookies."

He leaned forward and began pouring. "Yes, that's great. Let's have a little nosh."

The teapot was in the shape of a swan, and there was a matching creamer, white china cups, and sugar packets just like they had at restaurants. The cookies were shortbread, and when Hannah picked one up she couldn't help noticing that even *it* was beige. It was tasty, though, and gave her mouth something to do other than talk.

"Good?" her father said.

She nodded.

"I want those cookies," Christy said, impatiently, and the baby started whimpering then.

Asher took a cookie for himself and then scooted the box over to Christy so she could reach in and take them as she pleased. "So?" her father said.

Duke's whimpers grew, coming quick, becoming louder and louder, only magnifying the silence in the room. "Stop it," Christy suddenly growled into the baby's ear.

Asher shot up from the couch and walked over to them. "Honey, let me have him," he said, obviously embarrassed.

"I've got it," Christy said.

"He's not an *it*."

"I've got *him*, damn you." Christy was on her feet too then, patting Duke hard on the back while he howled and squirmed on her shoulder.

"Don't damn me. Not in front of Hannah. I won't go through this again." Asher leaned forward, reaching for the baby, but Christy leaned back, resisting.

"Oh no," she said. "He's not going anywhere."

"Listen to your tone," he said. "Do you want him to be afraid of you?"

"You're right, you're right. I don't feel like myself, Ash."

"It's OK," he said. "Give him to me." Asher's voice was soft but his action was deliberate. He reached out and pried the baby out of his wife's arms. He rocked Duke back and forth, the baby's arms bright red from where they'd been grabbed. Asher was stepping side to side with the boy in his arms, trying to soothe him. *It's OK, it's OK, Daddy's here.*

Hannah watched Christy try to collect herself and calm down. "I'm tired. The baby's tired. Let me take him upstairs to sleep," she said.

"I'll take him," Asher said, heading toward the stairs.

Christy looked at Hannah. "I really am. I am. I'm so damn tired. I need some sleep myself." She walked away from Hannah then and followed her little unhappy family up the stairs.

Hannah didn't know what to do or say. Christy was never her favorite person, but she was never mean. Hannah adjusted herself on the couch. She took a sip of tea. She ripped open a second sugar packet even though her tea was sweet enough already and poured it into the cup. She took another sip and waited for her dad to return, which he did fifteen minutes later.

"All that baby needs is a little sweet talk. A lullaby—a song. Is that too much to ask?" He sat in his easy chair heavily and looked around the beige room. He looked older and sadder to her than he had in years.

Christy hadn't been herself since the baby came, he admitted. He told her that he'd been having nightly phone discussions with Hannah's aunt Emma, the psychologist, every night—he didn't know what he'd do without her. Sometimes, he confided, he even called Hannah's mother and asked her opinion. He found himself wanting to describe the situation to Nina, which really didn't make sense to him. He told Hannah that his sister had assured him that lots of women got depressed when a baby came, even when it was all they'd ever wanted, all they'd ever talked about. Parenting wasn't what they thought it would be. It was so much work. A new mother gets exhausted. Sure, Christy might seem sad or mean or impatient, but deep down she was really very happy and full of love. "Oh, I'm babbling," he said, catching himself. "I'm sorry. I haven't seen you in months and here I am going on and on."

"It's OK," she said.

"I talk to God, of course, but He doesn't talk back."

"I'm glad to hear it," Hannah said, smiling.

Upstairs there was the sound of a door closing, and then another slamming. Asher looked at the stairs.

Hannah told her dad that Christy didn't seem that bad to her. "I've heard that it's common for new moms to be cranky," she said.

"Enough about Christy," he said. He looked down at her leg, which was still propped up on the ottoman. "That's the biggest one I've seen yet."

"Yeah," she said.

"But it's the last one, right?"

"I hope so," she said.

1 0

NOT DRIVING was fine in Las Vegas, no need, and so Martin drank after work with the busboy Elmer. When their boss wasn't looking and the night-shift waiters had gone home, Martin and Elmer hid out inside the back of the restaurant after closing and slipped their first beers of the night from the miniature fridge they weren't supposed to know existed.

Elmer, who'd returned from Vietnam with a scar on his face—a keloid ring, like a second mouth right next to his lips—was so skinny it almost hurt to look at him. He reminded Martin of Sandy as a teenager. Skinny Elmer, all collarbones and pointy shoulders, all concave chest and cheeks, and big, dark eyes. Mr. Hero was the world's slowest busboy.

Martin liked Elmer fine as long as he worked in someone else's station. He'd been hanging out with him a few nights a week, going to casinos after they left the restaurant, playing blackjack or Seven-Card Stud. After a few games, they'd find a bar where they'd guzzle another drink or two and sweet-talk a couple of girls.

Time moved quickly, days became months became years, and one girl turned into another girl. They were drinking girls, easy in their halter tops and short skirts, which they happily stepped out of, easy in their chunky shoes or calf-high boots, and they were only passing through, with birth control pills in their pink purses, little tablets they sometimes pulled from plastic sleeves, popped out, and swallowed in front of him. The pills were a new thing, a discovery, and the girls were discoveries as well, each one so generous and agreeable, so far away from home, and Martin was agreeable too, always grateful in the beginning, with his head thrown back, accepting their mouths and bodies with all the grace he could muster up.

It was dangerous when he had one too many beers or when he lost money, which, despite his good luck, sometimes happened, and on those nights, he'd grow agitated and talkative and wouldn't want a girl. He'd think about home and his parents and Penny and even his friend Tony. He'd slur his words, stumble around the casinos, cussing and bumping into slot machines or waitresses, and Elmer would have to take his arm and steer him out of whatever establishment they were in, leading him down the street and home. He'd guide Martin to the couch and slip off his shoes. Martin would struggle, leaning up on his elbows, and try to confess, but his tongue was fat and his mouth was dry, and those first few very drunken nights only Hannah's first name would make its way into the room. Within months, though, Martin was elaborating: naming the street where he hit her and describing the dent she left in his fender. And within the year, Martin, in an especially intense blackout, told Elmer the whole story: how he'd driven away and left her there, the white sheet he draped over his car that afternoon, and how he dropped off gifts at the hospital for weeks. He told him about the snow globe and paper dolls, the strange cast the girl was wearing on her leg when he saw her for the last time, just days before he left town.

"Be quiet now," Elmer said, drunk and guilty too. He covered Martin with a blanket and got him a glass of water and a couple of aspirin, which he insisted Martin swallow, standing over his friend until he put the glass down. When Martin was finally snoring, Elmer talked to the dark room. "You haven't done anything worse than what I've done, you don't know what I did," he said.

In the morning, Martin woke up, not knowing how he got home or what he said or did, and he found Elmer asleep in the hallway outside the bathroom. They had mutual headaches and complained about the terrible taste in their mouths. They complained about the weather, not even nine a.m. and already ninety-five degrees outside. "Fucking desert," Martin said.

"It's worse than 'Nam," Elmer said.

"No one's shooting at us, though."

"Yeah, well." Elmer paused. "Why didn't you have to go? How'd you escape all that?"

"Flat feet and color-blind."

"Both?"

"Yep."

"Lucky you," Elmer said.

"Lucky," Martin agreed weakly.

Neither of them mentioned the conversation from the night before, Martin because he didn't remember and Elmer because he did. They headed to a diner down the street from the apartment. They sat at the counter, side by side, Martin spooning scrambled eggs into his mouth, Elmer chewing a piece of dry toast. They sat, sipping coffee, quiet as strangers.

Hours later, at work, Martin complained about Elmer's performance with extra venom. "You're too fucking slow," he growled. "Go bus Jack's station."

"And you, you're a—" Elmer began.

"I'm a what?" Martin said, suddenly afraid.

And Elmer walked away, but not before flipping Martin the bird.

11

WHILE DUKE slept upstairs, the three of them ate an uncomfortable dinner at the dining room table. Hannah and her dad were dressed in day clothes, but Christy wore a fuzzy yellow robe. On the wall, just above Hannah's chair, the baby monitor transmitted every sound the boy made. When they first sat down, he cried a little, and Christy ignored him and Asher jumped up and rushed to the monitor, leaning over Hannah while she peppered her steak. He shushed them both, which wasn't necessary because they weren't talking.

When Asher sat back down, he made an effort at conversation. It was all so stilted and made Hannah miss her mom and Azeem—even when they bickered or disagreed or roamed the house naked.

"I bet you're looking forward to getting out of that thing, Hannah. You've been through so much," Asher said, looking over at Christy. "Hasn't she been through a lot?"

"She has," Christy said unenthusiastically.

There was silence.

They cut their meat.

They chewed.

They passed the bowl of peas and avoided eye contact.

Christy buttered a piece of bread, her eyes moist, looking like she was about to cry.

Asher reached around Hannah to grab the mashed potatoes. He scooped an extra-big serving onto his already very full plate. "Have another slice of meat, Hannah," he said.

"No, no, I have enough," she said.

"She doesn't like it," Christy said, more to herself than to anyone else.

"I have enough, that's all," she insisted.

"Delicious," Asher said.

Hannah nodded in agreement, smiling weakly.

There was more silence.

And some more.

Christy adjusted her heavy breasts in the robe and sighed.

Finally, Hannah asked him about what it was like being a new dad, and he said, "Remember, I was yours," and Hannah said, "I forgot," not meaning that she really forgot but that it must have been different now because he was older and more attentive and living in a beige house in Irvine and his wife, who used to be too sweet, was sour and scary, but she just said, "That's not what I meant. I meant, he's a boy."

When Christy finished eating one piece of bread, she quickly reached for another. It seemed she was in a race. At one point, she reached into the basket, searched around, and found nothing. "There's more," she said, jumping up from her chair and hurrying away. Hannah heard the oven door squeak open and slam shut, Christy's slippers slapping on the kitchen tile, and then she was back at the table, setting the basket down. "There's more where that came from," she said.

"I'm sure," Asher said.

"What does that mean?" she snapped.

"There's more bread is what it means."

Christy reached into the basket, pulled a piece from the loaf, then used a flat knife to slather a slice with butter, and Hannah could see the tip of her pink tongue at the side of her mouth, anticipating.

"What are you staring at, Hannah?" Christy said, chewing and talking at once.

"Nothing."

"Just what's so interesting?"

Hannah was quiet. "I'm sorry," she finally said.

"If you're not staring at anything, there's no need to apologize," Christy said.

Asher leaned across the table and rested his hand on Christy's hand. "Don't be upset. Let's try to have a nice dinner."

"I'm not upset," she said, snatching her hand away.

"Let's just eat and enjoy Hannah's visit."

"Oh, you're right," Christy said, her voice cracking. "I *am* upset. And I don't know why. I don't know what's wrong with me. I'm just hungry—is that so wrong?" she said, tears streaking her face.

Hannah lifted her napkin from her lap and wiped her mouth. "I'm sorry, Christy," she said again.

"I need to keep up my strength—that's why I'm eating. I'm so hungry. You can't imagine how hungry I am," Christy said. "Breast-feeding is draining. I don't even have the energy to get dressed in the morning. I've got five of these fucking robes in different colors."

Christy wiped her eyes. She blew her nose into a napkin.

"Your mother didn't breast-feed you, Hannah. Did you know that?" Asher said, obviously trying to change the subject.

"I didn't know," Hannah said.

"I told Nina she should try to make it work, but one dot of blood on her nipple and she sent me out for formula. A mother should try," he said. "They say when a baby's breast-fed, he's smarter and has a better immune system. You're smart enough, certainly—but you might have been Einstein."

"I'm glad I'm not Einstein," Hannah said, feeling annoyed.

"You still into bugs? Still reading about insects?" Christy said, sniffling.

"She'll probably be a doctor or scientist," Asher said. "You want to be a scientist?"

"I don't think so," Hannah said.

"God knows you can be whatever you want to be."

"*God knows,* yes, *God knows,*" Christy said, mocking. "We know how smart you are. God knows I hear about how smart you are daily."

"She *is* smart," Asher said. "So I like to talk about how smart she is? When Duke's bigger, I'm sure he'll be smart too."

"He'll never be as smart as this one here," Christy said, pointing at Hannah with her fork, looking like she was going to cry again. "He won't be reading science texts at ten, I'll tell you that."

"Who knows what he'll be reading?" Asher put both palms flat on the table and spoke softly. "He's going to be fine, brilliant maybe, a scholar—who knows? And you're going to feel better too, honey," he said.

"I don't think so," she said weakly.

He glanced at her robe then, where a splatter of steak sauce rested just beneath her breast. Hannah could tell he didn't know whether to mention it or not. He paused. Took a sip of water. He couldn't take it, Hannah knew;

looking at the splotch was hurting him. "You've got a stain, honey," he finally said, pointing at her chest.

Christy looked down. She snatched the napkin from her lap and dipped a corner into her water glass. She was rubbing at the stain and rubbing at the stain, only making it worse. "Damn it," she said.

"Why don't you go upstairs and put on one of the others? You've got four pretty robes up there that aren't stained." Asher's voice was sticky-sweet, like he wasn't talking to an adult at all, but to a child.

"OK. Yes," she said.

"Good girl," he said.

"I'm sorry, Hannah," Christy said. "I'll go upstairs and change. Maybe I'll even take a shower."

"Good, good," Asher said.

"Your dad is right. I don't know what's wrong with me. I feel so fucking weird."

"Honey, please don't say the f-word. You never used to say that. It's Nina who likes that word," Asher said.

"Stop bringing up my mother," Hannah said.

"Sorry," he said.

Christy looked at him. "You know, Asher, it's just a word. It took me years to realize it, but it's just a fucking word. It's the least harmful thing I do these days, saying *fuck*." Her voice was strangely calm.

"I don't know why the three of us can't just talk to each other and enjoy each other's company."

"You're right. You're absolutely right." Christy said. "I'm going upstairs. I'll take a nice fucking shower and put on a different fucking robe."

"Oy," Asher said.

Once they were alone at the table, her dad finished off what were now certainly cold mashed potatoes. Hannah's appetite had disappeared. She moved her peas around with her fork and wished she was with her mom and Azeem.

Asher put his spoon down and looked at her. "It's *shpilkes*, is what it is. It's nervous energy. Christy's condition won't last forever, thank God. Her hormones need to level off, that's all. The doctor says it's temporary."

"I'm sure it is," Hannah said.

"A few more difficult weeks—that's all."

"You'll survive," she said.

"I'd like my cheerful wife back, that's for sure. I don't know who that woman is."

In the morning, while Christy and Duke slept, Asher talked to Hannah about Jesus. Her salvation had been on his mind a lot lately, he said. He wanted to discuss waiting until you're married and saving the unborn and the lifelong union, despite any problems, he had with Christy.

"Last night, you didn't know who she was," Hannah said.

"Didn't mean it," he said.

She looked at him.

"Even when a conflict seems insurmountable, it's not," he continued. "Not if there's love there. It's a mountain you climb. It's a wave you ride."

It was my mother you cheated on, Hannah thought while he spoke.

He wanted to talk about bright, sweet Heaven and Noah, those animals, and all that water spilling across the world. He quoted Minister Craig, repeated what the man said just last Sunday from behind the podium about sin and culpability.

"Isn't that the guy who predicted Duke would be a girl?" Hannah said.

"So he's not a fortune teller," he said.

Still, Asher wanted Hannah to see the beautiful stained-glass windows his church recently had cleaned and their shiny new pews and, mostly, he wanted her to see what he called *the light*.

"I'm a Jew," Hannah said.

"Well . . ." he said.

And then she thought about it. "Actually, I like science."

"The daughter of a dentist," he said. "Of course you do."

"A lot," she added.

"What does that have to do with anything?"

"I believe in science, Daddy."

He looked at her. He shook his head.

"I *believe* Darwin, is what I mean."

"You know, Hannah, you can ask Jesus into your heart and like science at the same time. You can believe Darwin too."

"Jesus isn't for me."

"*Mishegas!* He's for everyone."

"He's not," she said.

"You're young—you don't yet know what's for you."

"I know what's *not* for me," she insisted.

He shook his head.

"I'm an atheist," she admitted finally.

Her father got up from the couch and stood, staring down at her, his hand on his heart. "Be Jewish," he said. "At least be Jewish," he begged.

12

AFTER HANNAH'S visit, Christy's depression escalated. Asher found his wife hunched over the crib with her face just inches from the baby's face, screaming for him to *shut the fuck up*. Christy fell to her knees, sobbing and rattling the bars of the crib. Asher rushed over, horrified, and pulled his wife to her feet.

"Don't yank me," she said. "You get your hands off me!" she hollered. And then, just like that, she punched him in the face.

His eye was still black, he told Hannah on the phone. "Better me than my baby," he said.

He was talking to Hannah in a way he hadn't talked to her before, like she was his friend and confidant, and it made her feel mature and necessary. He was candid, using surprising detail, using words like *postpartum depression, hormones,* and *scientific studies*. He told her that Christy was in the hospital for what he hoped would be a brief stay. Christy was resting, he said. Hannah knew exactly what hospital he was talking about— the massive white building with the tall pillars and marble lions—the loony bin on the hill in Newport Beach. Everyone knew about that hospital. It was where the rich loonies went to rest.

So Christy was resting and Asher had to sit by her bedside and watch her rest and Christy's own mother and father were staying in the beige house and helping Asher take care of Duke and hopefully not telling him to shut the fuck up when he cried and they were staying until Christy was rested, well-rested enough to return home and not shout at the baby or shake his crib.

At first, Asher admitted, he didn't want Christy to go to the hospital, he wanted her to spend more time with Minister Craig, but when he suggested this, Christy called Minister Craig a fucking idiot, saying that she had already talked to Minister Craig and he was useless. She couldn't stop eating or screaming or wanting the baby to disappear, and whatever was wrong with her had nothing to do with Jesus.

Take me to that fucking place on the hill, she told Asher.
Get me the fuck out of here.

13

FOR THE first few years Martin was away, he sent postcards to Penny because the girls on the bar stools only made him miss her more. He sent cards with the Strip and the hotels and the slot machines and the farmers' market that went up on Saturday mornings, and then he found a mall with a specialty shop where they had handmade greeting cards from all around the world. He bought cards from Bangladesh and India and Japan, and he sent her those and wrote lies on them: *Within the month, I'll be here. I'm going here next.*

But he never left the Strip, and Penny got married and quickly divorced, and then she got married to someone else. This time for good, she wrote back. She had three children in four years and told Martin their names: Randall, Rudy, and Renee. She wrote that they lived across the street from a Buddhist temple and that watching the hairless men in their robes walking the temple dog sometimes made her sad. She told him that she was head nurse now and it involved a lot of responsibility. She was busy. She was very busy these days. She told Martin that she loved her husband.

Finally she wrote him a curt note on a thick piece of stationery, asking him to stop sending postcards, saying that her husband didn't like opening the mailbox and seeing Martin's signature and didn't appreciate the way he signed his name with the word *love*.

The girls Martin met were usually tourists, just passing through, a weekend, three nights, four nights at the most. He met them in bars and sometimes casinos. They liked to drink and often did things with him that they'd never have done at home, they said.

I don't know what's gotten into me, one claimed.

I'm never like this, another swore. *It's the lights, it's the gambling, it's the city.*

He looked at her skeptically.

Fine, she said. *I'm lying. It's none of those things.*

What is it, then? he asked.

It's you, she admitted.

But that one had only hours left. He promised to stay in touch, but after a few uninteresting letters back and forth, he abruptly stopped the correspondence.

Most of the girls had big hair, teased and puffy at the crown, flipping up at the sides, like Mary Tyler Moore's. More than one had a chipped front tooth.

If a girl lived in town, she'd end up wanting to *know* him eventually. He was guarded and distant, a young man who didn't want to be known, and when a girl asked him why he held back or whined that he didn't talk enough, he'd pull away even more, not answering her phone calls or stiffening at her touch. She didn't know shit about his life, she'd say, she didn't know where he went to high school, where he was from, what his favorite color was, or what his favorite item was from the buffet cart at Circus Circus.

"Do you like the crab cakes at the Flamingo or the salmon cakes at Harrah's?" some girl would want to know.

"Come on, open up," she'd whine.

Or, "You could be a killer," she'd say, teasing.

"Open up," she'd say again.

"*You* open up," he'd say, kissing her neck or ear, encouraging whoever she was back into bed.

The big-titted chubby one, Marla, was smart and pushy, though. He actually dated her for nearly a year. Her family was from Las Vegas and she grew up in a suburb on the outskirts of town. She was a senior at the University of Nevada, studying psychology and political science. And she wanted more school after that, good God, graduate school, which Martin thought was an oxymoron. She wanted to teach college one day, maybe even run for office.

Marla wasn't interested in how he felt about the Flamingo's crab cakes or Harrah's salmon, but she wanted to know if he was bullied as a kid or if he was the bully.

"Neither," he said.

"Oh, come on," she insisted.

"Neither," he said again.

"Everybody was one or the other."

Marla wanted to know why he showed up in Nevada all alone and why he'd stayed so long. She wanted to know why he never talked about his family or feelings. Where did he see himself in five years? How did he feel about the war? Did he ever get so sad that he couldn't get out of bed? She wanted to know why Martin's only friend was that skinny guy, Elmer, and she wanted to know how he felt about President Carter and the Panama Canal.

The girl didn't let up.

"Why won't you let me in?" she'd ask.

"Come on, tell me what you were like as a boy."

"What were you like as a teenager?"

"What did your parents say when you told them you were leaving?"

"Can't we just do what we're doing?" he'd say.

One night after sex, they were spooning on the couch, naked, and he was so relaxed, nearly asleep, when she started up. "Tell me your secrets, Marty."

He tried to ignore her and she asked him again.

"Damn it," he said, sighing, taking his hand away from her breast and running it angrily through his hair.

"I need to know where you come from—and not just the city, either. I know it's the beach. I know you grew up surfing and smoking pot, but I need to know more," she said.

He picked up the remote and turned on the television set, where young men who'd been soldiers were now hippies with long hair and ratty beards, holding signs and chanting protests.

"For instance, why weren't you drafted? I don't even know that." She stared at the young men on television.

"I'm fucking color-blind and my feet are flat. You happy now?"

"No, I'm not happy."

"This isn't working."

She took the remote from his hand and muted the TV. "A guy can't escape where he comes from. He has a history, and even if he's all clammed up, not telling anyone, he's still who he is."

"You've taken too many psychology classes, that's what's wrong with you." He snatched the remote back and turned up the volume. Sadie had hopped up onto the couch between the two of them, demanding to be touched. Martin rubbed her fur, her head and ears, and the cat purred loudly.

"I need some time alone," he said without looking at Marla.

With a huff, she got up off the couch.

He stood up too, and they were looking at each other.

"You're a dick," she said.

"Fuck you," he said.

"Fuck you, dick," she said.

And then, surprising himself, Martin pushed a naked Marla against the living room wall, her big tits bouncing, her mouth stretching into a horrified, blubbering circle.

"You crazy dick," Marla said, using her hands on the wall to gain traction and stand up. She swept up her blouse from the coffee table and put it on. "I tried hard with you, dick. And you know what? You *were* the bully," she said. "That's right, I knew it. A bully *and* a dick. You were. How many kids did you torment? The short one, the fat one?" She was really crying now, stepping violently into her jeans, and buttoning up her blouse. She buttoned it up all wrong, the collar uneven, and she was trying to fix it on the way out the door.

After he heard her slam the main door to his apartment complex, Martin sat down at the kitchen table and thought about things. Regardless of what she called him, he shouldn't have pushed her against the wall. He almost loved her, her soft body, each perfect curve, and he loved her brain and her mouthy opinions. On a good day, he even loved her questions. Sure, he had no intention of answering them, but it was good to know that she gave a shit. She was right, he was a dick, but he wasn't always such a terrible guy, and as a boy he certainly wasn't the bully—she was wrong about that.

He thought about Manhattan Beach. He thought about the hospital and Penny the nurse, who seemed to suspect his secret and seemed to forgive him. Leaving that little girl banged up by the curb would always be the worst thing he'd done, the thing he couldn't shake. But that little girl was a teenager now, probably fine, all patched up and probably even walking and getting into her own kind of trouble.

When Martin got caught at the restaurant with his hand in that secret fridge, the boss fired him. He took a couple of weeks off, gambled and hung out with a depressed Elmer, who was also fired, and then filled out a few applications for jobs. Within the month, Martin started waiting tables at a more casual seafood shack downtown. He liked it better, no more starched uniform or shiny shoes. He liked the way the creamy clam chowder smelled as he carried it to the tables, and he liked that the little old lady boss asked everyone to call her by her first name, Ilene, and that she gave the employees an endless supply of chowder and hot bread when they worked at least a six-hour shift.

Ilene had gray hair that she wore up in a messy bun. She wore funky floral dresses and dark nylons that she pulled up to her knees. She was sweet and approachable, always wanting to sit down and flatter you while you counted your tips.

"You're some kind of waiter," she'd say.

"What a bright future you have," she'd tell them.

Martin talked to Ilene the way he hadn't talked to anyone in years. He told her about his family's restaurants and how he wasn't sure he'd ever return.

He admitted he lied to his father on the phone.

He told her that he used to drink too much, but he was getting that under control.

He said he always wanted to go to school but didn't know what to study.

He told her about his cat Sadie's antics.

He said that he didn't know how to talk to girls his own age.

He told her he didn't drive.

He admitted he was afraid he would always be a disappointment.

At her urging, Martin signed up for morning cooking classes, which kept him out of the bars and casinos during the week. He found that he didn't drink as much at home. Sometimes just a couple of beers relaxed him fine and helped him to sleep.

He was surprised how much he loved the cooking classes, how he looked forward to the mornings when something particularly interesting was, as his teacher said, *on the menu*. He was learning how to make a mean omelet: flat, perfect eggs, how to chop onions and heat them into honey before folding them over with pink cubes of ham. He was learning how to whip cream into a sturdy point and bake a flourless chocolate cake, how to make French sauces, frittatas, roux and pilafs, a Thai-spiced fish.

"Tell me what you made in class today," Ilene would say when he arrived at work. He'd be putting on his apron and she'd stand there, listening carefully to each word he said.

Twice his family came out to visit, this last time a few days ago. His parents pulled up to the curb in a new light-blue Caddie with his sister and her baby, Billy Jr., in the backseat.

Martin watched them climb out of the car from the upstairs window. He stuck his head out and hollered hello and waved. They looked up at him, smiling, waving back.

Sandy, who now ate her food and was a normal, healthy weight, handed Billy Jr. off to Martin's mom. She walked to the back of the car and opened the trunk. It seemed she was struggling to pull out the two oversized suitcases and Martin wondered why his dad just stood on the lawn with his arms crossed. Getting the suitcases out of the trunk was something that his father had always insisted upon doing; even when Martin was a teenager and could help out, his father shooed him away.

After dinner his parents went for a walk on the Strip and he took his sister and the baby back to his apartment. She put Billy Jr. to sleep on the couch and they moved into the kitchen, where she told Martin that she was pregnant again and so happy. She explained that Billy Sr. was working long hours these days, that they were saving up to buy a bigger house and that's why he didn't come out this time. She said that she hoped they'd see Martin back in California this Christmas.

"You know the restaurant business," he said. "I can't get time off. It's busy season."

"It's sad that you never come home," she said.

They sat together at that table, drinking coffee, the cat purring in Sandy's lap, and he told her about cooking school, his new job and boss, and about Marla, pretending she was still his girlfriend when really he hadn't spoken to her in nearly a year.

"Where's she now?" Sandy asked.

"Visiting her folks," he said.

"I'd like to meet her."

"You'd love her," he said.

"Is she *The One*?" his sister said, raising her eyebrows.

"Possibly," Martin said.

Sandy told him how all that talk about cooking and omelets had made her hungry and coaxed him into making her some eggs even though it was ten o'clock at night and they'd had dinner only a couple hours earlier.

While she was finishing up, dragging her toast across the plate, she admitted that there was something she needed to tell him.

"What?" he said.

"It's about Daddy."

"What about him?"

"He's sick," Sandy said.

"Sick?" Martin leaned forward and looked at his sister.

"It's his heart."

"How sick?"

Sandy's face suddenly looked long and tired. She sighed and leaned back in her chair. "Mom wants you to come home, Marty. Dad could go at any time."

"He ate a big dinner. He's out gambling. They look so happy. It can't be that bad," he said.

"It is," she insisted. "The doctor wants to do surgery, but Mom thinks it's too risky."

"He doesn't *look* sick," Martin said.

"You can't see his heart," his sister said.

PART 3

1

HANNAH STOOD in the door frame. She looked at them and wondered what was wrong. Outside, skateboarders whizzed past the house, wheels loud on the pavement. One kid screamed another kid's name. Someone called someone a pussy. She shifted her weight from one crutch to the other, wondering if Azeem had decided to leave her mom or maybe they'd stopped loving each other. Or maybe they still loved each other but one of them loved someone else too, maybe he was insisting that they open up their marriage, and maybe her mom, despite the book written by that very happy couple, still didn't want to.

But that wasn't it.

He wanted her mom to describe the dream she'd had last night about Hannah's leg. It was important, he said. She should know these things, get ready for them.

"Tell her," he said.

"No." She took a sip of her coffee and stared straight ahead.

"You should tell her," he pushed. "I'm the psychologist."

"You're not a psychologist *yet*," she said.

"I'm studying. I know what's healthy. I understand mental health."

She shook her head.

"Honesty is important. Getting it all out in the open. A family should talk about things. It's important that she know. I'll tell her," he said.

"It was *my* dream."

"Describe it then."

"It's cruel."

"She needs to understand that there's more to it than walking."

Hannah shifted her weight again. "Tell me," she said.

"I had a silly dream," her mom said.

And he described it.

And he wouldn't stop talking.

169

And he kept talking even though he knew that he was hurting both of them.

The dream was about hamburger meat.

Hannah was seventeen, not fourteen, and she loved a man. The man was older, say twenty, and Hannah wanted to have sex with the man, but was too upset about her skinny leg.

It was ugly.

It looked like polio.

He wouldn't love her if he saw it.

It would scare him.

He would take one look and walk away.

Her mother went to the freezer and pulled out a pound of hamburger meat.

She let it defrost on the counter.

It was all she knew to do.

She carried the meat to Hannah's room.

She placed the meat on her atrophied calf while Hannah slept.

And she held it there, like that, until the meat stuck.

"Your mother did this," Azeem said, hesitating.

"Oh, dear God," Nina said.

"Your mother did this so you could have sex with the man and not be—"

"Stop it," her mother said.

"Do you understand?" he said.

Hannah was still standing in the door frame. She hadn't moved. The kids on skateboards were back, flying down the street, cussing into the sky. She heard the word *dickhead*. She heard *watch this*. She heard *fuck you*. She looked down at her cast, and then up at her mother, whose face was now gone behind her hands.

2

MARTIN'S DAD had collapsed and died at their newest restaurant, which ended up being his favorite of the three, his sister said on the phone. He was on his way to a table with a pair of tiramisus and a slice of raspberry cheesecake that he'd made himself. He was carrying the desserts on a tray above his head.

"Usually Dad didn't serve food, but he'd been excited to show off his new cheesecake," she said.

"How's Mom?" Martin said.

"She needs you," Sandy said.

The next morning he packed up his clothes and bought a bus ticket home. He called Ilene first, hoping for a quick good-bye. He wanted to leave the same way he'd arrived, quietly, without fuss. But Ilene started to cry, saying that she loved him like a grandson, asking him to please keep in touch, insisting he come by the restaurant so she could give him some sandwiches for the road.

Next, he called Elmer, who said that he'd always wanted to see California's beaches and girls. "When you get your own place, I'll be out for a visit," he said. "Maybe I'll even move out there."

"Why uproot yourself?"

"A change might be good for me."

"You're doing just fine here."

"Get me a job at one of your dad's restaurants."

"I have to go," Martin said, feeling like he was about to cry.

"Sorry about your dad," Elmer said.

"Thanks. I have to go," he said again.

"Wait, hold on," Elmer said. "They're *your* restaurants now. Right, buddy? You can just *give* me a job. You scored, man."

"Shut up," Martin said.

"Sorry, buddy. Sorry. Listen, let me wait tables. Let me prove myself, man. I'll help you run things."

"I'm hanging up," Martin said.

"I don't know why I can't ever catch a fucking break."

And Martin hung up the phone and let himself cry. He sat on the couch in the living room and looked at Sadie, who was curled up on the coffee table with a paw over her face, and cried some more. He cried and cried, hoping the neighbors couldn't hear him, but wanting to get it all out before leaving the house and getting on the damn bus.

Later, he lured Sadie into the carrier with a fingertip of tuna. He set a towel on the bottom and tossed in her favorite rabbit-fur mouse. He stopped by the restaurant and hugged and kissed Ilene good-bye. He accepted her turkey sandwiches and plums and chocolate chip cookies. "Everyone should eat cookies when someone dies," she said. "Sit down, Marty, visit with me one last time."

"I can't—bus leaves soon," he said, moving Sadie's carrier from his left hand to his right.

"Give me a second to say good-bye to Ms. Sadie then." She took the carrier from him and put her face right up to the bars, where Sadie was sniffing, her whiskers twitching. "Bye-bye, Sadie Lady," Ilene said.

Sadie meowed all the way to California. Sometimes she stuck her face to the carrier with the mouse in her mouth. When she meowed loudly, people turned to stare. *Fuck you*, he thought, *it's a bus, not a library*. Every now and then, he'd whisper to Sadie, passing her treats through the bars. An old man who smelled like garlic sat next to him. He popped mints into his mouth every few minutes. He'd reach into his pocket and pull one out. It seemed he had an endless supply. "Want a peppermint?" he said an hour in.

"No, thanks," Martin answered.

And the man sighed, saying, "Suit yourself," like Martin was really missing out on something.

Martin unwrapped one of Ilene's sandwiches, sniffed at it, and took a bite.

"What do you have there?" the old man said, peering over.

"Sandwich," Martin said.

The old man got off the bus halfway through the trip, and a woman Martin guessed was in her late thirties got on and took the seat next to him. She had a paperback of *Fear of Flying* that she kept open even when he suspected she wasn't reading from it, a barrier between the two of them that Martin thought was a fine idea. He wished he'd at least brought a newspaper. He bounced along in his seat and stared out the dirty window at the hills and mountains—miles and miles of the same hills and mountains.

They stopped at a diner and the driver gave them thirty minutes to eat. Martin didn't want to leave Sadie on the hot bus, so he brought her inside with him. He covered the carrier with his jacket, which only made her meowing turn into caterwauling. When the hostess gave him a look, he told her to put them in a back booth. "She'll quiet down in a minute," he promised.

From where he sat eating his burger, he could see the woman whom he'd guessed was in her late thirties. She was at the counter and Martin could make out her back and shoulders, her thick, straight hair. She wore a short-sleeve shirt and her arms were slender. Every now and then, a sleeve would fall off a thin shoulder, revealing her bra strap, and she'd pull it back up. He was looking at the woman, wanting to talk to her and wishing he'd been friendlier when she'd sat down next to him.

He wished he'd been a better son.

He wished he'd gone home when Sandy told him that his dad was sick.

Back on the bus, the woman picked up *Fear of Flying* again. He'd heard the book was almost pornography. Martin moved his eyes without moving his head, trying to sneak a look at the print. He thought he made out the words *fuck* and *cock* and maybe *pussy*. He looked at the woman's legs then, which were long and thin, covered in denim. He looked at her visible bra strap and felt a boner coming on. He adjusted himself in the seat and turned to the window again.

An hour later, the woman put the book down, looked at him, and said, "Do you ever think—"

He turned from the window and looked at her. "What?" he said.

She seemed disappointed, as if she thought he might have had a different face, one she could talk to. "Never mind," she said.

"Come on," he said, smiling.

"Forget it." She picked up her book again and didn't put it down until they reached the bus station in Los Angeles.

3

NINA AND Azeem arrived in Palm Springs an hour early for Phillip's fiftieth birthday party. Phillip was a friend from The Elysium, a former British television star, famous in his day but retired now and out of the limelight. A longtime member of The Elysium, Phillip was the best volleyball player at the camp and had recently been elected to the board of directors. He lived in Palm Desert, just fifteen minutes from where they were now. They'd bought him a fancy volleyball, which was wrapped up in a pretty blue box with a white bow, sitting on Nina's lap. She had slept nearly the whole way there with her head against the window and now she was achy. "I slept funny," she said, rubbing her neck. "What did I miss?"

"A lot of brown mountains," Azeem said. "Oh, and a dead dog a few miles back."

"I dreamt that I was clothed at The Elysium. No matter what I did, I couldn't get my clothes off. I was pulling and tugging. They were glued to me or something."

"Was I there?"

"I'm not sure," she said. "Everyone was annoyed at me for staying in my clothes. I tried to explain the situation, but they were hostile and wouldn't listen."

"So much for 'clothing optional,'" he said.

"They wanted me to go home. Some woman actually told me to leave." He laughed.

"It was upsetting. Sort of like the dreams I used to have about getting caught naked at school. My dreams are so vivid lately." She paused. "I wish you wouldn't have told Hannah about the hamburger meat."

"She's stronger than you think," he said.

"Strong isn't the point." Nina couldn't get the image of her daughter, after a painfully quiet few seconds, spinning around on her crutches without saying a word. She jumped from her chair to follow her, but Hannah was fast on those crutches, flying down the hall, and by the time Nina reached her bedroom, the door was already shut. Nina stood, calling her daughter's name, but Hannah ignored her.

Later, when Nina tried to tell Hannah that it was only a meaningless dream, Hannah abruptly changed the subject, and Nina knew not to bring it up again.

"We're so early," Azeem said now. "What should we do?"

Nina looked at her watch. Phillip's birthday party started at seven and it was only five after six.

"I was surprised you slept. I had the radio on the whole time. A talk show on NPR," he said. "There was an Arab and a rabbi—" he began.

"Sounds like the setup to a joke." She yawned.

"Yeah, well, it wasn't funny. They started out talking about the conflict today and ended up arguing about the '72 Olympics."

"Munich." She shook her head. "No one handled that correctly."

They were past Palm Springs and nearly in Palm Desert. They'd be at Phillip's house in no time. Nina placed her palm on the hot car window. "It's terrible out there," she said.

"Look," Azeem said, pointing at a big thermometer hanging from a streetlight. "The sun's gone down and it's still 101 degrees."

"I'd be a nudist even if I wasn't a nudist in a place this hot. And if my clothes were glued to me, I'd go nuts."

It was too hot to walk the streets, too hot to stop and stretch their legs, too hot to get gas or think or window-shop, and Nina really had to pee. "I know it's bad manners to show up early, but do you think Phillip would mind? He's always so easygoing," she said.

Azeem shrugged. "Back home, you arrive when you arrive. You're invited, you show up. You're welcome no matter what time it is. We sit you down and offer you tea."

"Well, here," she started to say, and then stopped herself.

"Here, what?" he said, turning to her.

"Nothing," she said. "Maybe Phillip won't mind if we show up early. It's not like he has to get dressed for the event."

They decided to go straight to Phillip's house, hand him his birthday present, and just apologize.

They knocked on the door, and Nina was sheepish, apologetic, when Phillip greeted them. He had a towel wrapped around his waist, his dark hair was still wet, and there was stubble on his chin, a razor in his hand.

Azeem held the present out to him, an offering.

"What's this? I said no presents," he said, smiling.

"We couldn't resist," Nina said.

"Come on in." Phillip took the box from Azeem. "The caterers are in the kitchen, but you're the first guests here."

"I'm sorry we're so early," Nina said.

"Really sorry, Phil," Azeem added.

"The drive didn't take us nearly as long as we thought it would."

"No traffic. We're not used to that," Azeem said.

"No worries," Phillip said. "I'll set you up in the bonus room with a couple of drinks while I finish up a few things. When the others arrive, I'll let you know," he said, kindly.

"May I use your bathroom?" she asked.

"Certainly." Phillip pointed her down the hall.

When Nina returned from the bathroom, Azeem was already naked in the bonus room, sitting on the black leather couch and sipping what looked like lemonade. "It's spiked," he said, setting the drink down.

Nina stepped out of her shoes and skirt and underwear. She unbuttoned her blouse, took it off, and turned her back to Azeem so he could unclasp her bra. She opened their bag and scooted Azeem's sandals over, making room for her own. After carefully folding up her clothes, Nina set them on top of the shoes and zipped up the bag.

She was about to sit down next to Azeem when she noticed Phillip's family photographs on the wall. There was a lovely picture of his wife, Janet, who had died a year earlier in a car accident and whom Nina used to sit with sometimes at The Elysium. In the photo she was waving, standing by a pair of palm trees, smiling big like she had all the time in the world. There was a picture of his two adult sons sitting at a table playing chess, their bare chests visible. And some other people Nina didn't recognize— all of them naked. Everyone in every picture was naked. Some of the people in the photographs wore hats and shoes, but never clothing. In one picture, a naked Phillip held a Chihuahua wearing a yellow sweater.

"Look at this. The dog's dressed," she said.

Azeem got up from the couch and stood next to her, looking at the dog.

Phillip knocked, and then popped his head inside the room. "Everything OK in here?" he said.

"We're admiring your little dog," Nina said.

"Barney died two months after Janet. I think he died of grief," Phillip said.

"I'm sorry," Nina said.

"Thank you. It's been difficult, but I'm better every day," he said, not seeming better at all. "Make yourselves comfortable. People should be arriving soon." He closed the door and Nina could hear his footsteps in the hall.

Azeem sat down first and she sat next to him. She leaned forward and picked up her drink. The ice had melted, which disappointed her. The drink was strong and sweet; she could taste the lemons and sugar and vodka. She didn't really like hard alcohol, but decided to drink it anyway. It was a party and maybe it would help her relax.

Apparently Azeem didn't want to relax. He wanted to talk about the radio show again. He reiterated, saying that the rabbi and the Palestinian were discussing the ongoing Middle East conflict and he wasn't sure how they ended up talking about the '72 Olympics. "It was nearly eight years ago," he said. "Let it go already."

The comment made Nina feel sharply Jewish. She'd long ago given up being religiously Jewish and certainly wasn't unsympathetic to the Palestinian plight, but when Azeem brought up Israel, she felt uncomfortable, and worse, she worried that on some level, way down, he hated her just a tiny bit. She didn't hate him, though, but felt guilt and maybe a little fear, which she didn't quite understand. When they weren't talking about Jews and Arabs, Nina believed that they were almost able to forget what they were.

She was ambivalent about Israel and when she discussed it with her mother or sister on the phone, she found herself getting angry at their certainty, how positive they were. They said things about Jewish territory and Arab anger that made her cringe. She'd sympathize with the Palestinians and defend them, one time even hanging up on her mother when she'd said, "Arabs are a pill." "I'm married to a pill," she reminded her. "And I love that pill very much," she'd said before slamming the phone down.

Still, when Azeem brought up Israel, she felt defensive, like Jews all over the world were her blood relatives and she needed to protect them.

She took another long pull from the drink she didn't really want. Soon they'd be at a party and this was how they were preparing for it, getting in the mood? "Are you excited to see your brother? He'll be here in, what, a week?" she said, trying to change the subject.

But Azeem wasn't letting go. He told her that the rabbi's nephew was one of the athletes who died. "The rabbi shouldn't have been commenting on the event."

"Why not?" she said.

"Obviously," he said, irritated, "he was too close to the situation."

"Maybe the boy's death earned him the right to talk about it." She set down her glass and looked back up at the Chihuahua in the sweater.

"Bullshit," he scoffed.

When guests rang the doorbell, Nina was thankful. A smiling and newly shaven Phillip popped his head inside the bonus room again and invited them out to join the others. As they stood up from the couch, Nina whispered to Azeem. "It's a party," she said. "Let's talk about party things and have a good time."

"OK," he said, snatching up his drink.

More guests arrived. The Harrisons, who she recognized from The Elysium. Two couples she didn't know. Phillip's mom and dad, who were in their late seventies and surprisingly youthful. Mitch and Mica showed up with their parents. Mitch had brought along a handsome young friend who was heartily shaking hands with everyone and saying their names out loud. "I want to get all your names right," he said, smiling big.

Unlike the bonus room with its black couches and dark rugs, nearly everything else in the house was white. White rugs and white couches and white chairs and white lamps and white bookshelves. There were splashes of red too, pillows and two red, high-backed chairs in the corner of the room that Mitch and his happy friend quickly claimed as their own.

The Harrisons requested a tour of the house. Phillip pointed the rest of the guests to the backyard and then led the couple up the stairs.

Outside, there was a pool shaped like a perfect circle and a square Jacuzzi. The caterers and servers were clothed, passing out food to all the naked guests. Nina was alone, sitting on a lounge chair that was shaded by a palm tree, and from where she sat she could see the steam rising from the Jacuzzi. It looked like the hoses were on full blast, the bubbles breaking the water. A very skinny woman, whose body looked twelve but whose face looked fifty, was stepping into the hot tub. An older man held his hand out to her.

Azeem stood at the bar ordering drinks. He looked over at Nina and waved and smiled. He wanted to be nice now. She waved back.

A husky man came up and stood behind Azeem and the two of them started talking. Azeem was laughing and Nina could hear his laugh from where she sat. She loved his laugh, and it made her smile hearing it. She watched him accept an appetizer from one of the servers. He stabbed something with a toothpick and put it in his mouth. She watched him scratch his chest. She wondered if they'd make it as a couple or if too much was pulling them apart. She watched him watch a pair of women walking by. One of the women wore a baseball cap backwards and heavy red lipstick. The other one wore bikini bottoms but no top. The husky man watched them too. She wondered if it was only a matter of time before Azeem opened up their marriage on his own or if he'd already done so.

Phillip's dad had a head of thick white hair and a neatly trimmed white beard. He sat at a table with his wife and a group of older women, passing a joint around. There was a teenage girl about Hannah's age, one of the guest's daughters, who was visiting from London and walking through the party by herself, saying a cheerful hello to everyone. The girl was lean and tall and seemingly comfortable with her nudity. Nina thought that she probably had grown up with nudists. Kids like Hannah, whose parents came to the lifestyle later, were usually inhibited, and when they joined their parents at the camp, did so reluctantly. If and when they took off their clothes, their tan lines gave them away. The seasoned nudists called them "cottontails."

If Azeem were to open our marriage, he'd want to do it here, is what Nina thought. He'd want that naked woman or that one. He'd want her or her. He might even want the teenage girl. He'd want the one with the long braids or the one with the straight blonde bob. He'd want the tan one sitting at the edge of the pool dangling her feet, her tan calves half-submerged.

Azeem had a fresh drink now and had moved out of line with the husky man. The two of them were standing a couple feet from Nina, within earshot. She could hear Azeem talking about the Munich Olympics and the Israeli athletes, and the husky man was obviously uncomfortable, scratching his cheek and nodding, looking around the yard, searching for someone, anyone else to talk to.

Nina didn't know why Azeem insisted on talking politics now, here, with these people who just wanted to drink their fruity drinks and smoke pot and eat their jumbo shrimp and little meatballs and skewers of chicken, who didn't want to think about Israel or the Gaza Strip or Palestinians, who just wanted to chitchat about nothing and swim in the pool and watch Phillip blow out the candles on his cake and open his gifts, who just wanted to sit in the Jacuzzi until they ran out of words and the pads of their toes and fingers wrinkled.

4

AFTER THE funeral and reception, after family and friends and long-time customers had all gone home, after Sandy, Bill, and the kids were on the road, Martin's mom's face changed, her cheeks fell, and the stoic expression she'd been wearing all day disappeared. "I'm going to bed," she said wearily, even though it was only seven p.m. He was on the couch, petting Sadie, when his mom leaned down and kissed him on the top of the head.

He gave Sadie one last gentle tweak of the ears, then got up to straighten up the house. Sandy and Bill had done most of the work already, but there were still a few things Martin could do. He stretched plastic wrap over the casseroles the neighbors had dropped off and put them in the fridge. Sadie followed Martin around while he picked up the few remaining napkins, cups, and little plates. Sadie sniffed at a cube of cheese that had fallen on the floor and he let her eat it.

An hour after his mom had kissed him good night, Martin went to her room to check on her. The door was ajar, and when he knocked and stepped inside, he found her under the covers, sitting up in the near dark, staring straight ahead. "You all right?" he said.

"No," she said.

He stood there, quietly.

"I've got nothing."

"That's not true," he said.

"What will I do now, Marty?"

He sat down at the foot of the bed. "You'll do what you have to do," he said. "You'll grieve and then you'll get on with things. You'll keep the restaurants going."

"No," she said firmly.

"No?"

"You'll do that." She leaned forward and patted his thigh. "He wanted you to come back and take over."

"I'm here," he said.

And she wanted to talk.

Of course she wanted to talk.

She wanted to go over it again.

"The restaurant was full," she said. "People were in line, spilling out the front door. You know how your dad loved that."

His father had used his hip to bump open the swinging doors that led from the kitchen into the main dining area. He took a few healthy, robust steps, but right before he'd reached the customers' table, he collapsed and fell to the floor, the tray flying through the air, his rich desserts a mess in the corner.

"I'm all alone," she said, starting to cry. "I don't even have any real friends. It was just us, your father and me."

"I know," he said.

"Other women have friends. They do lunch. They go shopping. I only wanted to have lunch with your father." She pulled a piece of Kleenex from the box on the nightstand and blew her nose.

"You'll make friends," Martin said.

She shook her head. "I'm glad your dad was doing what he loved to do, and that there were happy people all around him."

Martin nodded, imagining that the unlucky customers who watched his father die were not smiling, but horrified. He imagined many were particularly disturbed by their proximity, but he didn't tell his mother that.

"I'm glad he wasn't alone," was what he said.

5

NINA HATED sacrificing her weekends at The Elysium, but because of this particular cast, she hated leaving Hannah home alone for long periods of time even more. If it was a walking cast and Hannah could get around on her own, fine, but it wasn't. It was a very heavy toe-to-groin, the heaviest yet. And Megan and Becky were both away for the weekend and Nina wouldn't leave Hannah alone—what if the house caught on fire or someone broke in and she couldn't defend herself or get away?

Azeem rushed over to the cupboard and pulled the plastic bag from a shelf. He carried it over to where Hannah sat on the couch. "If you wear this on your leg, you can get in the camp pool. Please, please, pretty please," he said, standing above her, smiling, excited, and waving the bag.

"No way," she said.

"You can keep your clothes on." He looked to Nina for backup.

Nina shrugged.

"Lots of kids keep their clothes on," Azeem insisted.

Hannah looked at him skeptically.

"Well, I've seen a clothed kid—haven't you, Nina?"

"Oh, yes, that one," Nina said, catching on.

"You shouldn't lie," Hannah said. "You're both really bad at it."

Then they were on the couch next to her, Azeem on her right, still holding the bag, and her mother on her left. Azeem leaned forward and attempted to fit the bag over Hannah's leg, but it was a sorry fit and he finally gave up, sighing, leaning back on the couch.

"It's OK," Hannah said. "I don't want to get in the pool with a bunch of naked people anyway."

She could play gin rummy all day and sit on a blanket and read and hang out with those kids she'd heard so much about. Think of the story she'd have to tell Becky and Megan. Wouldn't they be impressed?

"Grossed out is more like it," she said.

"Come on, Hannah," Azeem pleaded.

She was wavering, knowing they could sense her bending, finally bending, and knowing they'd never quit now.

"We're nakeds," he said. "You don't have to be a naked, but you can join us for the day."

"It's nudists, Azeem," Nina corrected him. "I've told you a hundred times."

"Nudists, then," he said.

If she joined them, they said, they'd take her out for Lebanese food afterwards in Santa Monica where they'd probably see movie stars, and they'd stop at a bookstore on the way and buy her two new novels and that book she wanted about the black-winged damselfly.

"I want this one about worms too," she said.

"Anything you want," Azeem said.

"And I don't want to tell Rebecca and Megan. When they come over, you can't mention it. No teasing."

"Fine," Nina said.

"OK," Azeem said.

Hannah sighed, giving in.

"Terrific!" Azeem said. "Hannah's coming with us to the naked camp."

6

SO THIS was The Elysium. This was where they came on Saturdays and Sundays, where they shed their clothes and all they had then was skin. They displayed their two asses, his penis, her breasts, their arms and shoulders and backs and legs, their calves and thighs, her mother's triangle of dark fur.

So this was the grass they walked upon.

So this was what all the fuss was about, why they rushed out of the house on weekend mornings.

And the naked people were everywhere, of course. They were in groups or they were cooing couples or they were alone. They were walking or perched on beach chairs or sprawled out on blankets. Some of them were sitting with their bare asses directly on the lawn. They were standing by the pool, a family. A man was sitting cross-legged in a yoga position, while a woman knelt behind him, rubbing sunscreen on his back, her huge breasts swinging from side to side. A woman in only goggles and a bathing cap dove into the deep end. A couple holding hands trudged up the hill. Two men sat under a tree together, one of them strumming a guitar. An old man stood alone, eating a sandwich. A few women about her mother's age played a board game several feet away from Hannah.

She was alone, on a blanket with an open book in her lap. She was reading about baby worms that lived in the guts of cockroaches, how when the cockroaches were eaten by rats, the worms grew and had sex in the rat's intestines. There were worse places she could have been, Hannah thought. She could have been in a rat's ass losing her virginity.

She was, of course, the only one clothed in the whole damn place. Regardless of how conspicuous she was, no way was she taking off her jeans or T-shirt. Several people stared at her. One old man smiled. One of the women playing the board game caught her gaze and nodded hello. A little boy dropped his father's hand to point at Hannah. He looked startled and maybe afraid, as if he'd never seen a clothed person before.

She tried watching the people who weren't watching her. She held the book in front of her face, pretending to read, peering over its pages. Her crutches were lying next to her with two bottles of water, a deck of cards, her mother's box of raisins, and a jar of peanuts. There was a half-eaten banana going brown beside her that she didn't feel like finishing. She couldn't wait to be sixteen with a driver's license and couldn't wait to be out of the cast. She'd make her own decisions about how to spend her Saturdays. She could go to her dad's house for an hour or two without having to spend the night. She hoped her dad was OK. She wondered if Christy was getting better in the hospital, if she'd ever be her cheery self again.

Her mom was visiting with some women across the way and Azeem was in the pool, doing laps. He said he'd be back and that he wanted to play cards with her when he returned. She didn't know if he really wanted to play with her or if it was a mercy game.

She watched her mom with the other women. She was laughing, hard, her hand reaching up to cover her mouth.

Women's bodies were still full of secrets, even here, is what Hannah thought, looking at her mother and the others, the four of them making a half circle around an oak tree. Her mother looked comfortable and happy, happier than she'd looked in weeks. She was laughing again, her head thrown back, at something one of the women said. From Hannah's blanket, she could see their four very different bodies: short, tall, medium, and incredibly bony, shoulder blades and hip bones jutting out like little plates. They were naked, yes, but exposed only to a point. Men and boys, though, they didn't have a choice—everything was out there and vulnerable. She turned to watch a pair of men heading toward the volleyball courts. One man's penis was incredibly large, smacking at his thigh, and the man next to him, who held the white ball under his arm and who was so much taller than Big Dick, had a little tiny thimble of a thing. She wondered if the thimble bothered him, and then thought probably not—he was here, wasn't he?

She was near enough so that she could make out Azeem, who looked so small, like a miniature man, doing laps in the pool. There were children standing waist-high in the shallow end. A woman wearing a visor sat with her feet dangling in the water. Next to the pool was the Jacuzzi, which was as big as the pool itself. Up the hill and to the right stood the health food stand that her mom had told her served carrot juice and carob milk shakes—all the breads were brown and the fruit fresh. It was a hut with a thatched roof surrounded by little picnic tables. Hannah was restless and decided to go get something. She put her book down and was reaching for her crutches when two naked teenagers appeared at the foot of her blanket. She saw their toes before she saw the rest of them. *Anything but this,* she thought.

They introduced themselves as Mitch and Mica, the twins her mother had talked about.

"Hi," Mica said, twirling a piece of her dark shiny hair around a finger. "Whatcha doing?" she asked, as if they were any three teenagers anywhere and not two naked ones and one very clothed one with a big cast on her leg. Mica wore nothing but dangly earrings and a choker, a tight necklace made out of turquoise beads. It was pretty, though, and Hannah wished she was a clothed girl instead of a naked girl because then she could stare at the choker without being forced to see the girl's happy little breasts.

"Hey," Mitch said, looking right at her. "Want a piece of gum?" He pulled a foil stick from behind his ear.

"No, thanks," she said.

"Want to smoke some pot?"

She shook her head.

He too had a choker on. It was made of puka shells. Hannah tried not to look at his body, which was lean and hairless and tan.

"Your mom's a cool woman," Mica said.

"She told us about your accident. Can't believe the guy just left you there." Mitch unwrapped the gum and put it in his mouth. He was chewing loudly and she thought she saw a bubble of spit escape from the side of his mouth.

"It was a long time ago," Hannah said.

"Yeah, but still," he said. "People like that should be punished. They're dangerous. Look what he did to you."

Hannah didn't respond. She hated it when people said things like that. It made her think that they were judging her life's worth. She grabbed her book with one hand and was using her crutches to stand up. She was momentarily eye level with the boy's penis. She wanted to die. She wanted to be anywhere but there, looking right at it. "I was just leaving," she finally said. "I'm hungry and I have to study. I'm going to go get something to eat."

"We'll go with you," Mica said, eagerly.

"No, it's fine. I have some reading to do." She patted the book for proof. The twins looked at her, disappointed.

"I'm sorry. I've got a test on Monday—summer school," she lied.

Mitch looked at her skeptically.

"Your mom didn't mention it," Mica said.

"I've got some really good weed in my bag," Mitch said.

"Another time," she said. "I'll be back another day. It's OK here. It's not that bad. We'll talk then. We'll smoke then," she continued, babbling and nervous. She let her weight fall on the crutches and spun around, wondering how long it would take her and if it would be difficult to get up the hill. She took a hop and then another one.

"Want us to wait for you?" the girl said.

"You sure you don't want us to come along?"

"We can keep you company."

"No, no, it's OK. I'll be back another day," Hannah said, lying again and, again, hopping away.

Hannah was breathless by the time she reached the snack stand. She could walk pretty far on crutches, but not straight uphill. She looked down and thought she could still see the pushy twins by her blanket. She wondered if her mom knew that her favorite two teenagers in the place were stoner kids and hoped they'd be gone when she returned.

She stood behind several people in line. They were naked and they were hungry. Every butt was different. One woman's was shaped like a heart. Another looked kind of square, like two boxes or two marshmallows pushed together. A few had pimples on them, but most didn't. The woman with the heart-shaped butt scratched it without ceremony, as if it were her arm.

Behind the counter, the woman had only one breast, a puckered scar where the other breast had been. She held an orange above a plastic cup, squeezing it into juice. The scar was thick and looked fresh, recent. She wore a blue bandanna as a scarf on her head. Hannah tried not to stare. She knew what it was to be stared at. She tried to imagine what the woman had been through and what she was made of, coming here, to a nudist camp of all places. She wanted to talk to her and believed they could communicate, that they knew some of the same language. What did perfect Mitch and perfect Mica with her pretty blue beads know about any of it?

No one would admit that she might not walk again, but at night she heard her mother and Azeem whispering to each other, or one of them looked at her with a certain kind of pity, and she knew that it was very possible that this cast too would come off and that they'd fit her for a brace and she'd limp and eventually her foot would twist and they'd leave that doctor too and meet another, one with promises or hope, one she was sure to disappoint, one who would inevitably disappoint her.

She didn't even want to think about her mother's dream. So what if her leg was skinny when the casts came off? People who'd had broken legs and worn casts for months had told her that the broken legs were always skinnier than the other ones. They said they were surprised, but that within weeks their limbs plumped up, and regardless of her mother's dream and Azeem's pessimism, she wanted to believe that.

The woman with only one breast didn't smile when she handed Hannah her cranberry juice, but she smiled at the regulars she already knew. Hannah sat at a picnic table in front of the hut. She drank her juice and every now and then she'd look up at the woman and try to catch her eye.

A very tall, skinny man stood in line with another man. They looked around thirty, Hannah thought. She watched the skinny man elbow his friend, gesture with his chin at the woman's scar. When they got to the front of the line, their eyes stayed fixed on the menu board.

Hannah finished her juice and then waited in line again and ordered a cheese sandwich. She thought about asking the woman an innocuous question, but didn't say anything because the woman barely looked at her as it was. Even when she handed Hannah the sandwich, she did so quickly without thanking her the way she thanked the others. Hannah decided that it was her clothing, her jeans and T-shirt and one shoe, that offended the woman.

Why so hardcore? she wanted to say.

Aren't there other, more important things? she wanted to ask.

She sat down at the table again and ate her sandwich, watching the line shrink, and when no one was there and the woman was alone, she approached her, smiling. She said, *Hey,* and said, *How are you doing?* and said, *What's it like working here?* and said, *Do you like working here?* and said, *Nice weather,* and said, *My parents come here and begged me to come.*

She wanted to say, *What's your story?* and *What happened?* and *Did it hurt?* She wanted to tell her about her mother's dream, about hamburger meat, she wanted to ask the woman how she really felt about all these bodies, about two-breasted women with long life spans and those men who wouldn't look her in the eye, but if the woman barely acknowledged simple questions like *Do you like working here?* how could Hannah expect to get the answers to the questions that really mattered?

7

MUSTAFA'S FLIGHT into LAX had been delayed. It was nearly ten p.m., and after a bland dinner of prewrapped turkey sandwiches, Nina, Azeem, and Hannah had moved to an airport bar. If Nina wasn't at a party, she rarely drank, yet tonight she was sipping a glass of red wine and already thinking about ordering another.

The airport and the bar were mostly quiet except for the occasional burst of activity when a plane arrived. There was an arrival now, a cluster of travel-weary people with shoulder bags moving past the bar's big windows, looking for the luggage carrousel. Most of them seemed lost or unsure, following the few who happened to be the first off the plane or the fastest walkers. Nina imagined that the people in front were lost too, perhaps their confidant strides were lies, and they were as confused as the followers. She thought about the open marriage Azeem had promised not to talk about, but was talking about more and more, how certain he was that it would add another dimension to their marriage—an informed cheating, he was calling it. She wondered if she'd eventually cave, if she was nothing but a follower too.

A middle-aged man swatted his screaming toddler's shoulder, which only made the boy cry harder. A couple of giddy girls, teenagers, obviously excited to be in Los Angeles or excited to be home, walked arm in arm. And a woman as tall and lean as a fashion model powdered her pretty face as she strode past. Nina was thinking that her legs were long and that if Azeem had been looking at her, he'd certainly want to fuck her. And the woman behind her. And the older woman in sweatpants with the long gray hair. And the squat woman with the immovable bob. And her. And her. She knew he wasn't picky. "I'm attracted to almost everyone," he'd admitted more than once.

Mustafa was in the sky now, somewhere over the Pacific Ocean, heading toward them. He was wearing a bracelet identifying himself in both Arabic and English as an epileptic. She imagined the boy was worried, nervous, and hoping to be cured, his overly optimistic brother promising as much. Nina was thinking that when they brought him home tonight, she'd have his health to worry about along with yet another mouth to feed.

Azeem had expressed concern that the stress of flying might bring about a seizure, a bigger seizure, more intense than all the seizures that had come before, and Nina imagined Mustafa's fit, his fluttering eyes and flailing limbs, the focus of everyone around him, all eyes on the whipping, jerking boy he'd suddenly become. She pictured him in his traveling clothes, his best slacks and button-down shirt, with instructions in his pocket: *Take off my glasses, loosen my tie, don't restrain me or put anything in my mouth, put a pillow under my head, please talk to me sweetly when I come back.*

Azeem had bought a deck of cards at the magazine shop across the way and he was happily playing gin rummy with Hannah. It was early in the game and already clever Hannah was winning, three aces face-up on the table in front of her. It made sense that they got along so well, Azeem being twenty-eight to Hannah's fourteen, and Nina being thirty-nine to both of them. They teased each other and joked around like siblings. Sometimes Nina felt like everyone's mother.

The bar was dimly lit and smelled like popcorn, onions, and beer. The three of them sat at a square table in the corner where the light was best. A band of it came shining out from the back kitchen and lit an area just above the table, hitting their hands and the cards they held. Nina and Azeem sat on one side with a chair between them for Hannah's outstretched leg. The bottom half of her daughter's cast rested on the chair, her pinkish toes just a foot or so from Nina's face. Just the sight of those vulnerable toes was enough to make Nina feel sad.

"It was great to have you with us on Saturday. I know you weren't comfortable, but it takes time," Nina said.

"I don't want to feel comfortable there," Hannah said.

"Oh, it wasn't that bad, was it?"

"Not my thing."

Nina took a big swallow of the wine and looked around the bar.

Azeem glanced at Nina's glass before focusing again on his cards. "Why are you drinking?"

Nina looked at the wine in front of her, her lipstick stains, some three in a row, a series of insincere smiles. "It tastes good," she said.

"You OK?" Hannah wanted to know.

"I'm the mother," she said.

"I'm just asking. Damn."

"Don't say *damn*," Nina said.

"You let me say *fuck*, why can't I say *damn*?"

Nina sighed. She leaned back in her chair. She thought about getting on a plane herself, going somewhere far away and alone. "Say *damn*, say *fuck*, say whatever you want."

"Damn," Hannah said. "Fuck."

Azeem laughed and Nina shot him a look.

"What?" he said.

"Nothing," she said. Then, "Did you tell Hannah not to mention the fact that we're married?"

"I know," Hannah said. She paused. "You'll tell Mustafa eventually, right?"

"Sure, yes," Azeem said.

"You don't sound so sure," Hannah said.

"Let's play," he said.

"I don't know how long I can sit here. I'm restless," Nina admitted.

Azeem smiled at his cards.

"Not that kind of restless," she said.

"What kind?" Hannah chimed in.

She ignored them both then, slid the menu out of its wooden pocket at the edge of the table, and pretended to read from it.

"I hope my brother is OK," Azeem said.

Nina imagined Mustafa sitting between two irritated strangers, a man trying to read a magazine, a woman with a fitful baby on her lap, both of them unhappy with Mustafa's thighs, which were surely spreading into their seats. Their own thighs were reasonable. They pushed their plates away when they'd had enough. And now they'd paid for that little seat that was so much smaller because the boy was so big. She imagined an anxious, hungry Mustafa in the middle seat with a tranquilizer melting under his tongue and felt sympathetic, yes, but also repulsed. The last thing she wanted to do was take the boy to the nudist camp and see his sad body naked.

She wondered if she'd like him and if he'd like her and if Azeem would ever confess that he was married. She wondered if he'd brought pictures of the neighbor girl his parents had picked out for Azeem, if Mustafa would show them to his brother in front of her and Hannah, or if he'd wait until she left the house to break them out. She wondered if Azeem would admit to the boy that they were a family, that this wasn't something casual and temporary, or worse, convenient, but something permanent and based on love. Perhaps the boy would eventually tell his mother and the charade would be over. She wondered what Mustafa felt about his first big trip, his first time on a plane, going to a land he'd only seen in movies and on the postcards Azeem sent. Perhaps he was thinking about Azeem's promises: Disneyland, the mall, beaches and buildings, and a doctor who would finally cure him.

Nina had insisted that Azeem wait a few days before telling his brother about the nudist camp. She wanted him to be sure to stress that clothing was optional. Tell him he can sit on the hill with Hannah, both of them bundled up in winter coats and hats, if he'd prefer. He didn't have to go with them if he didn't want to. He could go to the movies or he could stay home and read. "Don't tell him it's what everyone does here," she had said. "That's misleading. If you don't stress that it's unusual, he'll think everyone in America prefers to be naked."

"Maybe they do," Azeem had said.

"You know what I mean. Let him know that we're different."

Now she finished off the wine and decided on a second. She stood up to get another and Azeem pulled on her skirt. "Easy, Nina," he said. "Get some water."

"I'm thirty-nine years old," she said, shaking free, staring down at him.

"Didn't you tell me once that Jews aren't big drinkers?" he said.

"Asher said that, not me."

Azeem looked at his cards.

Asher *did* used to say, "Jews rarely drink because we make terribly nervous drunks. We leave that to the goyim." When she thought about Asher these days, it was usually about Christy's mental health, but sometimes she'd hear his ridiculous generalizations in her head. "Jewish men don't beat their wives. That's for the goyim," he used to say. "Jewish men can't swim. The goyim? They're like fish." Or "Jewish women are awkward, even when they're beautiful." Or "Jewish women are best when they're not too skinny." And finally, he said, "Jewish men don't cheat," and then he left her for a tall, skinny shiksa he'd been cheating with for years.

When Asher picked up Hannah for a visit, when he stood on the porch and reached out to Nina for Hannah's overnight bag, she'd say hello, how are you, all the perfunctory polite phrases, but if she was in a bad mood, she might zoom in on him, focus, and ask about church or Jesus, and he'd answer her without the slightest bit of irony: *Jesus is terrific, life-changing, I'm full of love now.*

Full of love, huh? she'd say.

Not that kind of love, Nina. Not anymore. You know what I mean. Loving Jesus ensures that I'll have a happy afterlife.

I want to be happy now.

Now? What's now?

And she'd be stunned and baffled by the way one man had completely changed into another man. And by then, Hannah would be standing behind her, ready to go.

People change, it was true. They'd convinced Hannah to join them at the nudist camp. And, sure, it wasn't a perfect day for her, maybe something she'd never do again. She stayed in her clothes and said she'd felt like a leper. On the way home she claimed that she'd rather visit her crazy stepmother in the hospital than suffer through another afternoon avoiding the stoner twins, and Nina had reminded her that she had also played cards with Azeem and seemed to relax, and in the late afternoon, the two of them had sat under a tree together and watched Azeem lose three games of tennis in a row.

The wine was tasty and going down easily, and even though Nina preferred antianxiety pills to liquor—medicine prescribed by a doctor, always prescribed—she could understand why people drank so much of it. She'd been taking her *tablets,* as she called them, on and off, mostly on, since Hannah's accident. Now, though, she was *off,* out of pills and feeling everything: irritation that Azeem had quit his job to study full-time, anxiety about her daughter's leg, anger that he'd described her dream about the hamburger meat to Hannah, and anger at herself for not doing enough to stop him.

She sipped the wine and listened while Azeem made excuses, his brow furrowed in mock concentration. "It's because English is my second language. That's why I'm losing," he said.

Hannah laughed. "It's not Scrabble. It's not about words. It's cards," she reminded him.

He mumbled something in Arabic, but smiled at her.

Hannah looked at him mischievously. "Get ready," she said.

"No. Oh no. Please, no," Azeem whined.

"*Yes,*" Hannah said, dropping down a jack, queen, and king of clubs.

Nina felt a little jolt of parental pride.

"*Gin,*" Hannah said gleefully. "You're no match for me. I need some competition." She looked around the nearly empty bar as if she might find some there. A man and a woman, oblivious to the three of them, sat on a couple of stools, sipping drinks, talking to each other in low voices that barely carried across the room. Every now and then the woman let out a loud and startling laugh.

"One more game," Azeem said.

"You're no better at gin than you are at tennis."

"One more, please, please."

Hannah shook her head, playing hard to get. Nina watched her daughter use her fingers to fish around in her glass for a maraschino cherry. Earlier Hannah's face had lit up when she saw the bowl of those bright red cherries at the bar, and the bartender, a cheerful, smiling man with pink cheeks, noticed her crutches and dropped a couple in her soda. Now Hannah popped one in her mouth, held the stem between her lips and twirled it with a sensuousness that surprised Nina. Nina took a big drink of her wine and wondered if Hannah was still a virgin.

8

HANNAH HAD seen Azeem's pictures where his brother's face was as huge as a stop sign, all folds and skin, so she was surprised that Mustafa was no longer heavy. She had fantasized about the two of them becoming as close as siblings. She'd hoped that Mustafa would be the older brother she never had. She hoped that his illness would inspire a kinship and give them something in common. More than once she'd imagined him stepping off the plane, very round, yes, but with a sincere smile and a hug just for her. He'd wrap her in his big, soft arms and they'd be fast friends. She'd told herself that he'd want a younger American sister. She'd hoped that his weight, which probably made him feel self-conscious and embarrassed, and his limited use of English, and the three years between them, were only minor obstacles.

She could tell from Azeem's eyes that even he didn't recognize the young man walking toward them. He looked nothing like the pictures. He'd lost half of himself. Still, he looked older than his seventeen years, with a high forehead and stubble all over his face, in slacks that were bunched up at the waist and a sweater many sizes too big that hung from his shoulders.

Despite Hannah's hopes, she felt her smile fade and her muscles tighten. She didn't like that he'd lost all that weight and kept it a secret. People should know whom to expect. She didn't like his plaid shirt or old-man slacks or the way he just stood there letting her stepfather gush and cry and kiss him. He wasn't kissing back and there was something standoffish about the rigid way he held himself. Hannah suddenly felt very shy and, worse, left out. With each kiss and Arabic word, she felt Azeem leaving them and going home.

Azeem's eyes spilled over and he was kissing Mustafa on the face, each cheek, the top of his head, where Hannah had just spied a bald spot the size of a half dollar. What seventeen-year-old boy has a high forehead and a bald spot? she wondered. This new teenage brother looked twenty-five.

"These are your friends, yes?" Mustafa said in what appeared to be his best English.

"What did he say?" Hannah said.

"Shh," Azeem said. "Say it again, Mustafa."

"These are your friends, yes?" he repeated, each word very slowly, and looked right at her.

"Hi," she said.

"We're very *good* friends," Nina said, looking at Azeem.

Her stepfather held his brother by his shoulders and spoke quickly in Arabic, kissing his face, pulling him to his chest for a hug, and then pushing Mustafa away to look at his face again. Azeem was crying, but Mustafa's face revealed little about his feelings. This went on for several minutes, with Nina and Hannah standing and watching. It was uncomfortable for them. They didn't know what to do with themselves. Hannah felt gawky and graceless, like any face she made was the wrong face, like she didn't know what to do with her arms. Her cast felt even heavier than it was and her toes seemed to be going numb.

It was obvious that Azeem and Mustafa wanted to be alone.

"Well . . ." her mom said, but no one seemed to hear her or respond.

It was a long, awkward wait at the luggage carousel, the brothers talking excitedly while Hannah and her mom stood to the side, talking to each other with only their eyes. At one point, her mom looked at the brothers and tried to interject, which only made it even more uncomfortable, both of them looking at her like she was a fly or a gnat.

Most people were carefully watching the metal chute spitting out the suitcases, and Nina and Hannah were watching it too even though they had no idea which bag belonged to Mustafa.

"Oh dear," her mom whispered. "This is going to be a long visit." Maybe Azeem overheard the comment or maybe he felt bad, suddenly realizing that he wasn't including them, because he turned to them and tried to translate the last fifteen minutes of their conversation into a few words. "Mustafa's telling me about school and about how he lost so much weight," he said.

"You look great," Nina said.

"Talk slowly," Azeem instructed. "He knows a lot of English, but you can't talk quickly."

"You . . . look . . . great," Nina repeated.

"Shows something about his character—what my brother's made of," Azeem said. "Shows what he's capable of doing when he sets his mind to something positive."

Nina looked at Azeem. What was he talking about? He didn't even sound like himself.

"Not that people have to be thin," he added.

Nina and Hannah were nodding in unison, feeling foolish, when Mustafa's huge suitcase went moving right past the four of them. Mustafa pointed at it and muttered something under his breath without moving to follow his bag.

"Oh, let me," Azeem said, bolting after it, leaving the three of them alone to nod and smile some more.

Everyone except Mustafa carried something. Azeem dragged the big suitcase and Nina slung the stuffed overnight bag over her shoulder. She was struggling, leaning to one side as they walked through the airport. Azeem had strapped Mustafa's camera around Hannah's neck and arm.

"Don't do that," Nina said.

"I'm fine," Hannah said, offering her neck.

"She likes to help out," Azeem said.

Nina looked at Mustafa, thinking he would offer to take the camera, but he didn't say a word. "Hmm," she said. "You sure you're OK, Hannah?"

Hannah nodded and Nina let it go.

It wasn't the camera's weight that bothered Hannah, but the intense smell of Mustafa's overly sweet cologne on the strap. She'd told her mom she was OK, but truthfully she was relieved when they arrived at the car and handed the camera back to him.

Hastily, Azeem moved things around in the trunk: a notebook, a bottle of water, and the picnic basket they used at The Elysium. Azeem handed Nina a plastic bag that she held open while he dropped trash inside of it. He was shaking his head, seemingly embarrassed by the way they lived.

Nina's wine buzz had morphed into a headache, and she was in no mood for Azeem's impatience. She gave him a look that told him as much.

"You should probably let him ride in front," Azeem said, softening.

"What? Oh," Nina said.

"He just arrived. It was a long flight."

"Fine," she said begrudgingly. It was *her* car. She didn't belong in the backseat of her own damn car.

Hannah and Mustafa stood behind them. She was thinking that his head was kind of square and his chin jutted out too much and his wool sweater was even more old-man-like than his slacks, little balls dangling from the fabric like earrings, and he needed a shave. She was thinking that he didn't like the way she looked either, that she was as much of a disappointment to him as he was to her. She was thinking that getting through the next six weeks was going to be an uncomfortable hell, when Mustafa leaned in and uttered his first full English sentence just to her. "Where can I buy hashish?" he said.

She looked at him, surprised.

And he pressed his thumb and finger together and lifted them to his mouth, pretending to take a hit of a joint.

"I know what you're asking for," she whispered.

Again with the thumb and finger together, again with the inhaling, exhaling.

"*I know*," she said.

"Yes?"

"I don't know who sells it," she said, which wasn't really true, but she didn't want to get in trouble with him, not this soon, and what was he thinking, asking her something like that before he even knew her?

Nina turned around. "What are you two kids talking about?"

Hannah didn't know how much of the conversation her mom had heard and didn't know what to say.

"Hannah will show me around," Mustafa said.

"Of course she will," Azeem said. "Everyone get in the car. Let's get this young man home and fed."

9

THE BROTHERS spoke to each other in Arabic for the first few days, even in front of Nina and Hannah, which made them uneasy, especially when one brother said something apparently very funny and they both started laughing.

"Mustafa's English will only improve if he speaks it while he's here," Nina said.

"I suppose so," Azeem said.

"And it would improve more quickly if he spoke it to you too," she said.

"Give him a week or so."

The four of them were sitting in the den. Mustafa was sitting where Azeem usually parked himself, in the big chair. He rested his arms on the overstuffed armrests and stared at the TV.

Hannah had a book in her lap but looked up, nodding enthusiastically at her mom's suggestion. "Yes, yes—even to you, Azeem," Hannah said.

"It would be great if we could all communicate," Nina said. "We would be like a family."

Hannah thought she saw Azeem bristle at the word *family*. Of course, he hadn't told Mustafa exactly what was up between the three of them, who they were to each other.

The nightly news was on with the volume down low, and Mustafa seemed most interested in the screen during commercials, especially when a young woman was putting on lipstick or dancing around in a short skirt.

"You're right—both of you," Azeem decided, suggesting that Mustafa use the English he was taught in school. "You'll be fluent when you go home," he said.

"Flu?" Mustafa said.

"Flu*ent*," Azeem corrected him, sounding like Nina. "Don't worry about it, Mustafa. Talk to us in English from now on."

Mustafa looked confused.

"Let's start tomorrow. First thing in the morning, you'll talk to me in English."

"To you?" he said, pointing at Azeem.

Azeem nodded. "It'll be good for you. You'll know English very well when you return home."

Mustafa shrugged and turned back to the screen, where a bubblegum commercial had begun. The four of them stared dumbly at the TV set. A cheerful song played and a beautiful blonde woman with a huge pink bubble growing from her mouth raised her eyebrows suggestively.

"Good country," Mustafa concluded.

Later, when they went to pick up a pizza, Mustafa told Azeem that he'd lost the weight by eating only a quarter of what he desired. When he wanted two bowls of couscous, he allowed himself a small cup. When he wanted ten falafels, he allowed himself two and a half. When he wanted four skewers of lamb, he ate one. He gave up dates, feta, and flatbread, his favorite. He was always wanting more and never satiated and went to sleep thinking about food and dreamt about food and woke up thinking about it too.

Azeem was sympathetic. "I understand wanting more," he said. "It's something that gives you pleasure, so you do too much of it. It makes a kind of sense. I always thought your weight had something to do with the medicine, though," Azeem said. "No?"

Mustafa shook his head.

"What do you think of Nina and Hannah?" Azeem asked him.

"Very nice," Mustafa said.

"You're not talking to them much. I know it's a new place. And it's much harder using the language in conversation than it is at school. I remember when I first arrived. I barely said anything to anyone. I had only Arab friends."

"What's that?" Mustafa asked.

"I only had Arab friends," he repeated.

"No, I mean, what's *that*?" He pointed at a Jack in the Box on the corner.

"A fast-food restaurant."

"A what?"

"They give you food. Fast."

Mustafa laughed.

Someone cut them off, swerving into their lane, and Azeem called the other driver an asshole.

They were quiet for a block until Mustafa asked, "Who is the woman to you?"

"Nina's my girlfriend," Azeem said.

"How long?"

"A few years."

"That's a long time."

Azeem shrugged. "It's the way things are done here." He cleared his throat. "Tell me more about your weight loss," he said.

Mustafa admitted that he used a smaller plate and forced himself to eat slowly. He said it wasn't easy, that there was always a gnawing emptiness in his stomach. He felt it, even now, telling the story, anticipating the two puny pieces of pizza he'd eat while the rest of them ate until they were satisfied.

"Mom didn't tell me that you'd lost weight."

Mustafa said that he made his parents promise not to tell Azeem because he wanted to walk off the plane and surprise him. "You were surprised, right?" he said.

"I *was* surprised. And I've got a surprise for you too." Azeem pulled into a parking spot near the entrance to the pizza place and turned off the car.

Mustafa could smell the garlic and cheese wafting in from the open window. He was unlocking the car, ready to step out, when Azeem stopped him.

"Wait a minute. Let's talk here first. There's something I want to tell you about, a place we go on weekends," he began.

10

AZEEM BLAMED his brother's reticence on the language barrier, but Hannah felt that was an excuse. She thought he'd be friendlier and would make more of an effort. She thought he'd ask her other questions before asking where he could score drugs.

Now that he'd been with them over a week, though, she was getting used to his presence. Sometimes he did more than grunt hello at her. One morning they actually sat together at breakfast and tried to converse. Or she tried to converse and he offered her short answers in between bites of oatmeal.

She tried telling herself that his request for drugs was a way of establishing trust, a test, and perhaps she'd failed, let him down—maybe when she abruptly said she couldn't help him, he felt insulted.

All he wanted to do, though, was talk to his brother and on the phone to his family and friends, and when Azeem and Nina were out of the house, he wanted to go in the backyard and be alone.

He asked her again and again for pot, calling it *Mary Jane* and *bud* and *happy seed* and *marijuana,* pronouncing the latter surprisingly well, which made her think he'd practiced the word at home. She imagined him preparing for his trip to America, standing in front of the bathroom mirror and saying *marijuana* out loud.

One early evening when Azeem and her mom were in the kitchen preparing dinner, she sat with Mustafa at the table and tried to make conversation. "This table is for picnics," he began. "It's a picnic table, right?"

"It is," she said. "They think it's contemporary."

He looked at her.

"Modern," she said. "New."

He nodded, understanding. "My brother has changed."

"I guess so." She smiled.

"His studies, the place they go on the weekends. How do you say? Unusual," he said, finding the word.

She laughed.

He leaned in. "I like to buy marijuana," he whispered.

"I know," she said. And just then her mom appeared with a steaming roast, Azeem behind her carrying a basket of bread. "Dinner is served," Azeem said happily.

Mustafa asked her silently in the backseat of the car—again with the pressed fingers at his lips, again with the inhaling and exhaling. Again she shook her head.

"You know, if I get caught—which I won't—I won't tell your mom. I won't—how you say—*snitch*."

She wondered where he heard the word *snitch*.

She wondered if she could trust him.

She felt herself starting to cave.

That night he knocked on her bedroom door, stuck his face inside and asked her with just his facial expression and shrug.

And she invited him in. And she put down her book and he sat at the foot of the bed. And she told him that she'd ask around. She told him she thought that Head, whose real name was Steven and who lived just three doors away, had stash he was selling. Head, who actually nicknamed himself, was an eleventh grader, the football star at school, who was even more famous for being the best pot dealer around—*best* meaning that he didn't overcharge you or add oregano to his product.

No, she wouldn't buy it for him, even if he gave her the money.

It was enough that she'd look into it.

Because she could get in trouble, that's why.

Stop asking.

And no, absolutely not—she wouldn't go with him to Head's house.

He'd have to go over there alone.

"You can tell him I sent you, if it makes you feel better," she said.

Hannah didn't smoke pot herself, at least not regularly, but she had tried it a few times with Rebecca and Megan. It seemed everyone everywhere was smoking it, though, even the twins at the nudist camp. She couldn't imagine smoking pot *there*, how nervous she'd be, and how funny their naked bodies would become then.

Mustafa told her that he wasn't ready for the nudist camp yet. He wasn't nearly as opposed to it as Hannah had been, but he needed time to adjust to America first, he said. "Hannah and I will stay home and acquaint ourselves," he told Azeem, which Hannah thought meant: I'll smoke pot and Hannah can try to talk to me and I can ignore her and she can go to her room and read her stupid bug books and I'll watch American TV.

On Saturday morning, after her mom and Azeem had left for The Elysium, Hannah called Rebecca and begged her to skip the movies and mall just this once so she wouldn't have to be alone with him.

"What does he look like?" Rebecca said.

"Like a weirdo," Hannah said.

"Why should I come, then?"

"To see *me*."

"Is he cute at all?"

"No," she said.

"You owe me," Rebecca said.

When Mustafa returned from Head's house with his baggie of pot, he was in a much better mood. And he cheered up even more when Rebecca, in short-shorts and stretchy blue tube top, walked through the front door.

He told the girls that he'd scored *island bud*. The pot was from Maui and very good, Head had told him. Mustafa was beaming, smiling and animated. It was a side of him Hannah had never seen. "Let's all smoke this pot from Maui," he said.

"Yes," Rebecca said, enthusiastically.

They sat in the backyard and smoked. Mustafa took the first hit and passed the joint to Rebecca. She was smiling at him and giggling before the first joint was gone, and Hannah didn't know what was so funny. After she was stoned, though, she realized that Mustafa was indeed a comedian.

He leaned back in the lounge chair with his fingers interlaced, his hands behind his head. He closed his eyes and exhaled loudly. He had on a navy blue T-shirt that said something in Arabic across the front and Hawaiian-print shorts, which Hannah thought very appropriate since the pot was from the islands. Stoned, she found this amazing, incredible, and told them about her observation.

"You're right," Rebecca said, amazed too. "I wonder what it means."

"It means I belong here," Mustafa said.

Hannah knew on some level that it meant nothing, but stoned everything seemed connected and powerful. "I didn't even know you liked it here, Mustafa. I can't tell," she said, looking at him.

"Very much," he said.

They were quiet for a few minutes.

"It's not that I don't like you," he finally said.

"It's not that I don't like you too," she said.

She didn't know what they had just said to each other or what it meant, but she thought maybe it was a step forward.

"You really fit in, Mustafa," Rebecca said.

Hannah looked at her, amazed. What was she talking about?

"I'm very happy here," he said. "Now that I've scored Maui Wowie."

They all laughed at that, and couldn't stop laughing. They laughed and laughed until their stomachs hurt and their throats ached, and when they finally stopped laughing, they realized they were ravenous.

In the kitchen, they prepared peanut butter and jelly sandwiches. The girls drank orange juice and Mustafa finished off the milk. With his busted-up English, he managed to compliment and insult them at the same time, telling them that Rebecca had the more attractive face of the two but that Hannah had the better body. No one had asked him and Hannah decided that regardless of their moment in the backyard, he was still a weirdo.

After the peanut butter sandwiches, they ate everything else in the fridge, even a green bell pepper, which Hannah had never realized tasted so sweet. They sliced the pepper into strips and dipped it in tahini. They ate spoonfuls of chocolate ice cream and hunks of cheese.

Rebecca could barely understand Mustafa and was continually saying, *What did he just say?* Still, in the bathroom, she admitted that she thought he was cute, in his own way. Hannah was surprised.

"You told me he was huge," Rebecca said.

"He *was*," Hannah insisted.

"Did you tell me he was a fatty so you could have him to yourself?" she wanted to know.

"God, no," Hannah said.

"Because all you have to do is say it and I'll keep my hands off of him, but he's foxy," she said.

When they got back to the living room, Hannah looked at Mustafa carefully, searching his face and body, trying to see what her friend saw, and she couldn't. He had a hand under his T-shirt and was scratching his chest. "I don't get it," she whispered to Rebecca.

In the early afternoon, Mustafa fell asleep on the couch, so the girls moved to the dining room.

"What's with the picnic table?" Rebecca asked.

"It's new," Hannah said.

"Seems like it belongs outside."

"Azeem thought it would be interesting. He likes to be interesting."

Rebecca considered this. She rubbed her finger over the surface and said, "Has it been shellacked?"

"Yeah," Hannah said, embarrassed.

"Mustafa doesn't look like the boys at school," Rebecca said.

"You can say that again."

"You don't think he's foxy?"

"Not really, no."

"He's interesting—like your stepdad."

"He's OK, I guess."

"Want me to call Pablo and ask him if he wants to come over and smoke pot with us?" Rebecca asked.

"Yes!" Hannah said.

Rebecca picked up the phone and started dialing.

The doorbell woke Mustafa up. He stretched and yawned and sat up on the couch. Pablo was all smiles, white straight teeth and perfectly pink lips. Dark T-shirt and shorts, black flip-flops. His cast had come off last week and already his right leg was almost as tan and strong as his left one.

Rebecca whistled. "Your legs are looking good, Pabs," she said.

"Pabs?" Hannah said.

Rebecca shrugged.

Pablo pulled a six-pack of beer from a paper bag. He twisted off the caps before handing bottles to the girls. "You want one?" he asked Mustafa, who shook his head no.

"No beer," Mustafa said. "Just pot. Drinking beer takes away from feeling the pot."

"Whatever you say," Pablo said.

"That's what I say," Mustafa said.

"OK then," Hannah said, nervously.

Even though they obviously didn't like each other, Mustafa offered Pablo a joint, which he happily accepted and immediately smoked. After he'd dropped the roach into his Coke can, Pablo pulled out his harmonica and offered to play for them. "How about some Bob Dylan?" he said, looking directly at Hannah.

"Yes, yes," she said, more excited than she'd meant to sound. "I mean, if you want to."

Rebecca looked at her.

Mustafa looked at Pablo.

She looked at Pablo too.

"Play for us," she said.

They'd heard him play before at school, but never like this—his playing, like the bell pepper, had never been so sweet.

Within the hour, Hannah was sitting alone with Pablo in the backyard, side by side on the lounge chairs. Rebecca and Mustafa were in the den doing whatever they were doing. Pablo had sunglasses on, his harmonica by his side. The weather was perfect, not too hot, and a slight breeze cooled Hannah's skin. She looked at Pablo's leg, which was nearly as tan as the other one, and by next week, she was sure, they'd be identical. She asked him how it felt to be rid of the cast.

"It's great," he said. He looked down at her cast. "I mean, I get to do the things I used to do, you know?"

She nodded.

"Feels nice out here. I'm glad I came over," he said. "I'm glad Rebecca called. Why didn't *you* call?"

"I don't know your phone number," she lied.

They were quiet and it was excruciating for Hannah, but her mouth was dry and she couldn't think of anything interesting to say.

"Your brother's pretty funny," Pablo said.

"He's not my brother," she said. "He's my stepfather's brother."

"Then he's your uncle," he said.

"I don't think of him like my uncle," she said.

"Your step-uncle then."

Hannah was mad at herself. This was her big chance and here she was disagreeing with him, barely saying more than a few stupid words at a time. Her tongue felt like cotton and she was nervous, thinking that he was bored and probably hating her, even though he was smiling.

"It's really hitting me now," he said. "I'm too stoned to move. That was some good shit."

"Want something to drink? Another Coke?" she offered.

"Fuck, yeah," he said.

In the kitchen, she opened the fridge and pulled out two cans of Coke. She grabbed a bag of potato chips from the cupboard too.

Even after all these years, it was a challenge to carry things while using crutches, but she had developed methods. She held the chips, securing the bag with her chin and chest, and set a can on each hand rest, and hopped back out to Pablo without too much trouble.

He stood up, flustered, his cheeks red. The harmonica fell to the ground and he left it there. "I should have helped you. I'm sorry. What was I thinking, just sitting here like an asshole. I'm stoned. I'm sorry," he said again.

"I get around fine," she said.

He looked down at her cast. "How much longer do you have to wear that thing?"

"Three weeks," she said.

"Can I sign it?"

"You already did."

"I know," he said, picking up the harmonica and putting it in his pocket. "I want to do it again."

"Maybe later," she said.

She sipped her soda and he gulped his down. He had the bag of chips in his lap, his hand in the bag. He was staring at her and then he wasn't staring at her. He was eating potato chips and forgetting to share. She thought this was adorable somehow and she watched him eat, noisy and with enthusiasm. There were pale crumbs on his perfect lips. His arms were golden brown, hairless and muscular, and she wanted to touch them. He put the empty can down on the table in front of them and smacked those perfect lips, satisfied.

They stared at each other.

"Your face—" he said, looking at her hard.

"Yours," she said.

He scooted his lounge chair closer to hers and it made a horrible scratching sound on the concrete.

"Kiss me," he said.

And, just like that, she did.

11

HIS PARENTS had turned Martin's old apartment into a storage space. It was like a garage above the garage. When his mom fell asleep, he went outside and up the stairs to check it out. He opened the door with his old key and found a room full of discarded things from the restaurants: old sinks, countertops standing on their sides against the wall, and a trio of rusty toilets where Martin's bed used to be. The room was musty, too cluttered to walk around in, but he scooted in between a sink and toilet and stood in the middle. He thought about the many nights he'd spent in this space unable to sleep, thinking about the girl he'd hit. He decided he hadn't changed at all—he was still the very young man in the dented car, hiding from himself. He wondered where the girl was now, if she could walk, and if she still thought about the person who'd hit and left her there.

It wouldn't be easy being in his thirties and staying in his sister's old room. He ripped down the Partridge Family and Donny Osmond posters and tossed out the dried-up corsage from her prom that was on the dresser. He told himself that his living situation was only temporary and that once he'd helped his mom sort through his dad's things and get used to being alone, he'd rent an apartment and move out. He'd find his own place, maybe something in Los Angeles if he could figure out the bus system, or maybe something closer, overlooking the water.

Sandy and her husband had bought a four-bedroom house in La Mirada with a big backyard and orange trees. More square footage for your money inland, his sister said. Martin's mom wasn't happy that Sandy and her grandkids were now an hour away, and she complained about it frequently. "Right when I need her the most," she'd say. "She was always selfish. Remember when she wouldn't eat?"

"I remember," he said.

"Remember when she told her father to fuck off?"

It was strange hearing the word *fuck* come out of his mother's mouth. He smiled at her. "I was already in Vegas by then, but you told me all about it."

"Dad didn't like Sandy's boyfriend, which made sense. That fellow didn't come to the door when he picked her up. He'd honk at the curb. What kind of manners . . ." she said. "And *fuck off* is a terrible thing for a daughter to say to her father." His mom looked at him. She paused. She seemed to be enjoying saying the word *fuck* and Martin wondered if it might become part of her vocabulary. "At least I've got you, Marty."

"Yeah," he said, sadly.

"It's you and me now," she continued.

"I'm only here for a short while," he reminded her.

"Nonsense," she said.

"It's temporary," he insisted.

"Where else do you have to go?"

She irritated him, but Martin felt sorry for her too. He'd find her late at night in the living room, with the television mute, staring out the window at the dark front yard at nothing. She slept late, well past the usual six a.m. sharp that he remembered from his childhood. Sometimes she'd come into the kitchen at noon and refuse coffee or even toast. She didn't fix her hair anymore but wore it clipped back with barrettes way too young for her, silver things with butterflies or daisies on them.

"Maybe you'll stay forever," she said.

"I'm here for a visit, Mom. A short while, until you feel better."

"You're not married—what else do you have to do?" she said, matter-of-factly.

She was old, so much older than he remembered her, the years and his father's death having changed her features—her lips thinner and her cheeks hollow, dark half-moons under her eyes. He was surprised at the deep lines running up her cheeks, and she had a nervous habit of pulling at the loose skin under her chin.

She pulled at that loose skin now, sitting on the couch with her legs tucked under her. They'd eaten dinner together and she hadn't bothered dressing. It was only dusk and she was already in her robe and slippers. The streetlights had just come on and she was pestering him about not driving—even offering to buy him a car with some of the life insurance money, and wanting to know what had happened to make him so afraid of getting behind the wheel.

"I'm not afraid," he snapped. He was sitting in his father's chair, reading a magazine his dad had left behind, an article about the Miss Universe pageant, where the stage collapsed right after the winner was crowned. While his mother continued talking, he was imagining all those beautiful girls spilling to the floor.

"They have pills for your nerves. I've been prescribed some of those pills, although I suppose you're not supposed to drive after taking them," she said.

"It's not nerves," he said.

"What is it, then?"

"I don't fucking know." He slapped the magazine closed, giving up, and dropped it on the coffee table.

"Watch your language, Marty."

"I'm a grown man."

"Maybe—but you're living in my house."

"Not for long."

"Maybe forever."

"Stop saying that," he said angrily. "Say it again and I'll be out by the morning."

"Well," she said, taken aback. "You too, huh? What did I ever do to my children to deserve this?" She tightened her robe at the neck and shook her head.

He needed air. He needed to get away from her before he really told her off. "I'm going for a walk," he said. His boots were by the couch and he leaned forward and grabbed them.

"Where are you going?" she said, softening.

He shrugged angrily. It was none of her damn business. He was lacing up the boots and not looking at her.

She asked him if he could stop by the pharmacy to pick up a prescription for her. She couldn't sleep, she said, she couldn't eat, and the doctor had promised that the little white pills, the ones she thought he should take too, would help. It was why, she said, she'd been so agitated. She was pulling on the loose skin under her chin again. "I'm sorry, Martin. I know I'm making this worse for you. Something pops into my head and the next thing you know it's coming out of my mouth. I can't seem to swallow it. It just comes out. I'm sorry," she repeated.

"OK, OK," he said, picking up his wallet and keys. "Give me the prescription," he told her.

12

THEY TOOK Mustafa to a female doctor in Fullerton who he kept calling Nurse. Finally, after Nina corrected him for what seemed like the tenth time, he called her Doctor Nurse. They took him to doctors in Huntington Beach and Oceanside. On the way to San Diego they stopped for fast food and Mustafa ordered the smallest burger on the menu. After the appointment at the La Jolla hospital with a doctor who was suffering from some terrible tic himself, they went to Sea World and spent a somber afternoon with the trapped dolphins and otters and whales.

Their last stop of the week was at UCLA, where an epilepsy specialist Azeem had read about in the newspaper only confirmed what Nina had been telling him all along. There was no cure, even here in Los Angeles, Dr. Schultz said, and the most exciting, cutting-edge thing he knew about in epilepsy research was an experimental drug that they'd been studying for only a few months. He had high hopes for the drug, but it wouldn't be available for at least another year to the general public.

"My brother will be home by then," Azeem said.

"I'm sorry," the doctor said.

At the car Azeem whispered to Nina that because Mustafa had just received bad news maybe he should sit in the front seat on the way home. "And just for the ride back, we'll be talking in Arabic. The boy's upset with the bad news," he repeated.

"It's not really news," she said.

"I have hope, Nina, so it's news to me," he snapped.

She opened the back door and climbed in. She was getting to know the backseat of her own car very well. The seat belt and ashtray. The hump between the two seats where she rested her arm. The headrests she stared at and, finally, the backs of their heads. Her legs felt cramped and she wished she'd sent them to the doctors without her.

Last night after dinner, Mustafa had placed a flat palm on his stomach and said the spaghetti was very tasty but didn't seem to agree with him.

He was nauseous, he said, so Azeem suggested he sit in the front on the way home from the restaurant.

Azeem insisted he sit in the front seat the whole way to San Diego too because he'd have a better view of the ocean. "You live here," he'd told Nina. "You see the ocean all the time."

On the 405 freeway, the two men talked about Dr. Schultz. Nina couldn't understand what they said, but she heard the doctor's name every now and then. Nina was used to doctors not having answers, and from what she could tell, Mustafa's situation wasn't nearly as dire as Azeem had led her to believe. He hadn't had one episode and he'd been there nearly two weeks. Azeem had told her that he'd had episodes at least weekly, sometimes more than one a week. Now, she wondered if he'd lied just to get her to fly him over. If he'd lie about that, she thought, he'd lie about other things.

She leaned forward between the two seats up front and said, "You've been feeling pretty good since you've been here, yes?"

"Yes," Mustafa said, turning to her.

"Interesting," she said.

"What are you saying, Nina?" Azeem caught her eyes in the rearview.

"He's just doing so well," she said.

"And?" Azeem said.

"And nothing," she said.

In the conversation that ensued, she could have sworn she heard Mustafa mention the name Raina, but when she leaned forward again and asked Azeem about it, he gave her an angry denial. "Jesus, Nina," he said. "Stop it," he told her.

When they got off the freeway, Azeem turned to her. "I've always thought that the doctors up north would know more. We'll take a trip to San Francisco," he said. "We'll stop at Stanford. I'd love my brother to see the Golden Gate Bridge."

He turned to Mustafa, who was saying something to him in Arabic. "Yes, you're right," Azeem said.

Nina asked what they were talking about. She looked out the window at two girls about Hannah's age, riding by on bikes. A little boy rode his Big Wheel on the sidewalk. A woman sat on the porch with a little white dog in her lap. The light turned green and they moved forward.

"Mustafa was just saying that a lot of Americans jump off that bridge."

"I don't think of them as Americans," she said. "I think of them as people. Just sad people."

"But they *are* American," Azeem said.

Don't be petty, she wanted to say. *Don't be a liar,* she wanted to say. "I suppose so," she said.

13

TONY STOOD behind the counter, a pharmacist like his dad. Off to the side, Martin watched him work and thought about all the years he'd wasted in Las Vegas. He wished he'd done something during those years to become someone new. Tony *was* someone new, all cleaned up in his white jacket, his shiny black hair that used to grow into wild curls combed to one side, gelled and neat. Martin wondered why his mom hadn't told him that Tony was her pharmacist. Maybe she wanted him to be surprised.

His old friend was attentive and thorough, handing a very old man a white bag of pills, leaning over to explain to the old guy not to mix that drug with this drug, and not to drink grapefruit juice with that one there. He pulled a vial of pills out of the bag and tapped on the lid to make his point. "Promise me, Clayton," he said.

"I promise," the old man said.

At the front of the line, Martin surprised him.

"Damn," Tony said, smiling big. "Holy shit," he said. He gestured to another guy in a white jacket to take over for him, and then stepped through the little gate to hug Martin properly.

"How long have you been back?"

"Just got here."

"Are you staying?"

"I'll stay awhile."

"I want to catch up. Murphy's was torn down, but we can grab a coffee down the street."

"A coffee?"

"No booze for me."

"Really?"

Tony nodded.

"You look all doctor-like," Martin said. "Who would have thought you'd clean up like that?"

"Hey, listen," Tony said. "I heard about your dad. I'm real sorry."

"Thanks," Martin said.

"I always liked your dad and his restaurants. He gave us free food. I remember those cheeseburgers and vanilla milk shakes. We'd be all stoned and he wouldn't say a thing, just feed us."

"Yeah."

"He never gave us shit for anything we did. Remember that time we took his car to Huntington Beach to meet those chicks? Remember we left a bag of seeds and half a joint in the front seat? I used to get so fucked up," Tony reminisced, obviously enjoying the memory. "Anyway, your dad was a good guy. How's your mom holding up?"

"Not great." Martin sighed.

"That's too bad."

"I think she's crazy now," he continued. "She acts like I've moved back to marry her, like I'm going to stay in that house forever."

Tony laughed.

"It doesn't help that they spent every fucking minute of their lives together."

"Send her my best," Tony said. Then he held up his hand, proudly displaying a wedding band. "Married Annabelle a year after you left."

"Congratulations."

"Two kids and a dog. It's a good and boring life. What about you, Marty?"

"Left a girl in Las Vegas," he said, lying.

Tony's eyes lit up. "What is she, a dancer, a showgirl?"

"Marla's a student."

"Tell me she's a showgirl—let me have a fantasy."

Still the same old Tony. Martin shook his head.

"Why didn't you bring her along?"

"She's got classes, a life in Vegas."

"Always breaking some girl's heart," Tony said.

They were quiet, looking at each other.

"You're still good-looking," Tony said then. He patted his own soft belly. "Me, I've gone to fat."

"You look fine," Martin said.

Tony shook his head. "*You* look fine," he said. "We can find you someone new who lives out here just like that." He snapped his fingers.

"Don't worry about me," Martin said.

The other pharmacist skittered out of the gate then, all flustered. He held a notepad and a pen. "I've got a question, Dr. Tony," he said nervously.

"I'll be there in a second," Tony snapped, shooing the guy away.

"*Dr.* Tony?" Martin said, smiling.

"Yeah, I know," Tony said. "Anyway, I have to get back. They don't know heart meds from asshole meds. Want to get some coffee after work?" He talked over his shoulder. "I get off in fifteen minutes."

"Hey, wait a minute," Martin said, pulling his mom's prescription out of his shirt pocket. "I need to fill this."

14

IT WAS obvious to Hannah that Mustafa felt immediately at home at The Elysium and was more than eager to take off his clothes, pull off those pants, rip off his shirt, and gross her out. She didn't think he was stoned yet but was certain that he had joints in his bag. She wondered if he'd find the teenage nudie twins and get stoned with the two of them.

And sure enough, right after her mom and Azeem made their way down the hill, Mustafa happily, quickly, stepped out of his clothes. He stood before her and tried to engage her in conversation and she felt he was taunting her. For a guy who'd lost all that weight, his skin was surprisingly tight. She imagined the pounds melting away and his skin snapping right back into place.

It was strange enough between them when Mustafa was clothed, but now, standing in front of her with only his watch on, with his uncircumcised penis and little balls, she felt sort of nauseous. She was sitting on a blanket and he was standing up, his hairy crotch, those little balls swinging in front of her. "Go swimming or something," she said.

"You're not friendly today," he said.

"You're naked," she said.

A pair of women in just their bras and tennis shoes walked by. They were holding rackets and one of them had sweatbands around her wrists.

"Why didn't you invite your friend Rebecca here, to this good place?"

"She doesn't even know about *this good place*. Please don't mention it to my friends. I don't want them to know. Promise me."

"What about Pablo? Does he know?"

"No," she said, raising her voice.

He looked at her and said nothing.

"I'd die," she said.

"You're shamed," he said.

"It's *a*shamed," she corrected him. "And it's not that. It's just none of their business. Everybody doesn't need to know everything. I'm sure you don't tell people everything."

"I disagree."

"Did you tell Rebecca that you used to be big?"

"No, but you did. Thank you much."

"Sorry about that," she said, meaning it.

"I think you should tell your friends about here, Hannah. I think it's a very good place," he said again, looking around at all the naked bodies.

"You don't tell your brother that you get stoned every day. He'd probably like to know that," she said, threatening.

"Too bad you're in a cast," he said.

"Yes, it is."

"You can't swim or anything." He looked at his watch.

"Thanks for reminding me," she said.

He shrugged and walked away, down the hill, and she noticed that his ass was almost as hairy as Azeem's.

She fell asleep on the blanket and when she woke up the naked twins were standing above her. "Can we sit with you?" Mica said. And the two of them sat down before she had the chance to answer. Their bare asses were on her blanket and Hannah decided that she'd wash it as soon as she got home. They'd obviously been swimming. Their hair was wet and Mica had twisted hers to one side and was wringing it out on the lawn.

"I didn't like coming here at first, either," Mitch said.

"You look pretty comfortable now," Hannah said, trying not to look at their bodies.

"But we were born like this," Mica said.

"Naked?"

They both laughed. "Our parents were nudists before we were born, so we grew up with it," Mica said.

"They'd have parties with naked people—it wasn't a big deal," Mitch said. "To our friends it's a big deal, though. They think we're weird. Well, they think I'm weird because of other things too." He pulled up a blade of grass and stuck it in his mouth.

Mica did the same, and they were both looking at her, chewing.

"My mom teaches high school English," Hannah said, out of nowhere.

"A *nudist* English teacher," Mitch said.

"Do your friends know?" Mica asked.

"No way."

"I understand."

"Show her what you brought her," Mitch said.

Mica reached into her bag and pulled out a turquoise choker. "Your mom said you liked it," she said.

"You didn't have to do that," Hannah said, touched. "That's so nice of you. It's beautiful." And it was. The beads were small enough to be dainty, but big enough to get noticed.

"Can I help you put it on?" Mitch said.

She must have looked startled because he quickly added, "It's not sexual. I mean, you're good-looking and everything, but—"

Mica cut him off. "He's a homosexual," she said, nodding, proud.

"I'm queer," Mitch said.

"That's good," Hannah said, feeling like an idiot. "I mean, it doesn't matter to me. It's normal. It's fine." She knew her words were coming out too fast. She felt like a fool. "I'm sorry," she said. "No one's ever come out and just said that. I don't care, though. Honest."

"I didn't think you would," Mitch said. "How about getting stoned with us later?"

"I don't know," she said, wavering.

"Think about it," he said. "Now let me put this on you."

She offered Mitch her neck and he reached around and put the necklace on, clicking the clasp.

"Perfect," he said. "Don't they look great with her eyes?"

Mica nodded.

"Thanks," Hannah said, touching her new choker.

"Last time you were here, you ran away from us," Mitch said, smiling.

"I was hungry," Hannah said. "I went to get a sandwich."

"The woman who works at the snack stand is our aunt," Mica said.

"She's back in the hospital," Mitch said.

"I'm sorry," Hannah said.

"I've never understood why people say they're sorry when they don't have anything to do with what's wrong. No offense," he said. "It's just one of those things I think about. And why are people afraid of queers? There's a queer on the football team at school, but no one knows he's queer. *I* know because he tried to kiss me in the boys' bathroom. If they knew, he wouldn't get to play."

"That's terrible," Hannah said.

"There's a couple nudists here who won't talk to my parents anymore since I announced I was gay." He looked around the camp and pointed to a middle-aged couple at the pool. "The Harrisons. Those two think nudity is great, getting stoned terrific, but a guy with a guy freaks them out."

"It's not right," Hannah said.

"Your brother's pretty funny," Mica said.

"He's not my brother."

And just then Mustafa came rushing up, all worried. His forehead was sweating, his hairy chest glistening, and his penis bounced against his thigh. "I can't find Azeem," he said, out of breath. "Have you seen my brother? Where's your mom?"

"I don't know where your brother is," Hannah said, "but my mom's right there." She pointed across the way to where Nina was sitting with that same group of women she was visiting the last time Hannah was here.

"He said he'd play tennis with me at two." Mustafa glanced at his watch. "He's late," he said.

15

NINA FELT it in her body, in her stomach and chest, before she found them.

She'd been talking to Kendra about her job and students, telling her that no matter how many times she read Shakespeare, the beauty astounded her, and then Kendra was talking about being a warden in an all-female facility, describing one inmate in particular whom she cared about and believed in, how she understood why the woman might want to shoot her husband in the leg, how aiming right at his thigh was different than trying to kill a man, and it hit Nina suddenly where Azeem was and what he was doing.

"Excuse me," she said, leaving Kendra midsentence.

She walked down the hill to the Ankh Room, which was really many rooms shooting out from a getting-to-know-you lobby full of beanbag chairs and furry rugs. She went through the lobby without looking at the people who were getting to know each other, and straight to the room where she and Azeem had made love the second time they visited the camp.

He was on his back. She saw half of his sweaty face, one glistening shoulder, and his legs shooting half off the cot. A woman moved on top of him. Her waist was noticeably small; tiny even, but it was her ass that Nina couldn't stop watching. The ass was enormous, jiggling, quaking, moving, and falling over Azeem's thighs and covering his middle torso completely.

He looked at Nina with an open mouth, ready to say something. "No, no," Nina said. "Don't talk. And don't stop what you're doing." Her voice was steady and calm. "Don't worry about me," she told them.

And they didn't.

They didn't stop, but continued, and the woman, whose face Nina couldn't see, held up her finger. "Give me a minute, give me a minute," she said, breathing hard.

Nina sat on the beanbag chair in the corner, giving the woman a minute and then another minute and then another. She watched the two of them like she was watching a movie. She watched the woman shudder, her toes curl, that myotonic tension, before she stood up and approached them. "Get out of my house," Nina said calmly.

Azeem was still hard when the woman got off of him.

"This isn't your house. It's the Ankh Room. I'm not in your house. This is everyone's house," the woman said, standing up.

They faced each other then. Two ridiculously naked women, Nina thought. There were no clothes to hurry on and nothing much to do, so the woman stood there a minute, not sheepish at all, glistening—a perspiratory reaction, Nina thought to herself. And then she said it out loud, *a perspiratory reaction.*

Azeem was sitting up on the cot, not talking, staring at them, breathing hard and shaking his head. He ran a hand through what was left of his hair.

"He said you wouldn't mind," the woman said, glancing back at Azeem, who only shrugged. Her voice was unemotional, and when she walked away from them, Nina could have sworn that she heard, from those huge ass cheeks, the tiniest fart escape.

At the car, Nina insisted on driving and told Hannah to sit in the front seat next to her. At first Azeem and Mustafa talked quietly in the backseat, but mile by mile their voices rose and Nina was tempted to turn around and tell them to shut the fuck up. She tried to talk to Hannah about Mica and Mitch, and admired the pretty turquoise choker they'd given her, but it was difficult to act normal and focus.

There'd been an accident, a three-car collision on the 101 freeway, and traffic was bumper-to-bumper, which meant more time in the car with him. Cars skidded to a stop behind them and Nina barely flinched. Mustafa nearly jumped into the front seat when one van came in too close. He screamed like a baby girl and Nina looked in the rearview mirror and rolled her eyes so that Azeem could see. She hated them both. She felt like an idiot. It didn't matter to Azeem that she hadn't agreed to an open marriage or not, he'd opened it on his own, he'd opened it with that tiny-waisted woman with the huge farting ass. And who knew how many other women there had been. Maybe he'd fucked a hundred and was walking around with syphilis and gonorrhea and crabs. Maybe he'd given her a venereal disease. Just the thought of it made her want to bathe. She'd take a hot shower when they got home and in the morning she'd call to make an appointment with her gynecologist to check things out.

"Did you know that Mitch is gay?" Hannah said.

"Oh, good for him," she said.

"Good for him?"

"What did you say, honey?"

"I said Mitch is gay."

"That's not nice," she said.

"I mean, he told me he was gay. He's not ashamed. It's who he is."

"Oh," she said.

"I like him a lot," Hannah said.

"That's great he's comfortable enough to tell you such a thing. Ten percent of the population has those tendencies, you know." Nina paused. She looked into the rearview mirror again and caught Azeem's eye. She shook her head so he could see, then looked at the road again. She couldn't concentrate. She could hear Azeem talking in the back and she could see Mustafa nodding vigorously.

She thought about pulling over on the freeway and telling them both to get out of the car.

"What's wrong?" Hannah said.

"Nothing. I'm fine."

"Something happened, Mom. What happened?"

Nina ignored Hannah's question. She felt sick to her stomach. Duped. Used. She imagined he only stayed with her because she supported his hairy ass. "What are you two talking about back there?" she said suddenly.

Azeem leaned forward between the seats. "Calm down, Nina," he said. She felt her face heating up and tried hard not to cry.

"My brother is hungry, that's all," he said.

"Feed him," she said.

He laughed nervously.

"Why don't you fucking feed him, Azeem?"

"Don't do this, please."

"Sit back," she said. "Let me talk to my daughter."

And then she stared straight ahead and didn't say a word.

16

THE NEXT morning, while Mustafa slept, Hannah's mom and Azeem sat her down in the kitchen and told her that that they were now platonic, that yes, they were married, but wouldn't be by the end of the year. They were waiting for Mustafa to go home before they broke up. Her mom had promised to take him to specialists, and *she,* unlike some people, didn't break her promises. They asked Hannah to please not tell Mustafa. It would only create drama and he wouldn't understand, they said.

"He doesn't even know you're married," Hannah said.

"That's true," Nina said, looking at Azeem. "That you insisted the marriage was a secret should have clued me in. I should have known. What was I thinking?"

"Nina, please," Azeem said wearily.

"Why would he care that you're getting divorced?" Hannah pressed.

Nina looked at Azeem then and said, "You see?" She got up from the table and left the kitchen, muttering to herself down the hall.

Azeem didn't want to break up with her mother, he wanted Hannah to know, but he wanted to sleep with other women. There, he said it. It was nothing to be ashamed of, he believed, and he'd said it out loud, and Hannah was still alive and breathing.

"Isn't my mom enough for you?" she asked him.

"I only *love* her," he said.

"So she should be enough," Hannah said.

"I only love her," he repeated.

"You want what my dad wanted." Hannah felt her eyes filling up. She didn't want to cry but couldn't help it.

"It's different," he said.

"No, it isn't," she said. "Why isn't she enough?" Hannah said, her voice rising.

"You'll understand later. When you grow up and meet someone and you're together for years and years. You'll see," he said.

But she didn't think she'd see any such thing. She had kissed Pablo when he asked her to kiss him. She had leaned forward in her chair and moved toward his pink lips. His tongue came at her, a perfect, sweet thing. He had called her the next night and the night after that. He played his harmonica into the phone. He listed the things they'd do together when her cast came off. *I want to ride bikes with you,* he'd said. *I want to dance with you.*

"Where will you go?" she asked him now.

"My cousin's apartment in L.A. Or I'll rent a place." He paused. He looked out the window, then back at her. "I want to be there when the cast comes off. I want to see you walk."

She ignored that comment.

They sat for several minutes without saying anything.

A door slammed.

Another door opened.

Someone was taking a shower. They could hear the water moving through the pipes.

"If you leave her, who will you be to me?" she finally asked him.

"I'll still be your stepfather," he said.

"No," she said. "You won't be that."

17

MARTIN AND Tony sat in a booth in the far corner and shared a pot of coffee. They ordered cherry pie from a woman Tony recognized from high school. He thought maybe she was the one he felt up in a coat closet at a party in the tenth grade, but it might have been her friend. "I remember sitting on the ground and the coats and jackets hanging in my face, but I don't remember if it was her or not." He shook his head. "I was so fucked up, I could have been feeling my mother's titty," Tony said, laughing.

Martin laughed too.

The two of them talked and talked.

When the waitress Tony might have felt up was done with her shift, she let them know that another waitress was taking over for her. "Do I know you?" she said to Tony.

"Maybe," he said. "Did you go to Manhattan Beach High?"

"I'm from Portland," she said. "But you sure do look familiar."

"You do too," he said.

They tipped her before she left and didn't move from the booth. They asked the new waitress for more coffee and told her that they were almost out of cream.

Martin talked about Las Vegas, about Ilene and Elmer and Marla, about the casinos and how often he won money. He admitted that he drank a lot and smoked a lot and fucked a lot of girls. He told Tony about cooking school and how much he liked preparing food. He liked the smells and spices, working with his hands and making something out of nothing. He said that from now on he wanted to be in the back of the restaurants with the skillets and ovens and people who were creative. He wanted to chop onions and smell garlic frying in the pan. And then he admitted that Marla wasn't his girlfriend. He hadn't talked to her in months, he confessed.

Tony said he'd stopped drinking and joined AA. The meetings saved his life, no shit. Sure, the people and their long-winded stories bored the fuck out of him sometimes, but their intentions were good and they needed to vent. We all need to vent, he said. He told Martin that he ran into a fire hydrant one midnight and smashed Martin's old car and all he remembered was water, all that water shooting into the sky, and that he sat there fucked up in the fucked-up car and decided he'd had enough. The judge decided that Tony had had enough too, and sentenced him to thirty days in jail and six months of community service. He cleaned up hospitals and met patients who'd been hit by drunks or women who'd been beaten up by drunks, or kids who'd been left by drunks, or drunks themselves who were all messed up physically and now trying to sober up.

"You couldn't walk away from that and be the same man," Tony said.

They sat for hours.

They ordered another pot of coffee and a second piece of pie each.

Tony said he loved his wife but that she wouldn't let him touch her. He said she drank wine at night, a glass, two at the most, which didn't seem to be a problem for her, and that it played with his mind sometimes. He said there were two different Tonys in his head having a conversation at all times: One Tony knew that to take one drink was defeat and the other Tony was always messing with him, saying, *Hey, look at your wife, look how she has a glass of wine and doesn't need another, look at her control, look at her pretty hand reaching for the wineglass, look at her lipstick on the rim, look at her head thrown back, that neck you used to know, look how relaxed she is after that glass of wine, so content, and look at my kids who won't go to sleep without a story and a glass of warm milk; even they have something to drink that soothes them.*

"I think about the valium I prescribe every fucking day," Tony said. "The muscle relaxants and painkillers. I think about buying a six-pack and sitting in the car drinking in my driveway until the sun comes up. I think about it, but I don't do it."

"Fuck, man, that's hard," Martin said.

"We've all done things when we were wasted, Marty. Isn't that right?"

Martin ignored the question. He sipped his coffee and didn't look at Tony. He looked at the wall above Tony's head, an autographed picture of some actor or entertainer he didn't recognize.

Tony scraped his plate with the fork, lifted a bite of pie to his lips, but stopped. He held the fork in the air while he said it. "I know what you did."

"What?" Martin said.

"I put it all together after you left, man. The car, the way you stopped driving and started taking the bus, the dented fender. The girl the whole neighborhood was talking about."

Martin put down his coffee cup and exhaled heavily.

"You need to come clean." Tony ate what was on his fork, staring at Martin. He was chewing his pie, looking right into Martin's eyes. "You need to come clean, man."

18

NINA DIDN'T forgive Azeem, but she wanted to get through the next month without fighting or incident. Soon Mustafa would return home and Hannah's cast would come off and she'd insist Azeem pack his bags and move out. It didn't matter that he swore on his brother's health that he'd never do it again. It didn't matter that he tossed the *Open Marriage* book into the trash can and said he was sorry.

Even though she was angry, she kept her promise and went with them to more doctors. They went back to UCLA to see another specialist, one who doubted the first one and claimed that a curative surgery would eventually be available. They'd take out the smallest piece of a person's brain, a piece you wouldn't even miss, and the seizures would stop, he said. They took Mustafa to San Francisco for the weekend, up and down the coast, visiting multiple hospitals and various doctors.

The doctor in San Francisco was especially blunt. He'd examined Mustafa and ran his tests and examined the results. They were sitting in his office for the consultation. Mustafa had said he wanted to stand, so Nina and Azeem sat in the two chairs facing the doctor's desk. There were plaques and diplomas along one wall, and Nina could see that the doctor had graduated from Harvard. On another wall, there were pictures of his smiling family. The doctor was pleasant enough but serious, sitting in a big leather chair. He picked up the plastic brain from his desk and held it in both hands. "The brain is complicated. Epilepsy is complicated," he said. "It's not going away anytime soon. I don't expect a cure in your lifetime," he said, looking up at Mustafa.

"I expect a cure," Mustafa said.

"It doesn't hurt to have hope," the doctor said, putting the brain down. "But I'm a realist and there's too much that we just don't know."

"But we'll know eventually?" Azeem said.

"Perhaps," the doctor said. "But you must remember that this here is the most complex part of us." He looked down at the brain. "When a person loses a leg, he's still himself, still thinks the way he thinks." He paused. "I'm sorry I can't help you people more," he said.

Like Mustafa, Azeem wouldn't give up hope. There had to be a cure somewhere. He did his own research, asked around, and at the advice of one of his professors, started reading a book called *The Sexual Mind*. He was, of course, in complete agreement with the author's theory about illness. Patrick Anderson believed that sexual repression made human beings ill. He blamed cancer and diabetes and arthritis and epilepsy on the deliberate suppression of one's sexual urges. He claimed that people could cure themselves of all sorts of conditions by giving in to such urges and accepting pleasure. The more pleasure, the better. Sexual satisfaction equaled physical health. It was like the theories he'd heard about illness and laughter, where someone with cancer sat in a hotel room for days on end, watching funny movies and stand-up comedians, and suddenly went into complete remission, only Anderson's theory was about orgasms and satiation.

Azeem sat Mustafa down in the den and told him about *The Sexual Mind* and the author's theory. He explained that Mustafa alone could control his disease. He handed the book to Mustafa, which he flipped through while Azeem spoke. Azeem promised that if Mustafa came often enough, freely, without inhibition, the seizures would stop completely.

Mustafa loved Azeem's suggested medicine and took to masturbating every day, all hours of the day and night, sitting, stroking, curing himself in every room of their suburban home. Mostly he did it when they were sleeping or when he was alone, but one time Hannah returned from Rebecca's house and found Mustafa on the couch, going at it. He waved her away, and she'd felt his irritation—it wasn't that she'd caught him doing something private or inappropriate, but more that she'd interrupted his favorite TV show.

Days went by, weeks went by, and Mustafa didn't have a seizure, not when he was tired or hungry, not even when he came down with a summer cold. Azeem was thrilled, insisting it was worth it—each embarrassing moment and extra load of laundry.

Even Nina and Hannah started to believe. It started to make sense to them. They were a fractured family, but one who believed in the orgasm, a family that had witnessed its power.

No one understood why, the week before he left, while sitting in a fast-food restaurant, holding a dripping burger in his hand, Mustafa started to shake, the burger falling into his now quaking lap, the terrible sounds coming from his throat and chest and somewhere deeper. No one understood his flailing hands and jerking shoulders. And they were all let down, the four of them who'd believed for weeks in the orgasm, who'd hoped it would save their lives.

PART 4

1

THE WINE rack in the kitchen was full of expensive Santa Barbara reds, bottles that Martin's mom and dad had purchased during their last road trip together. A month before his father's death, they'd stayed at a beach-front hotel and taken a jeep tour of the wineries in the region.

"It was beautiful," she told Martin. "Heavenly," she said. "Your father never looked better."

Every night for the last week, his mom waited for the sun to set before pulling a bottle from the rack. She'd stand a minute, marveling at the label. Stonecraft Valley, Eagle's Perch, and her favorite, Blackwood Estates. She'd shake her head. Her eyes would go moist and she'd be remembering some last moment she'd had with Martin's dad, he was sure.

If Martin happened to be in the kitchen, she'd feign weakness and ask him to open the bottle for her. She'd look up at him, imploring and sad. It wasn't that she couldn't do it herself, Martin knew, but that she hoped to tempt him. He also wondered if her displays of weakness or dependence were meant to keep him under her roof.

They had a system. After he popped the cork, he'd drop it in her waiting palm. She'd look at it a moment, mesmerized, before holding it up to her nose for a sniff. Then she'd proudly show him the stain. "Look at that, Marty," she'd say, holding the cork in front of his face. "See that color?"

"Yeah, it's red," he'd say, unimpressed.

"Not just red."

She'd swirl the wine around in the glass and tell him about its legs. "See that pretty bleed. Just look at that."

Even though wine hadn't been Martin's drink of choice, he didn't want to talk about it or think about it or watch it *bleed* down the glass.

"No one likes to drink alone," she said, repeatedly.

"Then stop," he said.

"Don't be silly," she said.

One night, after a couple glasses of what she called a *very impressive cabernet* from Blackwood Estates, she admitted that she didn't think Martin had a drinking problem. She always thought he'd made a big deal out of nothing. "You drank moderately, like a normal person, certainly like a normal teenager or young man, and then, one day, for no apparent reason, you got all cranky about it," she said.

"For no apparent reason, right," he said, his voice rising.

"Your father never thought you had a problem, either," she said.

It was late, after eleven p.m., and they were sitting in the living room in front of the television. Martin in his dad's chair and his mom on the couch with her feet up, slippers crossed on the ottoman. She was getting drunk, slurring her words. On the coffee table in front of her was a bag of pretzels she hadn't yet opened, a square of dark chocolate wrapped in foil on a napkin, and her third glass of that *simply terrific red*. The room was dark except for the light coming from the television. Johnny Carson had just finished his monologue and a commercial for toothpaste was starting up.

"Johnny is a good-looking man," she said. "I wouldn't mind getting to know Johnny."

"Please, no," he said.

"What?" she said. "I'm still a person. I'm still alive, Marty."

He said nothing. He looked at the screen and pretended to be interested in toothpaste.

"You know, I spent the last thirty-five years not thinking about the way men looked. I mean, I saw men—they come into the restaurant all the time, obviously—but I never really *looked* at them."

"You were happily married," he said.

"That's true, but some women still look. I think most do."

"I guess."

"But now," she continued, "as much as I miss your father, there's half the population I can look at."

"Jesus," he said. "That's a lot of looking."

"You know what I mean."

"Not really," he said.

"I miss him, of course—don't get me wrong, Marty. He was everything to me, your dad. I suppose at some point I'll need to move on, though." His mom leaned toward the chocolate. "Want a piece?" she asked him.

"No, thanks," he said.

"Chocolate will have to do for now," she said, smiling sadly.

He heard the crinkling of foil and the hard snap as his mom broke off a piece of candy.

She was talking and chewing at once. "You were the first one who talked to me about moving on, Marty. You said it yourself." She picked up her wine and took a sip. She ran her finger along the rim of the glass and didn't look at Martin.

When he'd talked to her about moving on, he'd meant her life in some generic sense and hadn't meant to encourage this plan of hers to ogle *half of the population.*

"Up until this point my life had been all planned out," she continued. "And after I recover, there will be all this possibility."

"Recover?" he said. "From what? Are you sick?" He leaned forward, suddenly worried.

"From grief."

"Oh, good—I mean, I don't want you to be sick."

"Grief's a sickness, Martin—don't minimize it. Or it *feels* like a sickness. You're lethargic, everything aches—not just your heart."

"Yes, you're right. I just didn't want you to have a disease."

When she drank, she seemed to him anything *but* grief-stricken. She seemed more like a slurring, sloppy woman on the mend.

"I thought you and Dad were happy," he said.

"I thought I was . . . I mean, I *was.* But now, there's possibility—a surprise waiting."

Martin didn't want to think about his mom's surprise. He didn't want to lie awake in bed tonight thinking about his dad, about how easily one man was forgotten once his widow had sucked down a few glasses of wine.

2

HANNAH WAS uncomfortable and confined in the front seat of Pablo's dad's truck, her cast at an awkward angle in front of her, her foot pressing against the floorboard. A cardboard lemon dangled from the rearview mirror, but the truck still smelled like his dad's cigarettes. Pablo, squinting and leaning toward the dashboard, drove slowly, like a little old woman, and she wondered if perhaps he was nearsighted.

"Can you see all right?" she said.

He turned to her, surprised, like he hadn't known she was his passenger. "Oh, yeah, yeah," he said. "The truck's dirty—that's all." He cleared his throat, leaned back in his seat, but was still squinting. Hannah reminded herself that the drive to Rebecca's house was a short one. It would be worth it. Rebecca's parents were away for the weekend and they'd have the place to themselves. Rebecca had promised them fruit punch and vodka and leftover Chinese food, she'd promised them time alone, just Hannah and Pablo, and even though Pablo was squinting and she was cramped in the passenger seat, Hannah felt like someone's girlfriend, and perhaps she was, sitting next to a boy she'd liked for years.

She tried to ignore his squinting and the dirty windshield, tried to put her concerns and reservations to the back of her mind: Pablo hadn't called her in a week, and when she finally called him, he asked her to hang out, yes, but was rushed and impatient on the phone. She tried not to dwell on the fact that he hadn't really helped her into the truck, just opened the door and taken her crutches from under her arms and tossed them into the back without giving her his usual boost.

"When this truck is mine—which it will be one day—it's going to be spotless. My dad's a slob," he said, turning on the wipers and squirting cleaning fluid with a flick of his wrist.

Hannah smelled ammonia and felt her toes going numb.

"You OK?" Pablo said, looking over at her. "You look uncomfortable."

"I'm fine."

"We're almost there," he said.

The cardboard lemon swung from side to side and the windshield wipers squeaked. Hannah shifted in the seat, trying to get comfortable, but it was no use.

He drove even slower down Second Street, passing dress shops and restaurants and bars, the parking meters and palm trees that lined the block, at what Hannah thought was parade-speed.

It was late summer, late afternoon, perfectly warm outside, and Belmont Shore was abuzz, busy with shoppers and families, people carrying bags and parents pushing strollers, young people spilling from bars onto the sidewalk, arms around each other's waists or shoulders.

Hannah wore a short-sleeve white blouse and jeans with the left pant leg cut off. She had a whole drawer of jeans and pants that she'd had to slice up to accommodate the toe-to-groin, but these jeans were her favorite pair and she'd miss them when the cast came off and she'd have to throw them out.

A group of older girls in cutoff shorts and halter tops stood outside of Hamburger Henry's, colorful combs sticking out of their back pockets and cigarettes hanging from their glossed lips. Three shirtless boys with wet hair clutching surfboards walked past the truck.

"It's not like we're in Huntington Beach. I don't know why they carry those things around here." Pablo paused. "Hey, I know those guys," he said, excited now, swerving over to the curb.

Hannah leaned back, startled, her cast bouncing on the floorboard.

"The one in the middle, he's a dick," Pablo said out of the side of his mouth.

Hannah thought about her dad holding a surfboard. She imagined him walking down the street, a man among boys, and missed him suddenly. She'd talked to him last night on the phone and he'd told her that Christy was out of the hospital and almost back to normal.

Pablo leaned over her, his shoulder hitting her chest. "Hey, Brian," he shouted out the window.

"Hey," Brian said, adjusting his board on his hip and moving toward the truck.

"Are you still a dick?" Pablo said, laughing.

"Pretty much," Brian said. He looked at Hannah. "Don't I know you?"

"Maybe," Hannah said quietly. He had a patch of sand on his chest, buck teeth, and eyes so blue they troubled her.

"You're the chick with the leg," he said.

She said nothing.

"You've been in a cast since you were born, right?" He laughed, looking at Pablo, who didn't laugh with him. "How long you been in a cast?"

She ignored him, looked at the windshield, the smeared dirt and bird shit, wishing that Brian would go away.

Pablo pulled away from the curb without saying good-bye. "Told you he was a dick," he said.

They were quiet and Hannah wondered if Brian's comment had embarrassed Pablo. Why would he want to be with a girl who'd been in a cast since she was *born*?

"You weren't born in a cast," he said.

But she was mad at him too. She didn't want his sympathy. She knew it was wrong to implicate him with a boy he didn't even like, but she couldn't stop herself. It seemed as if all boys were one boy, all of them dicks.

Still, she wanted *this* dick to like her.

"Maybe we should go to the beach sometime," he said.

"That would be great," she heard herself say, and as soon as the words came out of her mouth, she regretted them. She wasn't sure how her leg would look at the beach, especially before it had the chance to heal and match the other one. By the time it looked normal—which Hannah told herself was inevitable and only a matter of time—it would probably be December and too cold for the beach.

"You can watch me surf," Pablo said, smiling. He clicked on the radio and found a blues station that he said was his favorite. Most kids at school were dicks and they didn't know dick about music, he told her. He had one hand on the wheel and the other in his lap, tapping his thigh, keeping rhythm with what he called a very bitchin' harmonica solo.

At the end of the block, he turned down the radio so that the music was barely audible. "Becca told me that Mustafa spazzed out at a Jack in the Box. Said he went all body-snatcher and shit." He sounded eager to hear all about it.

"When did you talk to Becca?" She turned to him, surprised.

He shrugged.

"I just told her about Mustafa last night."

"Tell me about Mr. Spaz," he said.

"He's not Mr. Spaz," she said.

Pablo, slow as he was going, went over a pothole and her cast bounced against the floorboard again.

And then it was quiet in the truck and she wished he'd turn up the music.

And then it was still quiet.

She rolled her window down a couple of inches and then rolled it up.

She shifted in her seat.

And then she found herself talking about Mustafa, telling the story as if he *were* Mr. Spaz, just that and nothing more.

She found herself describing his seizure with enthusiasm, in detail, talking about his flailing hands and jerking feet. She was outside of herself, watching, she was two girls: the first girl gesticulating and excited, and the other one hating that first girl. She was upset, realizing that Pablo was enjoying the story, but what upset her more was how much that first girl relished in the telling.

She heard herself laughing when Pablo laughed.

She heard herself embellishing—the burger didn't just fall from his hand onto the table but flew across the room and landed in the corner. Azeem didn't catch Mustafa's body on the way down, but Mustafa fell to the floor and hit his head. She described the sharp crack of his skull striking the tile. "He could have died," she said.

The more she talked, the bigger Pablo's eyes got, the more engaged he was, and the more he seemed to like her.

The world was split into two groups, the damaged and the whole, the sick and the well, and no matter how much she wanted to be in one group, she knew she'd always be in the other. She could make out with a whole boy and even get him to like her, but she would always be a damaged girl.

She didn't want to think about all that now, though.

She wanted to be someone's girlfriend.

She wanted to be a girl on the beach.

She wanted to sit on the sand, smelling like coconut lotion, glistening and enviably tan, and watch Pablo surf. "My dad surfs," she said suddenly.

"It's cool when old men go out there. I've seen those old guys," he said.

"He's not *that* old."

Pablo shrugged. "Is he good?"

"I'm sure he's not as good as you are. I hear you're really good."

He told her that what she'd heard was true, he *was* good, but not good enough to go pro. He wanted to be a musician, anyway. He hated school and sometimes he even hated the beach and all the dicks who went to the beach and their dick girlfriends too. After he graduated, *if* he graduated, he said, he planned to live in the spotless truck and play his harmonica on the street for change until he was discovered.

She let him chatter on without interjecting and realized that she didn't know him—she didn't like him or like herself right now. She thought about telling him her stomach suddenly hurt and asking him to take her home, but decided to stay quiet.

"I'll get me a pillow and a blanket and a hot plate," he said, oblivious.

"You'd like that?" she said, weakly.

"Fuck yes."

"I wouldn't like that," she said, realizing that it didn't matter to him what she liked or didn't like because his plans didn't include her.

"I'll live in a parking lot in downtown L.A and sleep in my truck. I've got a cousin who's sleeping in a van now," he said, proud.

"Poor guy."

"What? Ernesto's doing great."

"Everyone needs a home."

"You don't get it," he said. "I'll live *here*." He patted the steering wheel. "I'll make friends with other people who love music as much as I do. I'll hang out with my cousin and play my harmonica on the streets until someone important notices me."

"Isn't this your dad's truck?" Hannah asked.

"It'll be mine by then—and it'll be clean," he said, emphatically. He turned the music up, louder and louder—a guitar squealing so loud that even if she'd asked him another question he wouldn't have heard her voice.

3

MARTIN RENTED an apartment a few blocks from the water. What they'd advertised as an ocean view was really a sliver of sea you could only glimpse from the low bathroom window. You had to be sitting on the toilet with your head cocked at an uncomfortable angle to see a damn thing.

When Tony came over, Martin sat on the closed toilet seat and demonstrated.

"Where?" Tony said. "I can't see anything."

"Fuck it," Martin said, standing up and rubbing his neck. "If I want to see the ocean, I can take a walk."

"There's a meeting tonight." Tony looked at his watch. "Starts in a couple of hours."

"Don't need a meeting." Martin was irritated. "I haven't had a drink in months."

"You want one, though, right? An icy cold beer? Some vodka and orange juice? Whiskey on the rocks? Remember how we used to sit for hours drinking whiskey? Didn't matter how cheap it was, we loved it."

Martin walked out of the bathroom with Tony talking to his back.

"Don't you want something cold and frosty?" Tony pestered. "It doesn't go away on its own. You have to confront it. Don't you want a drink?"

"Only when you talk about it, dickhead," Martin said over his shoulder.

"Let me know when it gets out of hand."

"Not when. *If.*"

They were in the living room, sitting on Martin's new couch. Martin rubbed his hand over the velvety fabric. "Bought this at the La Ramada swap meet, and those too," he said, pointing proudly at the red leather easy chairs across from them.

"Annabelle's been bugging me about new furniture. She wants a couch and a dining room set. She doesn't want the boy in the girl's crib. It's yellow—we bought a yellow one so that the next baby, no matter what it was,

249

could sleep in it. She wants, she wants, she wants. You're lucky, man," he said.

Martin said nothing.

"It's not like we can't afford it; we can. We've got enough money—it's not that."

"Get her what she wants, then."

Tony shook his head. "Seems to me that you should sit on a couch until the springs poke up your ass."

They were quiet a few minutes until Martin finally said, "Don't *you* want some whiskey yourself?"

Tony sighed. He shifted his weight and looked out the window. He breathed in. "Can't see the ocean from here, Marty, but you can smell it. Smells good," he said.

"Wouldn't you love a beer?" Martin pressed.

"Yes, yes I would," he admitted. "I always want one, but that doesn't mean I'm going to have one."

"How's that feel—me bugging you like that?"

"Shitty."

"Exactly."

"I'm trying to be a friend and sometimes I guess I'm just—"

"A dickhead," Martin said, interrupting.

"I was going to say an asshole, but dickhead works." Tony smiled. "Sorry about earlier."

"Yeah, OK."

"I mean it, Marty."

Sadie hopped up on the couch between them and they both reached out to pet her head at the same time, their hands colliding. They quickly pulled away and Sadie had to do without.

The two of them sat without saying a word, thinking about the beer they wouldn't drink, the many bottles of whiskey that waited for them lined up high on liquor store shelves all over town.

Tony got up from the couch and moved to one of the chairs. He cranked the handle on the side and shot back, disappearing from Martin's view, his shoes in the air. "*Damn*," he said.

"Don't break my new chair. Pull the lever toward you," Martin instructed.

Tony jiggled the handle and sat upright, his feet hitting the carpet. He situated himself. He ran his hand along the side of the chair. "Feels like vinyl to me. How much did you pay for these chairs?" he asked.

"Enough."

"I hope you didn't think you were paying for leather."

"Don't worry about it."

They were quiet again until Tony finally said, "Do you like being back in town? You OK here? How's work?"

"Great," Martin said, meaning it. "I'm the boss. I'm in the kitchen, making stuff. I'm trying out new recipes all the time. You and Annabelle should come by on Saturday. I'll get you a good table," he said.

"We'll get a sitter. You'll give us a deal?"

Martin nodded. "My dad hired a good crew. He had an eye for that sort of thing. Not sure if I'll be as sharp at hiring people when the time comes."

"You'll do fine."

"I don't know. My dad was a good judge. He could always pick them. He knew who'd be fast and who'd be slow."

"You got foxy waitresses?"

"I'm talking about busboys and waiters. But there *is* a redhead—" Martin began and then stopped himself. "Want some iced tea?" he asked.

"Sure."

"Or a beer?" Martin teased.

"Tea's fine. Tea's great. I've been sober five years," Tony reminded him. "How do you think I became a pharmacist? College and graduate school? I wouldn't have become anything if I kept going like I was going."

Tony asked him if he wished he'd gone to college. "You should have gone, man. It's not too late," he said.

"Cooking school was enough for me," Martin said, thinking that Tony was somehow managing to bore him and irritate him at once, thinking that maybe he'd go back to Las Vegas after all. Maybe he'd get someone else to take care of the restaurant. He'd open a Kettle's on the Strip and plan out the whole menu on his own. "I'll get that tea," Martin said, walking toward the kitchen. Sadie sprinted from the couch and followed him, the two of them leaving Tony alone to congratulate himself.

"Hey," Tony shouted after him. "Tell me about that redhead."

4

PABLO AND Hannah pulled up to the curb in front of Rebecca's house, and this time he made a point of rushing over to her side and helping her out. He pulled the crutches from the back and leaned them against the truck before offering her his hand.

Hannah had told Rebecca that Mustafa probably wouldn't join them, but still Rebecca looked disappointed when they showed up on her porch without him and, maybe more importantly, without his pot. "We'll have to drink *all* the vodka now," she whined.

"Hey, Becca," Pablo said. "Can you help me put the shell on?" He gestured to the truck, his future home, in the driveway.

Hannah wished she could have helped Pablo with the shell and was insulted that he hadn't even asked her. She knew she was useless in a toe-to-groin and would have been mad if he'd asked her to help in the first place. There was no way for him to win.

She stood on the porch watching Pablo and Rebecca haul the shell from the back, and when they zipped it up together, chatting and laughing, she imagined losing them both.

Rebecca sat too close to Pablo on the couch. She laughed too hard at his jokes and twirled her long hair around a finger. She looked mesmerized and impressed when he said the most innocuous things and Hannah was relieved when the phone rang and it was Mustafa, relieved when Rebecca trotted upstairs to her room to talk to him, leaving Hannah and Pablo finally alone.

They heard her bedroom door close and then her exaggerated laugh behind it. They heard her enunciating words, saying them too loudly, the way she always did when she talked to Mustafa.

"She really likes him," Hannah said, although she didn't think this was true and wasn't sure why she was saying it.

"She likes his pot," Pablo said, laughing.

"He's more than his pot."

"The burger went flying, huh?"

"I don't know."

"I thought you said—"

"I don't know," she snapped.

"Whoa," he said, backing up. "Let's be nice."

"I'm sorry," she said.

He came closer, talked to her in a sweet voice. "I like you, Hannah. I do." And she felt that he was trying to convince not only her but also himself.

And even though Hannah wasn't at all sure that she still liked Pablo, it was important that he like her, so she responded to his soft voice, moving toward him, letting him kiss her and kissing him back.

And he handed her the crutches, and she moved with him into the den, and tried to convince herself with her body and his body that they were still boyfriend and girlfriend. So what if they disagreed on the way over. So what if he wanted to live in his truck and play his harmonica on the street. People say all sorts of things they don't mean, she told herself. So what if she told him about Mustafa's seizure, if Pablo brought out the worst in her— it wasn't his fault that the worst was there.

In the den with the door shut, they couldn't hear Rebecca's voice, but Hannah felt like her friend was still with them. Rebecca was in the room, was on the couch with them—her voice and laugh in Hannah's head. Still, they kissed and kissed and kissed, and Pablo kissed her neck and touched her breasts, and Hannah kissed back, positioning herself just so, inviting his hand into her favorite jeans.

The back of Pablo's hand scraped hard against her cast and he cussed too loud. "Fuck," he nearly screamed, moving his hand from the left side to the right.

She only kissed him again, trying to pretend that her leg wasn't in the way. She was a girl whose cast was coming off in a couple of weeks, a girl who would then join the healthy, whole girls on their side of the room.

Later, when Rebecca finally got off the phone with Mustafa, she joined Hannah and Pablo in the backyard where they were sitting on wicker chairs, drinking a concoction of cherry punch and vodka. They'd already helped themselves to the Chinese food she'd promised them. Takeout cartons of fried rice and cashew chicken, half-eaten, sat on a side table between them.

"See you made yourselves at home," Rebecca said, smiling. She looked around the yard. "We need music. Want to help me with the speakers, Pab?"

Pab—what was with the Pab? Hannah wondered.

She watched and waited, dipping an egg roll into sweet sauce and lifting it to her mouth. Inside the house, Rebecca and Pablo worked together, hauling the three-foot speakers across the living room. Halfway to the screen, Rebecca lifted her speaker in the air, struggled the rest of the way. It was a ridiculous dance, Hannah thought, Rebecca's torso, shoulders, and face disappearing behind the speaker, and she was, for those few seconds, two red flip-flops, two perfect tan legs.

Pablo positioned the speakers at an angle so that they were pointing toward the backyard.

They sat outside until nearly midnight, drinking what was left of the vodka. The cherry punch stained their lips red. They listened to the Beach Boys until Pablo couldn't take it anymore and insisted Rebecca take those dicks off the turntable and put on a blues station.

Rebecca told them that it was fun talking to Mustafa on the phone. She told them he hadn't mentioned his seizure and that she hadn't really expected him to—they weren't that kind of close, she said.

The three of them talked about kids at school, kids they were looking forward to seeing when summer ended and school started, and kids they'd planned to avoid.

"I better get my own locker this year," Rebecca said. "Last year I had to share with Amy Owen. She pasted pictures of her stupid cat all over the door."

"All tenth graders get their own," Pablo said. He pulled a cigarette and book of matches from his pocket. When he popped the cigarette in his mouth and lit up, the flame illuminated the marks on his hand. They were worse than Hannah thought.

Rebecca shot up in her chair. "What happened to you?" she shrieked.

"Her cast," he said, looking down at it accusingly.

"Sorry," Hannah said.

"What did it do?" Rebecca wanted to know.

"It fucked me up."

"It's not a person," Hannah said, feeling drunk. "It didn't beat you up, Pablo. You're both acting like it's alive."

"What?" he said. "You're not making any sense."

"I am too," she protested, not at all sure.

But no one was listening to her. It was as if she'd disappeared.

"That looks painful, Pab," Rebecca cooed, leaning over and holding his wrist.

Hannah looked at Pablo's hand and felt embarrassed that something on her body had hurt him. "I'm sorry. *It's* sorry," she said.

"We've got a first-aid kit somewhere," Rebecca said, and then she was gone, rushing out of the backyard and bolting up the stairs.

Alone again, the two of them turned quiet. Hannah knew things were all wrong. She didn't like Pablo enough, and worse, he didn't like her enough, despite what they'd done in the den. "You drive like a little old lady," she said.

He was silent, picking at his scratches.

Then, Rebecca was rushing down the stairs, breasts bouncing in her T-shirt. By the time she got to him with the bottle of iodine and a handful of cotton balls, his hand looked even worse and he'd started to bleed.

Rebecca held the cotton ball to the bottle's mouth, and then she was leaning forward, dabbing at the tiny red dots, saying, "Here, let me help you, let me clean this up. He's hurt, Hannah," she said. "Can't you see Pab's hurt?"

5

MARTIN MADE the third restaurant his own and left the other two restaurants to Sandy and her husband, who were happy to take control of them. Kettle's served mostly Italian food and the first thing Martin did was add some menu choices. He made use of what he'd learned in cooking school. He added the Thai-spiced fish, even though his mom insisted it didn't fit with the rest of the menu. He added a flourless chocolate cake and a lemon meringue pie.

And he was drinking again, but was sure he had it under control. One beer a night—who would it kill? It was the only time he talked to people other than Tony or his mom or the men and women in the kitchen. He liked sitting after work with the waitresses and his one beer. He liked to keep the lights low and the red candles burning on the tables. Mostly he stayed quiet while letting the girls talk. They rolled up their sleeves. They unsnapped their barrettes and shook their hair free over their shoulders. They loosened the belts from their uniforms or took them off completely, draping them over chairs.

He liked them all, the brunette, the married redhead, and the one whose hair was a different color every other week: Cindy, Suzanne, and Suzy. It was hard to keep their names straight, but the redhead, Suzanne, her voice, the way she moved her hands when she spoke, the way she wiped off her lipstick with a napkin and her lips stayed pink, remained with him long after their little party of four had broken up. Images of her talking or laughing or even one night crying followed him as he walked home. The images followed him into bed and into his dreams.

He nursed one beer.

Another night he nursed two.

At first the girls asked him questions about his life.

Do you have a girlfriend?

Where do you live?

Is your friend Tony, the doctor, married to that woman he brought in on Saturday?

256

How is your mother getting on without your father?

Why did you move away?

And why Las Vegas?

He gave short answers. Sometimes he shook his head, saying, "I don't want to talk about me." After repeated attempts, they stopped asking. He liked that they didn't insist and that they let him sit with them while they talked and drank. The more they drank, the more intense their conversations became. Their laughter grew louder, they cussed and gossiped.

He listened to their stories of an unfaithful boyfriend, a husband who slept too much and ate too little, a miscarriage. He just sat and listened and stared at them or stared at the candle's flame, and sometimes he thought they almost forgot he was there, and that suited him just fine. He liked looking at them and he liked hearing their voices and he liked putting his fingertip in the hot wax, letting it dry, and peeling it off, letting the wax collect on the little napkin in front of him.

The girls talked about cheap tippers, the grapefruit diet, and birth control methods. Cindy or Suzy talked about church. Someone mentioned a shoe sale at the mall. Suzanne talked about the husband who was always asleep on the couch when her shift was over. She said that his breath had grown sour over the years and that lately he'd been refusing to eat what she cooked for him.

One night, after the restaurant had bustled with big spenders and generous tippers whom the girls were still talking about, Martin splurged and drank beers without counting. He used a key to open the bar and pulled a bottle of whiskey from a shelf. They drank and drank. He told the girls about his life in Vegas, cooking school, and his friendship with Tony. He ran a hand along the back of his chair and asked them if it was possible to tell the difference between expensive vinyl and cheap leather.

"Vinyl's never expensive, is it?" Suzy said, looking at Suzanne and Cindy for confirmation.

Both women shrugged and all of them started laughing, even Martin, who suddenly didn't give a shit what his chairs were made of. What mattered was that he had a place to sit.

When the laughter stopped, though, Suzanne wiped off her lipstick and started to cry. She told them about her husband again, how he was losing weight, becoming skinny. His face was gaunt and cruel, she told them. And he didn't say good-bye when he left the house for work. She missed those first few years of marriage when he wouldn't leave a room without kissing her, when he hungrily and appreciatively ate what she'd cooked for him.

It was after three a.m. when Martin found himself in the back of the restaurant with Suzanne. The other two kept up their chatter and he could hear their voices while he was kissing Suzanne and she was kissing him back, while he was unbuttoning the top of her uniform and slipping his hand inside.

"I'm married," she said, but she continued kissing him and let her hand fall to his crotch.

The four of them staying after work became the three of them—Suzanne always running home to her thin, sleeping husband.

It stung every time she said good-bye. When she rushed off or waved or when he heard the door click shut, he felt rejected.

Once, while he was setting a plate of pasta primavera under the hot lamps, she approached the counter and he tried to apologize for what had happened between them, when really it was a mutual thing and she'd seemed pretty happy while it was happening. He remembered how they'd moved to the cot in the back and how she'd wrapped her long legs around him and told him she'd been waiting for him for a long time, such a long time, she had said.

"I'm sorry about what happened," he said, leaning forward, feeling the heat from the lamps on his arms. "I mean, I'm sorry if you're sorry, which you seem to be. I'm not sorry myself."

Suzanne looked at him blankly like it hadn't been her that night and he hadn't been him and she didn't know what the hell he was even talking about. "Maybe you shouldn't drink so much," she said.

"What?" he said, surprised.

"You heard me," she said, grabbing the plate and spinning around, walking back to the dining room.

"Maybe *you* shouldn't," he called after her.

The next day Suzanne called in sick.

And the next.

And the one after that.

She had a cold that wouldn't let go, maybe it was the flu, she said, sniffling dramatically, coughing in between words. And then finally she just stopped coming in and didn't bother to call. He'd heard from one of the busboys that she'd been waiting tables at a French restaurant in Huntington Beach. And then Cindy told him that Suzanne and her husband were happy again and moving to San Francisco or San Diego, she couldn't remember which.

And then none of the girls stayed after work, each night with a different excuse. *I'm tired* or *I've got visitors from out of town* or *I think I'm coming down with something.*

He stayed after work alone, sitting in the corner in the near dark with only one candle burning, drinking beer after beer. He didn't keep track anymore and he didn't care. He didn't need those waitresses—they needed *him,* their jobs, he told himself. They were just waitresses and he was the boss. He was in charge of things. If he wanted to, he could fire them all and hire some new girls and ruin things all over again.

He drank until the bottles lined up in front of him, until he knocked one over and it crashed to the floor. He might have had six and he might have had seven. He might have had eight or nine.

He stepped over the broken glass and stumbled to the kitchen where he devoured what was left of the lemon meringue pie. He ate right from the tin with a spoon that still tasted like rice pilaf. He ignored the crust and scooped up the creamy yellow middle.

He woke up in his bed the next morning but didn't remember the walk home. The front door to the apartment was open and his keys hung from the doorknob. He found one shoe by the bed. When he opened the fridge, he found the other shoe on a shelf between the milk and eggs.

Still, he wasn't like Tony, he didn't need those AA people, those prying losers. He'd stopped drinking before and he could stop again. Cutting down was even easier. He thought about those first nights after work, sitting with Cindy, Suzy, and Suzanne for hours, nursing his single beer of the night. He could do that again. No more shoes in the fridge for me, he told himself. He didn't need to go to a fucking meeting, didn't need to stand up and identify himself as powerless, to confess his secrets to a bunch of nosy assholes.

6

HANNAH WATCHED the saw's spinning blade. She looked at the doctor's big hand holding the saw. She looked at his hairy knuckles and the thick veins shooting up his arms, and thought about all the doctors who had come before him, their many sets of hands and how they differed, how they were the same. She thought about the way her leg had been handled and touched and twisted by those hands, the casts they had made and removed, and how each time her leg popped free, it looked less familiar, less *hers,* thinner and more traumatized.

She thought about the time a particularly frustrated doctor had let go of her leg, dropping it like it was hot to the touch, how she wasn't ready, how she'd trusted and given him the weight of it. She thought about his repeated apologies after her leg had hit the examination table with a hard thud. She remembered her mom driving too fast, speeding toward the yellow lights, and cursing him all the way home.

She thought about the doctor who looked insane, who smiled continually, a big, exaggerated grin reminding her of a carved pumpkin, and the one who was always in a rush and liked to say *Let's make this happen. Let's get going. Let's get on our way,* as if the two of them were taking a vacation together.

She thought about the one who smelled like pastrami, who slid up to the examination table on his stool, too close to her face with his spicy, meaty breath. She remembered how he'd looked directly into her eyes, explaining each and every thing he was about to do to her leg in exhausting medical jargon.

She thought of their names, their nurses, and tried to remember their faces. She thought of the white powder that shot from their saws like snow when they lifted them from this cast or that cast or this one, supposedly, hopefully, the last one, the very last cast that Dr. Russo was preparing to remove now.

His bald spot, the size of a coaster, sat directly on top of his head and was surrounded by two white puffs of hair. His neck was thick with small red bumps traveling from his Adam's apple to his chin. Dr. Russo wore a blue coat instead of a white coat and it reminded her of the coats the guys wore who worked at the car wash by her house.

Her mom and Azeem were standing at her side, one on the right and one on the left. Her dad, who'd met the three of them there, was sitting in a chair he'd pulled up to the examination table and was touching her shoulder.

Her mom and Azeem had barely talked to each other in the car and Hannah had felt pressure to make conversation. She asked each of them questions and they gave her short, clipped answers until she gave up, sat back, and watched the other cars on the freeway. Two little girls waved at her from a back window. She looked at the center divider or she looked at the trees.

Now her mom reached out for Hannah, but she pulled her hand away, not to be mean but needing to hold the sides of the table for balance. She understood that they were eager and excited and nervous, just as she was.

In her underwear and a T-shirt with both of her legs stretched out in front of her, she was noticing again how dirty the cast was, exceptionally so, with big gray smudges like rain clouds and fraying edges at her thigh and toes. Having been dragged on the floor, the cotton at her toes was nearly black and she wished she'd had her mom cut the edges before they'd left the house. Hannah looked down at Pablo's drawing and thought about him, remembered the last time they were together in Rebecca's den and how far they went. She wished she hadn't complained about his driving.

Dr. Russo's office was so familiar to her, the life-size illustration of a body on the wall, the red and yellow and blue that represented the body's insides. A picture of a night sky was taped to the ceiling. She was supposed to look at the fake stars while he did what he did. There was a long cupboard against another wall, inside of which a skeleton hung from a hook. During Hannah's last visit, at her request, Dr. Russo had opened the cupboard and introduced the skeleton as Max. She thought about Max's many bones inside the cupboard. She wondered when he'd lived and how he died. She wondered how she'd die herself. She hoped she'd grow up and grow old first. She wondered what made Max decide to give his bones to science.

The doctors who preceded him were sometimes optimistic, but Dr. Russo had given his word, made a promise, and now as the whirring blades made their way toward the uppermost part of her cast, very near Hannah's crotch, he was either going to fail or deliver.

After he cut the first long line, he turned off the saw and looked at Hannah. With his chin he gestured to her crutches that were propped against Max's cupboard. "You'll need those things at first, but week by week you'll need them less."

"Hear that, Hannah?" her dad said.

"It's exciting," Azeem said.

After Dr. Russo cut the second line down the outside of her leg, he pulled out the scissors and cut through the gauze and cotton. The smell of her leg embarrassed her. It was a skinny, smelly thing. A thick purple scar wrapped around her ankle and Dr. Russo admired it. "Beautiful, just beautiful," he said.

Her leg was even thinner than she'd remembered it, uglier, it seemed, pale and scaly, and her toes, although freed from the cast, were still scrunched up together and curled.

The doctor and Azeem helped her off the examination table. Her dad stood up from the chair. She felt embarrassed in just her underwear, embarrassed by her skinny leg. After that afternoon with Pablo, after what she'd done with him, it didn't seem right that the four of them were looking at her now. She felt exposed and wished she'd had a robe.

Nina stood expectantly while the doctor and Azeem reached under Hannah's arms and stood her up. Hannah's dad had his hands on his hips, waiting. Everyone was nervous. Even the doctor didn't seem like his confident self.

Hannah's instinct was to hop. She didn't want to put weight on her left foot, expecting it to be sore and sensitive.

"Come on," Dr. Russo said.

"Come on, Hannah," her mother said.

"You can do it, sweet girl," Azeem said, and she could see that he'd already started to cry.

"It'll feel strange at first, maybe uncomfortable, but you'll get stronger every day," Dr. Russo assured her.

"Just a little bit of weight," her dad said, pleading.

There was a knock at the door and the receptionist stepped inside the room. "I'm sorry, Dr. Russo, your wife is on line four."

"Not now." He held up his hand. "We're busy here, Grace," he said.

"Sorry, sorry," she said, closing the door and rushing away.

Hannah gently placed her left foot on the tile.

She was surprised by how cold the tile felt, more intensely cold than it felt to her right foot.

"It's like ice," she told them.

"You'll feel temperature more acutely with that foot," the doctor said. "Hot will be hotter and cold will be colder. We expect that with nerve damage." He looked at Nina, who was nodding and holding back tears.

Hannah put a little more weight down.

She had to admit that her foot looked straighter than it had since before the accident.

Still, there was pain and pressure and all that cold. But she wanted so badly to walk, for them, and for herself.

She tried, one foot in front of the other, a few meek steps, but it hurt badly and she gave in to the limp.

"There," she said.

"Just a few more steps," Dr. Russo said.

"That's all I've got," she told him.

"It's great, Hannah. You did fine," Azeem said, picking her up and spinning her around in a circle. She was aware again of being in only her underwear and T-shirt. "Put me down," she said, but she was smiling at him and wiping his wet face with her hand.

7

THE NOSY assholes had become Martin's confidants. He'd been going to meetings with Tony on Monday afternoons and Thursday evenings. At the third meeting he'd stood up and introduced himself as an alcoholic and told an edited version of his story. He said he'd had a car accident and that he'd left the scene. This was years and years ago—nearly a decade, he told them.

"I hit a parked car and left without taking responsibility." He could feel Tony's eyes on him, see him shaking his head.

His sponsor, Jack, sat in the front row, nodding encouragingly. Jack was next to Tony, who was obviously waiting for more from Martin, his impatient expression saying, *Go ahead, tell us the truth.*

At the fourth meeting Martin admitted to the group that all of his sexual encounters occurred when he was drunk, that it was difficult for him to make it work without a drink or two, and that the girls in Las Vegas were usually tourists or married and unavailable here.

On the way home in the car, Tony smoked a cigarette and was obviously unhappy with Martin. "You didn't come clean," he said. "Maybe about fucking, but not about the girl you hit."

"I thought you quit smoking," Martin said.

"Don't you worry about me," he said.

Earlier, Martin had seen Tony bum a few cigarettes from an AA girl. Now he took a deep drag and the front seat filled with smoke. Martin coughed and rolled down the window, cold air rushing in.

"You know it's not right—that story you told in there. It's a lie, Marty. The program won't work if you're bullshitting everyone, if you're bullshitting yourself."

"I have to work at my own pace, man."

"You've got to at least tell Jack. Have you told Jack? He's your fucking sponsor."

Martin shook his head.

"If you're going to lie, don't tell the story at all. Talk about how you can't get it up without booze."

"Hey, wait a fucking minute. I *can* get it up. No one said anything about not getting it up."

"You told us you couldn't get a boner without a drink."

"That's not what I said. I hope no one thought I said that." He ran a hand through his hair.

"That's what I heard. Your dick doesn't work unless you're wasted. And the way you told the story made it sound like you'd had a fender bender and didn't want to have to call your fucking insurance agent."

"That's as far as I'm going to go."

"It's not far enough."

"Do you want me to go to meetings or not?"

"You have to do this right." Tony opened his window an inch and flicked the cigarette butt to the street.

"Fuck you," Martin said.

"Fuck you too."

"Go to hell."

"*You* go to hell, Marty."

They were quiet at a red light.

Tony turned on the radio. He pushed the buttons hard, moving from static to news to more static to Elvis Costello crooning "Alison." He angrily clicked the radio off.

"Hey," Martin protested. "I like that song."

"I like the truth," Tony said. The light turned green and he put his foot heavy on the gas, the two of them lurching forward.

"Easy," Martin said. "Jesus."

When they pulled up to the curb in front of Martin's apartment, Tony stopped short and Martin smelled rubber. He turned to Tony without taking off his seat belt. He didn't want to fight. Tony was his only friend in town and dickhead or not, he meant well. "You and Annabelle coming in on Saturday?" he asked, feeling like a pussy for not staying mad.

Tony pulled another cigarette from his shirt pocket and put it in his mouth. "I don't know," he said. He pushed in the car's lighter and stared straight out the windshield.

"My mom will be there—she'd like to see you again."

"Maybe," Tony said, softening.

Martin unbuckled the seat belt. He opened the door and stepped out, his boot in the gutter. He stood on the grass and put his hands on the top of the car. He leaned over and stared at Tony through the open window. "Thanks for taking me tonight, man."

Tony nodded.

"I mean it."

"Yeah, I know."

Martin tapped the hood a couple times, saying good-bye, and Tony waved at him without looking his way.

In bed, he smelled the ocean he couldn't see and pet Sadie, who was curled up and purring on his chest. He thought about Jack and Tony and the others, how during breaks they stood outside clutching coffee cups and smoking cigarette after cigarette.

The meetings were held in the back of a flower shop in a mini-mall in Torrance. Martin liked to sit by the door so he could smell the gardenias and roses while people told their stories—this man beat his wife and now she had only one eye, this teenager snorted so much coke that she had a hole in her nose that wasn't a nostril, this woman fucked her husband's brother. Martin preferred looking at the flowers to seeing the alcoholics' sorry faces.

He didn't believe in a higher power and he wasn't sure if he was technically an alcoholic. In Las Vegas, when Ilene had suggested he cut down on his drinking, he'd done so without having to confess a bunch of shit to a room of strangers. When he'd told himself to stop going out with Elmer and to stop fucking girls he hardly knew, he stopped easily. He beat off every night and didn't give a shit if he was alone.

He wasn't so sure that labeling oneself was a good thing.

God, Higher Power, and his least favorite, the Lord—you could call Him what you wanted to call Him, but He was always the same unbelievable dream to Martin.

· · ·

In the morning he met his sister for breakfast at a pancake house on Fourth Street and told her about the meetings. Sandy confessed over a big stack of banana waffles that she'd starved herself all through high school. She said group therapy was what saved her. "I don't know if you noticed, but I didn't eat at all back then. I lived off pretzels and Coke Slurpees and sugar-free soda."

"I did notice," he said, feeling guilty.

"Yeah, well," she said, cutting into the waffles with her fork.

"I'm sorry," he said.

"It's not your fault," she said. "It was me who wouldn't eat."

"I should have been a better brother."

"Are you making amends?"

He didn't say anything.

"Good for you," she said.

Sandy told him that she'd joined an eating-disorder group right after he'd left for Las Vegas and that several of the girls from her group were now dead. Only she and one other girl from that group had made it through. "In a way, it's worse than alcohol," she said. "You need to eat to live, but you don't need to drink."

She admitted that sometimes she looked at her baby daughter's fat little legs and soft arms and feared the girl would grow up with the same problems. And another part of her, the part she rarely acknowledged and didn't, until now, speak of, feared her daughter would always look like that—fat and pink and soft.

When she thought of withholding milk from her hungry girl, she started going back to group.

"Give it a chance," she told him.

The waitress came up to the table then, asking if everything was OK.

"Can we get some more coffee here?" Martin said, lifting his empty cup in the air.

"Right away," she said.

When the waitress was out of earshot, Martin leaned forward. His hands were clammy and his stomach ached. He could feel the sweat on his forehead and picked up the napkin to dab at it.

"What's wrong? Are you OK?"

"I don't know," he said.

"You don't look so well."

He put the napkin down and leaned forward, elbows on the table.

"What's going on?" she said.

"I want to tell you something," he said. "I need to talk to you."

"What? You're scaring me," she said.

"Remember that girl who was hit by a car?" he said.

"What girl? When?"

"Years ago, right before I left."

She put down her fork and looked at him.

"I hit her," he said.

"What are you talking about, Marty?"

"I'm telling you," he said. "I hit her and then I left her there."

8

THE NIGHT before Mustafa went home and two days before Azeem was to move out of the house, Hannah couldn't sleep. Mustafa had promised to write and keep in touch, and Azeem had promised that the separation from her mom was temporary, that he'd do his best to win her back. He'd live at his cousin's apartment in Los Angeles for a month, two at the most. They'd see a marriage counselor and patch things up. He loved her mom and he loved Hannah like a daughter. He'd be back, he promised, as soon as he could win back Nina's trust.

Hannah knew she should be relieved that the operation had been what the doctor called a success. Her leg was free, unbound, but it felt tiny and defenseless. Now, in bed, her thin pajamas weren't enough, the sheets weren't enough, and she was acutely aware of her leg's vulnerability. She hadn't told anyone, but she missed the casts, the protection and cover they had offered her. She pushed the blanket and sheets back and got out of bed, glancing at her crutches and deciding to leave them where they stood against her closet.

She walked down the hall to Mustafa's room. The steps were tentative and painful. She limped, tipped to one side, and held onto the wall.

It was after midnight and he was sleeping. With her ear to the door, she heard his heavy snoring. She knocked but didn't wake him. She knocked harder and opened the door a couple of inches. "Hey," she whispered. "Hey, Mustafa. I'm sorry to wake you," she said.

He bolted up in bed, looking around. "What's going on?" he said, startled.

"I'm sorry," she said again.

He composed himself, pulled the sheet and blanket up, and invited her in. "It's OK," he said.

"I wanted to ask you something before you go," she said, stepping into the room.

"Where are your aluminum friends?" Mustafa smiled at her.

"Left them in my bedroom," she said. "I held onto the wall. And it hurt like hell."

He nodded and yawned at the same time.

"I shouldn't have woken you up."

"Sit down."

"I know you're leaving in the morning. I didn't want to bother you, but I—" she began and then stopped herself.

"I'm not bothered," he said.

She stood there without saying a word, thinking that she could still go back to her room and leave him alone. He needed his sleep. His plane was leaving early in the morning.

"What, Hannah? Take a load off." He pulled his legs up, making room for her, and patted the space at the foot of the bed. "Sit down," he said again.

Mustafa's accent was still thick, but there was no mistaking his words. He liked colloquialisms and seemed pleased with himself when he'd used one correctly—or incorrectly. Hannah always understood what he said or meant to say even when he said something else.

"I wanted you to tell me again about your broken arm," she said.

"I told you. I had a seizure at school and fell down in the concrete."

"*On* the concrete," she corrected.

"On, in." He waved his hands around. "I fell," he said. "And broke my arm. Hurt like fuck."

She smiled.

"Just thinking about the pain makes me want to smoke a joint. You have one?"

She shook her head.

"I think I have one somewhere." He jumped out of the sheets, bent down, and picked his jeans up from the floor. He searched the pockets. He opened his wallet and searched his jacket. "Ah," he said, finding what looked like half a joint, holding it up for proof. "It's a fatty," he said, smiling.

"We can't just smoke it in the house," she said.

"Why not?"

"They're home. We'll get caught."

He grumbled something and opened the window. He sat on the couch. "Come over here," he said.

"You're leaving town, but I have to live with them. Or at least her," she said.

"Azeem and your mom are so moody these days—it would be good for them to get stoned. We should blow the smoke under their door and cheer them up."

Hannah laughed.

"Your mom would realize that my brother loves her even if he fucked that woman's big ass."

"He didn't fuck her ass," she said, smiling.

"You know what I mean," he said. "Anyway, it would be good for them to smoke some pot and loosen up. Hey," he said. "Are they married? I think they're married."

"They're married," she said.

"I knew it," he said. "Why didn't he tell me?"

"Because your family has a girl picked out for him."

"He's a different man than he was when he left. He's not right for Raina."

"Will you tell your mom?"

"Eventually."

"Good."

"Come over here," he said again, patting the seat next to him.

Mustafa was wearing surfer shorts that she didn't know he had, and though he looked sort of silly, she was happy he wasn't naked. She almost said, *I thought you slept naked,* and then realized how that would sound, so she kept quiet. Since the last seizure, he'd stopped going to the nudist camp and stopped masturbating obsessively too. "It's better when it's with a girl," he'd said soon after the seizure. "I don't need to do it morning, noon, and night," he'd told them all.

"Probably not," Azeem admitted.

"So much for your theory, brother," he said.

"The *author's* theory," Azeem said.

"You're the champion of it," Mustafa insisted.

"You've learned a lot of English since you've been here," Hannah said, impressed with the word *champion.* What would have been even better was if he'd used it as a verb. If he'd said, *Yes, brother, but you championed it.* She'd have to remember to teach him that before he left.

"I won't be pleasuring myself so much," he'd told them.

"Great," Hannah had said.

"Wonderful," her mom had said.

Now, Hannah and Mustafa passed the joint back and forth between them and when she coughed he handed her the pillow from his bed to cover her mouth. She smelled his scent on the pillow and knew that she'd miss him. She looked out the open window, felt the cool air on her face, and stared into the backyard at the trees and empty chairs. Far off, a dog howled, but mostly it was quiet.

"Tell me about your arm," she said again.

"That's all there is to tell," he said.

"Tell me how it was skinny."

"It *was* skinny."

"And tell me how it plumped up."

"It plumped up."

"How long did it take?"

"I don't remember."

"You must remember."

"Let me see your leg, Hannah."

She shook her head.

"That's why you're here."

"It's skinny now, but it's going to plump up," she said. "It'll take time, I'm sure."

"Let me see," he urged.

"No."

"We'll just sit here until you show me."

They finished off the joint and sat stoned without saying anything for a long time.

"Let me see," he said again.

She pulled up her pajama leg and there it was.

She thought she heard him gasp and then recover.

"Not *that* skinny," he said, looking at it. "My arm *never* looked like that," he said.

She quickly dropped the fabric and covered up her leg. She stood up to go.

"No," he said, sternly. "Sit down."

"I'm going," she said, feeling like she was about to cry and not wanting to do so in front of him. Still, instead of leaving she stood there, looking down at him.

"Come here," he said. "Come closer."

"No," she said. "Shut up, please, Mustafa. Don't say anything else." Her voice cracked into the room.

"The leg is just one piece of you. There are a lot more pieces," he said.

"Don't," she said.

"Listen," he said. And he lowered his voice so that she had to lean down and forward to hear him. "You've still got the good body," he told her.

"Rebecca's going to miss you," she said.

"My pot, maybe," he said.

And their lips brushed and they almost kissed and then they *did* kiss and then they *were* kissing and he had his arms around her, holding her, hugging her, and then she was crying for the first time in a long, long time, she was crying hard, and he was whispering something in Arabic, something sweet she could not understand but understood perfectly.

9

WHILE HANNAH was kissing Mustafa, Pablo was kissing Rebecca. Hannah found out because Rebecca told her on the phone. Pablo didn't want to face her, Becca said. He feels terrible, she told her. He wanted me to call you. He'd been drawn to her for months. "It was always me," Rebecca said.

"It's OK," Hannah said, and was surprised that it *was* OK. She had more important things to worry about now than whether or not Pablo liked her enough and whether Rebecca was loyal enough. She had Azeem, whom she missed, and Mustafa, whom she missed, and she had her mother, who missed and loved them both, and she had her father and Christy, who was supposedly cured, a new woman who was really just her former, too-cheerful self.

They were all coming over, her father and Christy from Irvine, Azeem from Los Angeles, and the five of them were going out to dinner in Manhattan Beach. A place called Kettle's that the Harrisons had recommended to Nina. They were going to celebrate what her mother called Hannah's nearly perfect gait, which was nowhere near perfect, which was barely passable.

Rebecca and Pablo didn't seem that important. It hurt, sure, and she wasn't happy about having to see them together at school, but if all went well, she'd be avoiding them and walking away from them, sans crutches, on two working feet.

She'd kissed Mustafa back and then kissed him again and felt more during those kisses than she had when Pablo touched her everywhere, and there was no explaining it, it just was.

In the morning, before he and Azeem left for LAX, Mustafa came into the kitchen to say good-bye. "Last night was something I should have understood from my first day here. I should have ignored your mean face and saw the real face," he told her.

"I told Pablo about your seizure," she said, putting down her glass of orange juice.

"So?"

"It wasn't right, the way I told the story . . ."

"It doesn't matter."

"It does."

"We're two peapods in a pod."

"It's two peas in a pod." Hannah was crying and laughing at once.

"I should have—" he began, but she interrupted him.

"I want to tell you about the word *champion*," she said.

"Tell me."

"It's also a verb," she told him. "Azeem *championed* that author's theory about sexual deprivation."

"I champion you," he said.

"I champion you too."

Azeem stepped into the kitchen. He picked up an apple from the fruit bowl and rubbed it on his pant leg before biting into it. He looked at Hannah and then around the room. "Hey, no crutches," he said, excited, juice running down the sides of his mouth. He reached for a napkin and wiped his lips.

"Don't get too happy," she said. "It hurt like hell just to make it down the hall."

Azeem walked over to her, mussed her hair, and kissed the top of her head.

Now, waiting for her father and Christy and Azeem to come over, she thought about Mustafa seizing on the concrete and breaking his arm. She thought of the car hitting her and changing the way she lived and moved in the world. For the first time in years she thought about the person who hit her, how he left her body where it fell, how he didn't attend to her body at all. She thought about her leg—just a piece of her, Mustafa had said, and then he kissed her.

It wasn't just a piece of her. He was wrong about that. It was one of her four limbs and it was fucked up and ugly and deformed. She hated that word and had always reserved it for other people, for babies born with twisted hands or feet. But it was a word that belonged to her now and he had told her the truth. The sight of it had made him gasp. He had to catch his breath and recover. It was wrecked and damaged, looking down at it made her cringe, and her mother's dream might well have been prophetic.

But the leg almost worked, she couldn't deny that it almost worked, that it was going to eventually work, do its job, it would eventually, one day, maybe even soon, take her away, it would take her to jobs and parties and restaurants, it would take her to a restaurant later that evening, in fact, to Kettle's for her celebration, where when she had to go to the bathroom she'd walk away from the table without crutches, leaving her four parents smiling and talking to each other, where she wouldn't need the wall, where she'd walk past two waitresses whispering in the backroom, where she'd walk past a busboy and a smiling chef, a chef whose smile would disappear when he saw her, whose skin would go pale, who would recognize her as his history, and who'd stand outside the bathroom waiting for her to open the door.

Her leg would take her past Rebecca and Pablo in the quad, to tenth grade, eleventh grade, and twelfth.

It would take her to college, to birthdays, and funerals.

It would take her wherever she wanted to go.

ACKNOWLEDGMENTS

MANY THANKS and much love to my family, especially my father, Aaron Glatt, my favorite storyteller, who says all of this is in the genes. For my brother Andrew Glatt, who's a lawyer and who said early on, "If you write anything remotely autobiographical, leave me out of it completely." Which I did.

To the Dinner Party Crew: Meghan Daum and Alan Zarembo, Heather Havrilesky and Bill Sandoval. Extra love and gratitude to Meghan, who read my work at a pivotal moment and offered much-needed encouragement.

To the gifted, lovely Emily Rapp, who spoke of it first.

To Leelila Strogov and Ernie Liang, who are the family we've picked out, and to Gwen Dashiell and Jessica Ware, who are more like my sisters than my friends.

I am indebted to the Civitella Ranieri Foundation for the gift of time and space; to California State University, Long Beach for a sabbatical I put to work; to my students, past and present; and to Suzanne Greenberg, who read an early draft and offered astute advice.

Much appreciation to Ron Hogan for his sharp eye and editorial wisdom, and to the loyal Andrew Blauner, my agent for the long haul.

And finally, to my husband, David Hernandez, whose own commitment to words has made our house conducive to writing, who turns off the phones and insists we get to work, and without whom the bad things wouldn't be as bearable and the good things wouldn't be as good.